BLUEWATER GANJA

THE NINTH NOVEL IN THE CARIBBEAN MYSTERY
AND ADVENTURE SERIES

C.L.R. DOUGHERTY

BLUEWATER GANJA

Bluewater Thrillers

Book 9

Caribbean Mystery and Adventure Series

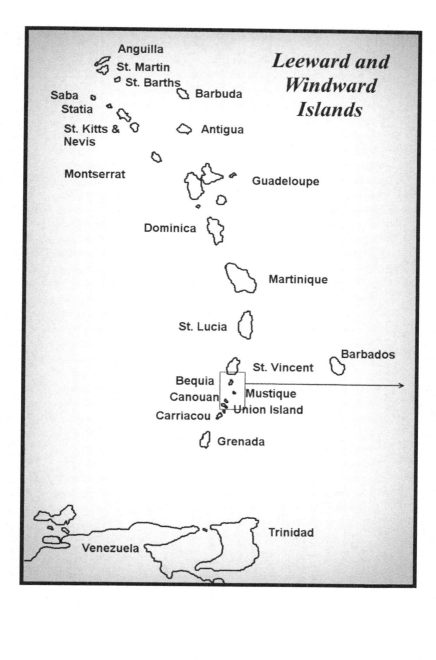

Leeward and Windward Islands

Anguilla
St. Martin
St. Barths
Barbuda
Saba
Statia
St. Kitts &
Nevis
Antigua
Montserrat
Guadeloupe
Dominica
Martinique
St. Lucia
Barbados
St. Vincent
Bequia
Canouan
Mustique
Carriacou
Union Island
Grenada
Venezuela
Trinidad

St. Vincent

St. Vincent to Carriacou

Bequia

Mustique

Canouan — reefs

Mayreau   Tobago Cays

Union Island   reefs

Hillsborough
Carriacou   Petite Martinique

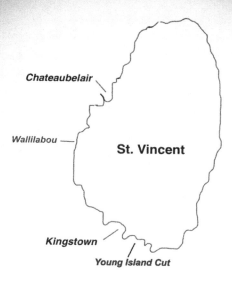

St. Vincent and Bequia

Chateaubelair

Wallilabou

St. Vincent

Kingstown

Young Island Cut

Admiralty Bay

Bequia

Mayreau and the Tobago Cays, St. Vincent and the Grenadines

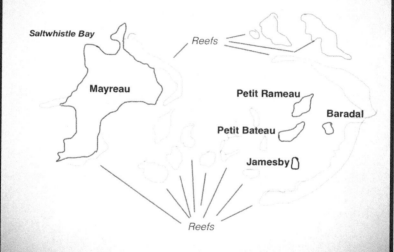

Saltwhistle Bay

Reefs

Mayreau

Petit Rameau

Baradal

Petit Bateau

Jamesby

Reefs

1
———

"CAREFUL! YOU'RE PINCHING," LIZ SAID, FROWNING.

"Sorry. I'm not used to such a smooth bottom," Dani said. "Just trying to get accustomed to how slick it is."

"Slides along like it's silk," Liz said, laughing.

"It's slippery, all right," Dani agreed. "Glad you did it; it feels way better than it used to."

"Her bottom was pretty foul," Liz said. "Freddy and the yard crew had to sand her down almost to the gel coat to get rid of the barnacle rings."

"Thanks for taking care of that while I was gone, Liz. She's sailing better now that she's clean — points closer to the wind, for sure. That's why I was pinching the jib."

"Both of us didn't need to hang around while they painted *Vengeance's* bottom. I thought some time with Ralph might cheer you up."

"Mm," Dani said. "It might have cheered me up, but —"

Liz didn't say anything. Dani would tell her about her time in Brazil when she was ready. Dani's love life was one of the few topics that wasn't up for discussion between them. Early in their friendship, Liz had made the mistake of asking about Dani's relationship with Ralph Suarez; she'd been surprised at how quickly Dani had rebuffed her.

"What's the story on the new guests?" Dani asked. Their agent, Elaine Moore, had booked a charter for them while Dani was in Brazil.

"A single father with a teenaged daughter," Liz said.

"Divorced? Or widowed?"

"Both, from what Elaine said."

Dani raised her eyebrows at that, turning to look at Liz and steering *Vengeance* by feel. She and Liz were *en route* from Grenada to Bequia, where they were to meet their guests. "Both?"

"The girl's mother was his first wife. She died several years ago, and he's been married and divorced a few times since then."

"Unstable," Dani muttered. "Can't have been good for the girl, having strange women come and go in her life like that."

"Are you speaking from experience?"

"Not really. I didn't have much contact with my various step-mothers until I was older and got to be friends with Anne."

"Did you spend most of your time with your mother after she and J.-P. were divorced, then? You were about this girl's age, I'd guess."

"No, I wasn't around either of my parents much after they split. How old is she?"

"Sixteen, Elaine said."

"That bodes ill for this charter," Dani said. "Just what we need: some sulky teenager with excess hormones."

"Oh, come on, Dani. She might be fun to have around. I wasn't sulky at that age."

"I'm sure you weren't, Pollyanna."

"Well, were you?"

"Was I sulky?"

"That's the question."

"I was too busy to be sulky. When I was sixteen, I was deck crew on the big Perini Navi in the Med, fighting off the advances of this shithead who had chartered her for six months."

"I'm surprised your father put up with that."

"He's a hands-off owner; he always leaves things up to his hired help."

"What about the captain, then?"

"No help there. He was worried about his gratuity."

"Were there other guests?"

"The shithead's wife, and several of his hangers-on. He was a famous Italian actor — played all these macho-man parts."

"His wife? She let that go on?"

"Thought it was funny. She was amusing herself with the captain, so she didn't care."

"Wow. So how did you handle that?"

"Invited him to my cabin one night. While he was groping me, I cut the crotch out of his pants with a filet knife and threatened to neuter him if he touched me again."

"That sounds like something you learned from Sharktooth."

"It was. The previous summer, when I was down in Nicaragua with him and Phillip."

"What were you guys doing there?"

"Contract work for the DEA."

"The DEA hired a 15-year-old girl? What kind of contract work?"

"They didn't know I was part of the team. The mission was to blow up as many coke factories as we could find and make it look like the work of rebel forces. That meant any time we got a chance, we ambushed the government troops, too. It was great fun."

"You had a strange childhood. Your father let you do that?"

"Of course not. He thought I was in Bequia with Mrs. Walker."

"Did you have any friends your own age?"

"Sure."

"Girls? Or boys?"

"Both."

"So what did you guys do for fun?"

"I told you. We blew up coke refineries and killed government soldiers. They were all part of the rebel militia — lots of teenagers did that."

"That's terrible, Dani."

"The soldiers had it coming. They were on the drug lord's payroll. They would have done the same to us."

Liz shook her head and studied the sails. "We're about to sail right over Kick'em Jenny," she said, referring to the submerged, active volcano to the northwest of Grenada. "You want to come about or fall off to go around it?" she asked.

"Let's fall off. We'll leave it on our starboard side and bank on the wind clocking through the afternoon to pull us back to the east."

"WHAT THE HELL am I supposed to do for two weeks, Mike?" Cynthia Savage asked, pulling the sheet up to cover her breasts as she sat up in bed.

Mike Conrad stared at the ceiling, hands clasped behind his head. "What do you mean, Cyn? Sounds like fun to me."

"Right. Stuck on some boat with my freakin' father? For two whole weeks?"

"He's not that bad, as parents go, is he?"

"He's so full of shit. I know what he's up to; he showed me the brochure for this charter yacht. It's run by two young women — both hotties, from the pictures."

"Well, that'll keep him out of your hair, won't it? Can't you let the old man have his fun?"

"It's gonna be a long, dry spell, Mike."

"So? Find yourself some guy; there's bound to be some people your age around."

"I doubt it. We're meeting the boat in some nowhere place — a little, tiny island. It's so nowhere, it's taking me a whole day just to get there. I gotta fly to San Juan and then to Barbados and then to somewhere called St. Vincent. Then I get on, like, a freakin' ferry boat to get to this little island. I leave here in the morning and I won't get there until after dark. Besides, I was thinking about weed, not sex."

"I heard of that place," Mike said, sitting up and fumbling for his pants on the floor beside the bed. He felt through his pockets until he found a joint. Sticking it in his mouth, he lit it with a match from the bedside table. He took a deep hit and passed it to Cynthia, watching as she dropped the sheet to take it from him.

She held the smoke in her lungs for as long as she could.

After exhaling in a long sigh, she took a breath and said, "This is some good shit."

"Mm-hmm," Mike said.

"What did you mean?" she asked.

"When?"

"You said you'd heard of that place."

"Oh, yeah. St. Vincent. They grow lots of weed there. Good stuff, too. My friend's parents have a house on Mustique. That's part of St. Vincent and the Grenadines."

"They grow weed there?"

"Yeah. Good shit. He brought some back once, the dumb bastard."

"Dumb bastard? You said he was your friend."

"Yeah. Dumb for smuggling marijuana. Really stupid; no way it's worth the risk when it's so easy to buy it here."

ED SAVAGE FROWNED at his secretary. "I'm not going to be here tomorrow, Linda. I'm headed out of the country for a couple of weeks with Cynthia, remember?"

She nodded. "I told him, but he said he didn't care about your personal problems. You're on a retainer, and he needs you."

"Damn it all. See if you can change my flights. I'll call Cynthia."

"I already booked you on new flights. Same flights, but for day after tomorrow."

"What about Cyn?"

"I didn't change hers; she's already flown the first leg, remember? I could — "

"No, that's all right. I forgot she was stopping over to see the McCarthys in Miami Beach tonight. Might as well let her go ahead; it's too late to change the charter arrangements. They can pick her up in Bequia tomorrow night and I'll join them the next day. No big deal."

"Should I call that charter broker for you?"

"No. No need, really. I'll just let Cynthia know. She can tell the women on the yacht. Shouldn't make any difference to them."

"Okay, then. I'll call his secretary back and confirm the meeting."

2

"Welcome back, ladies," the customs officer said. "Always good to see you. You got some guests this time?"

"Thanks!" Liz said. "We do have guests, but we're picking them up here."

"Ah! That's good; mebbe they spend more money in Bequia that way." He grinned.

"Could be," Dani said. "We'll come back and add them to the paperwork before we go anywhere."

"That'll be fine," the man said. "When they come?"

"On the ferry this evening," Liz said. "Joe's Taxi's going to meet their flight and take them to the terminal in Kingstown."

"Mm-hmm," the man nodded and stamped the paperwork. "I probably see you in the morning, then. Enjoy Bequia."

"Thanks. We always do," Dani said, stuffing the papers in her shoulder bag as she and Liz walked out onto Bequia's main street. A lone car crept through the surging crowd of pedestrians like a mouse in a room full of cats.

"We've got some time to kill," Liz said.

"I thought you'd want to go to Gloria's and stock the larder. Or at least to the Rasta market, for some fruit," Dani said.

"It's too early to go shopping. I could use some coffee and maybe a snack."

"Shall we go to Mrs. Walker's, then?" Dani asked, stepping across the 18-inch span of the open sewer that ran between the steps of the government office building and the street.

"Sure," Liz said, turning to the south. "Sewer's ripe this morning."

"It's that onshore breeze," Dani said. "Keeps it from draining until the tide drops. It'll be fine in an hour or two."

They walked down the street, keeping to the west side of the flower bed that divided what was intended to be a vehicular lane from the pedestrian walkway. Liz stopped every few feet to examine some blossom that caught her eye.

"The flowers take care of the aroma down this way," she said.

Dani acknowledged Liz's comment with a nod, but her attention was drawn to a display of model boats that one of the street vendors was setting up in the shade of the trees that grew between the walkway and the beach.

"Mornin', Dani," the old man said, a snaggle-toothed grin breaking through the grizzled beard that covered his face. A big yellow, green, and red knit cap flopped over his head, hiding his dreadlocks.

"Good to see you, Sam. You thought anymore about that model of *Vengeance*?"

He chuckled. "Workin' on it. It's back at the shop; should be ready in a few days, dependin' on how busy t'ings are. You in a hurry, gal?"

"No, but we've got guests coming aboard tonight. I just thought if you had it ready, we might make a sale for you."

"I 'preciate that, Dani. I t'ink it's a good idea, 'bout offerin' the guests a model of *Vengeance*. Soon come, but it don' do to hurry this kind of work, see. It takes time to do it right, an' tha's the onliest way to do t'ings."

"Okay, Sam. No hurry. You just let me know."

"Oh, yes. I will do that. You ladies goin' to see Mrs. Walker, I 'spect?"

"Yes, we are."

"Tha's good. Tell her I see her fo' lunch in a bit, please. Ask her can she save me a goat roti, if you don' mind."

"Okay," Dani said, turning to find that Liz was window shopping across the way at a craft shop that featured hand-made batik fabric.

"Looking for something in particular?" Dani asked.

"No, but I was thinking some throw pillows out of that cloth would brighten up the main saloon."

"Want to go in?"

"Another time; I'm fading. I need that coffee."

"LINDA?" Cynthia said, holding her cell phone to her ear as her eyes scanned the faces in the gate area. "It's Cynthia, I'm — "

"Glad you called, Cynthia. Your dad's been trying to reach you. He's been delayed; he wants you to go ahead to Bequia. He's got a meeting today, but he's scheduled on the same flights tomorrow."

Cynthia swallowed, hard. "He ... why didn't he call me?"

"He tried your cell, but he couldn't reach you, so he called Anna's parent's place in Miami Beach. You were supposed to be visiting her, remember?"

"Um, right. I ... uh — "

"Never mind, Cynthia. It doesn't matter to me, but you're busted. Better get your story straight before tomorrow, kid."

"Thanks, Linda." Cynthia disconnected the call and joined the line waiting to board.

Once she reached her seat, she stashed her bag in the overhead compartment and strapped herself into the window seat. She needed to rest after her marathon evening with Mike, but sleep eluded her. She was too preoccupied with what to tell her father.

She'd been dating Mike since her sophomore year, when he had been a senior. Her father had never approved of her taste in boys, and Mike was no exception. She had worked hard to maintain her relationship with Mike since he'd gone away to the University of Miami, but her father had not allowed her to accept his invitations to come to football weekends or fraternity parties.

She'd used the Anna McCarthy ruse twice before, but both times she'd included brief visits with Anna and her parents at their place in Miami Beach. This opportunity had come up on short notice, and the McCarthys weren't there. She'd gambled and lost, but she'd think of something. Besides, the old man was a hypocrite. He chased anything in skirts, and she knew he caught more than his share. Who was he to tell her who she could date?

She woke up when the plane's tires hit the tarmac. Rubbing her eyes, she got to her feet and retrieved her bag. As she stretched her legs on the walk through the concourse in San Juan's airport, she thought about what Mike had said about his friend buying weed in St. Vincent. Aside from the aggravation of getting her caught in a lie, this change in her father's plans could be an opportunity.

She passed an ATM on her way to her connecting flight and replenished her cash; she would buy some of that high-grade grass when she got to St. Vincent. If her old man were busy with the two babes on the boat, she would have plenty of time to herself. She might as well be prepared.

AFTER SEVERAL HOURS ON SMALL, twin-engine commuter planes, Cynthia enjoyed the fresh air when she stepped onto the tarmac of E. T. Joshua Airport in St. Vincent. Even though she broke a sweat just from breathing, it was a relief to be in the open. After a

100-yard walk during which perspiration soaked through her blouse, she was inside the terminal. It was still warm, but at least the air-conditioning reduced the humidity.

She showed her passport to an immigration officer and breezed through baggage claim to customs, thankful that she had only a carry-on bag. She walked through the green-flagged, nothing-to-declare lane into the arrivals area and stood for a moment studying the crowd of taxi drivers holding hand-lettered placards.

Spotting one that said "Mr. Savage," she pushed through the crowd to the man holding it and explained that Mr. Savage was her father, and that he would be arriving at this time tomorrow. The young man with the placard nodded and smiled.

"Welcome to St. Vincent, Ms. Savage. You still wanting to go to Bequia?"

"Yes, please."

"My name is Wilbur, and I work for Joe's Taxi. Your charter company arranged for the pickup. Let me take your bag, and I'll show you to the van."

"Thanks, Wilbur," she said, handing him the carry-on. "That your first name?"

"Yes, ma'am," he said, and led her toward the exit. A white mini-van with the legend "Joe's Taxi and Tours" painted on the side sat idling at the curb, the air-conditioning running full blast.

As Wilbur hefted the bag into the back, she noticed his slim, muscular build. "Please, Wilbur, don't call me 'ma'am.' You make me feel like an old woman. My name's Cynthia."

He turned and nodded, a grin splitting his dark, handsome face. "Okay, then. Cynthia it is. We got some time to kill before the ferry to Bequia. If you'd like, I can take the scenic route and you can see some of our beautiful island." He opened the sliding door and gestured for her to climb in.

She held his eyes for a moment, smiling, and then ran her gaze over his torso, lingering on the ridges of muscle under the snug, cotton polo shirt. She couldn't miss the gold charm in the shape of a marijuana leaf that hung from the slender chain around his neck and dangled just below his Adam's apple. She batted her eyes and looked back up at him. "Is it okay if I ride up front?"

"Sure," he said, his eyes taking in her curves. "Whatever you'd like, Cynthia." He closed the sliding door and opened the front passenger door, extending a hand to help her up the step into the front seat. "You must wear the seat belt, though, in front."

She nodded, smiling, and buckled herself in as he got in and pulled away from the curb.

"We have an agricultural economy here," Wilbur said, as he gestured at the lush, green countryside just outside the airport.

"I've heard about that," she said. "A friend told me that you grow some fine weed here."

He took his foot off the gas and turned to look her in the eye for a moment. Whatever he saw seemed to satisfy him. He returned his attention to driving, and said, "Weed?"

"Grass, bud, ganja, whatever you want to call it," she said. "Guess it's a good cash crop."

"Your friend smoke?"

"Uh-huh. You?"

"From time to time, mebbe. You smoke?"

"When I can."

He reached up and plucked a fat joint from over the sun visor. Lighting it, he inhaled deeply and passed it to her. "You can, now," he grinned, exhaling as he spoke.

She took a hit and passed the joint back to him. "That's good stuff all right," she said, as she let the smoke out after twenty seconds. "Locally grown?"

He bobbed his head up and down. "Like your friend said, we grow some fine weed here."

"Any chance you could help a girl with a problem?"

"Could be. Depends on the problem."

"Uh-huh," she said. "I thought you might be able to."

"What do you need? Weed's not a big deal, but other stuff's not so easy."

"Weed's what I'm looking for. I'm gonna be on a boat for two weeks, so I kinda need to stock up."

"No problem. You got cash?" Seeing her hesitation, he said, "I only ask 'cause I can stop at a bank machine if you need to."

"How much?"

"Twenty — that's U.S. dollars, not E.C. That'll get you a good stash. Enough for you to take care of a few friends, maybe, for a couple of weeks."

"How do we make it happen?"

"Easy. I make a phone call. When we get to the ferry terminal, you pay me, like you payin' for the taxi. There's a bar on the ferry. You order a Piton and some salted nuts. The bartender will give you the beer and a paper bag with the nuts and a baggie in it. No big deal."

"You've done this before," she said.

"Mebbe so," he said taking another hit and passing the joint back to her.

"Make your call, Wilbur," she said, as she raised the spliff to her lips.

FESTUS JACOBS SAT in the shade of the awning on the upper deck of the ferry as it idled against the dock in Bequia. He could see the people disembarking from here, and he knew they couldn't see him. The girl strolled down the ramp with that loose-jointed gait that marked her as stoned to those in the know. He'd spotted her earlier in the bar when she made the pickup. She must have sampled the goods on the crossing.

He didn't monitor transactions like this as a rule, but the Dragon Lady was interested in this girl. That meant money, and Festus believed in following money.

He saw her approach the two women who held a sign with the name "*Vengeance*" lettered on it; that must be the name of the yacht. They were making this too easy. He had expected to have to follow the girl to learn the boat's name, but now he didn't even have to get off the ferry.

He stood, turning away from the crowd ashore and looking out over the harbor. Removing a small pair of binoculars from his shoulder bag, he swept his gaze across the boats at anchor, pausing on the fanciest looking one. He put the glasses to his eyes and adjusted the focus, estimating that the boat was around 60 feet in length.

The hull gleamed white in the late afternoon sun, and the varnished brightwork sparkled like gold. The boat swung slightly with the breeze, and he was able to make out the beginning of the name picked out in gold leaf on the transom. Everything about the vessel screamed money, even the oversized U.S. flag that wafted in the gentle breeze.

There would be plenty of money from this one, and not much risk. Marissa Chen — the diminutive, middle-aged woman that everyone called the Dragon Lady — had enough of the senior police officers on her payroll to make this work. Festus could run small-time scams on his own, but just looking at that boat told him this would be too big for him and his cronies. He was happy to be working for the Dragon Lady on this one.

3

Cynthia had rolled a joint from her new stash and smoked it on the ferry. She was feeling mellow when she looked over the crowd at the foot of the gangway. She spotted the two women pictured in the brochure her father had shown her. One of them held a placard bearing a line drawing of a sailboat and the legend, "*Vengeance*." Going with the flow of the crowd, she took almost a minute to reach them.

"Hi," she said, stopping in front of them and dropping her bag. "I'm Cynthia Savage."

"Welcome to the islands, Cynthia. I'm Liz Chirac, and this is Dani Berger. Is your dad far behind you?"

"Um, he couldn't make it today. He got sucked into some kind of meeting with a client." Cynthia grinned, waiting.

"Is he still coming?" Dani asked after several seconds, frowning.

"Who?"

"Your father. Who else?" Dani snapped.

"Oh. I guess. Linda said he's on the same flights, um, tomorrow, I think."

"Who's Linda?" Liz asked, stepping forward so that she was between Dani and Cynthia.

"Linda? Oh, yeah. Linda Mason. She's his, um ... his secretary."

"You must be tired," Liz said, cutting Dani off as she was about to speak. "Let's get you back to *Vengeance* and get you settled. We'll show you around Bequia tomorrow while we wait for your dad."

"Mm, 'kay. Might as well," the girl said, yawning.

Dani picked up Cynthia's carry-on bag and stomped off to the dinghy dock, leaving Cynthia and Liz in her wake. She flung the bag into the dinghy, jumped aboard, and had the engine started before Liz escorted the girl down the dock. When they got back to *Vengeance*, Liz took the girl below and settled her in one of the midship staterooms.

"Let me know if you need anything, Cynthia," she said. "Anything at all. Drink, snack, extra bedding, whatever."

"I'm good, thanks, Liz," Cynthia said, closing the door as Liz left.

"Charming girl," Dani sneered, as Liz joined her in the cockpit.

"Give her a break, Dani. That's a miserable trip, and you know it."

"Especially for a stoner."

"Stoner?" Liz asked.

"She's wrecked," Dani said.

"Oh, she's just beat, I imagine," Liz said.

"Spaced out, bloodshot eyes — she's been toking. You tell her about zero tolerance?"

"No. Elaine would have covered that in the package she sent them."

"Don't bet that little Miss Congeniality bothered to read it, even if her father shared it with her."

"I'm going below to get a glass of wine. You need one, too. Want anything else?"

"No, but the wine does sound good."

Liz stepped below and returned in a moment with a bottle of chilled white table wine and two glasses. She filled one and handed it to Dani.

When Liz had her own glass in hand, Dani said, "I have a bad feeling about this one."

"Lighten up, Dani. You have a bad feeling about most charters. Sometimes I wonder why you're even in this business."

"It's because of the boats, not the people," Dani said.

"At least see what Cynthia's like after a night's rest before you write her off; two weeks could be a long time with your attitude."

"Hmph," Dani grumbled. "She's — "

The buzz of her phone interrupted her. She glanced at the screen. "That's odd. Sam sent me a text asking me to call him ASAP."

"Sam?" Liz asked.

"The model boat guy," Dani said, raising the phone to her ear. She listened for a few seconds, nodded her head, and said, "Thanks, Sam," before she disconnected the call.

"What's up?" Liz said.

"His nephew's a cop. Sam was showing him the model of *Vengeance*, and the nephew remarked that the drug squad from St. Vincent was planning a raid in Bequia later this evening. We're the target."

"What?!"

"The nephew heard the guy in charge of the drug squad calling his team together. He mentioned *Vengeance* by name, and told them they were headed for Bequia for a bust, that he'd been tipped by the regular dealer."

"So do you think — "

"No 'think' involved. Miss Cynthia bought herself a couple of ounces of weed on her way from St. Vincent."

"What are we — "

"Let's get under way. The best thing we can do is be gone when they get here. We can sort out the aftermath later, after we ditch her stash."

"WHERE ARE WE GOING?" Liz asked. "We don't have clearance papers to leave."

"As far out to the west as we can get," Dani said. "I figure we might make it outside the limit before they find us."

Vengeance was plowing through the long-period swells at almost ten knots, her diesel wide open and the Yankee jib drawing as she ran dead downwind in the 20-knot easterly trade winds.

"Then what? Are you thinking we'll clear out at Union or somewhere? We'll still have to go back to Bequia to pick up Ed Savage."

"We'll go back in the morning," Dani said. "After we make sure we're clean. Get in mid-morning, and drop the hook."

"How do you plan to make sure we're clean?"

"Take the helm. I'm going to wake up our little princess and put the fear of God into her."

"Dani, let me — "

"No. This is a job for the iron fist, not the velvet glove."

"Don't hurt her, Dani. She's just a kid."

"An almost adult kid who could cost us our boat, Liz. Don't worry; I won't hurt her, much. Not unless she's more aggressive than she seemed."

Dani went below, and moments later Liz heard a crash, followed by a scream of sheer terror. The scream ended abruptly with a resounding slap, and she heard Dani's voice.

"Shut up and listen to me, or I'll give you something to scream about. Where's your stash?"

Liz cringed as she heard a sob, and then soft words, followed by another solid slap.

She heard Cynthia's raised voice. "My father's a lawyer, and he'll — "

"Don't even start that. He's nobody in St. Vincent. They won't even let him visit you in prison, and if you think I won't have you locked up after I get through kicking your ass, you're dreaming. Besides, I'm betting he doesn't know you're a doper, does he?"

Liz heard a whimper, followed by Dani screaming, "Answer me, you little shit!"

"N-no. Please, if you don't tell — "

"Don't start trying to bargain with me. Hand over your stash, all of it, right now, or I'll make you hurt like you never imagined."

A few seconds later, Dani appeared in the companionway, a Ziploc bag in her hand. She opened it and emptied the contents over the side of the boat, holding the bag downwind and well away from *Vengeance* as she shook the last bits out. She ripped the bag into two pieces and tossed it into the water.

"Please," Cynthia sobbed, crawling through the companionway onto the bridge deck. "You don't know what he'll — "

"I couldn't care less," Dani said, cutting her off. "You have no idea how close you came to getting us all locked up. Whoever you bought that grass from reported you to the cops. We could still lose our boat and go to jail, and believe me, you don't want to go to jail in St. Vincent. Especially if I'm your cellmate."

"Why would — "

"Get out of my sight. I don't want to look at you right now; I need to think and make some phone calls to see if I can get us out of this mess. Go!"

Dani took the helm, and Liz moved to stand beside the distraught girl. "Come on below," Liz said, putting an arm around Cynthia's shoulders. "I'll make us some herbal tea, and we'll sort this out."

VENGEANCE, still running before the wind under sail, was about 25 miles west of Bequia and the big island of St. Vincent. Dani had shut the diesel down after she checked the radar and saw that no vessels were following them.

"You really scared her," Liz said, taking a seat beside Dani.

"Good. She should be scared. We aren't out of this yet."

"What's your plan?" Liz asked.

"What's she doing?"

"She's asleep. Once I got her calmed down and told her how serious the drug laws were down here, she started dozing off and spilled her tea. I got her settled in her berth and she was dead to the world in a minute or two. What are we going to do?"

"We'll go back to Bequia, but not until I can find out what's going on."

Liz chewed on her lower lip for a beat or two. "I'm not sure I understand."

"Well, she did ask a reasonable question. Or was about to, when I cut her off. I can only think of one reason why the dealer would have tipped the cops."

"You think he was trying to curry favor or something?"

"That's a possibility, but it's more likely that they were planning a shakedown."

"A shakedown? How would that work?"

"Oh, it's a fairly common scheme down here," Dani said. "The dealer lines up a crooked cop and tips him when a tourist makes a buy. The cop busts the buyer, but he keeps the whole thing off the books and takes a payoff from the tourist to forget about it. The cop and the dealer split the money. Cynthia was a perfect mark — a spoiled rich kid. They'd have locked us all up until her father showed, and then put the squeeze on him, big-time. Us, too, and they'd have impounded Vengeance in the bargain."

"How are we going to keep them from doing that when we get

back? If they're crooked, won't they just plant some marijuana on *Vengeance* and go ahead with their scheme?"

"They probably would, but not all the cops are crooked. Phillip's got a long-standing relationship with the Chief Superintendent. We'll stay out of their waters until he can get in touch and let us know it's safe for us to go back. I just hope Cynthia wasn't holding out on me. We may still get searched. If she's got more drugs, we're screwed."

"I don't think she has anything else, Dani. She was shaken up by this, worried about her father's reaction. She's already in trouble with him for sneaking off to meet a boy when she was supposed to be visiting a girlfriend and her parents at their vacation home in Miami Beach."

Dani's face split in a grin. "Now, that makes me like her a little better. How'd he catch her?"

"He tried to call the girlfriend's parent's place to tell Cynthia about his change in plans. When he got their voice mail, the message said to call them at their place in Atlanta, so he did. You can guess the rest."

"No wonder she didn't want him to know about the weed, then."

"Are you going to tell him? She's really worried about that."

"I'm not sure we'll have a choice. It depends on how things play out back in Bequia. If we manage to get clear, I guess there's no reason to add to her problems. Sounds like she's in enough trouble already. Maybe she'll learn something about the risks of dabbling in drugs."

Liz looked at her wrist watch. "It'll be sunrise before too long. Should I make us some coffee?"

"Sure. I don't think we'll be going to bed any time soon. Maybe if we're lucky, we can squeeze in a nap this afternoon before her father comes."

Liz stood up and stepped toward the companionway.

"Hey, Liz?" Dani said.

"Yes?"

"Bring the sat phone when you come back. I'll call Phillip after we have a cup of coffee. He'll be up soon anyway. May as well give him time to think about this before the Chief Super gets to work."

4

"WHAT DID HE SAY?" LIZ ASKED, PUTTING A PLATE OF SLICED FRUIT on the cockpit table.

"He agrees that it's probably a shakedown; he says there's been a resurgence of that sort of thing recently. Thanks for the fruit."

"You're welcome. So he'll call his friend?"

"Yes. He'll be back in touch. He thought we should stay lost for the time being, though."

"Hmm. Think we'll be able to get back in time to meet Ed Savage?"

Dani shrugged. "I hope so. Otherwise, we'll have to tell him what's going on. We should probably prepare Cynthia for that, just in case."

"Prepare me for what?" Cynthia asked, rubbing her eyes as she stepped through the companionway.

"Have some fruit," Liz said. "And there's coffee, if you want."

"No coffee, thanks. But the fruit looks yummy. What's going on? Where are we, anyway?"

"We're about 20 miles from Bequia," Dani said, "waiting for things to settle down."

"I feel like a fool. I thought weed was okay down here, with the Rastas and all."

"Yes, well, there's certainly enough misinformation in the media to give you that impression," Liz said.

"Cynthia?" Dani asked.

"Yes?" Cynthia dropped her fork and began twisting her napkin, cowering as she turned to face Dani.

"Sorry I was so rough on you last night. I didn't think we had time for any drawn-out discussion after my friend tipped me to the raid."

"Okay, I didn't know; Liz explained ... "

"She told me," Dani said. "Look, I was your age not so long ago; we all make mistakes. It's part of growing up. I did a lot of stuff that I didn't want my parents to know about."

Cynthia put down the napkin. Her face relaxed a bit, and she forced a smile. "Like what?"

"There'll be time for that later," Dani said. "Right now, we need to deal with the fallout from this drug thing."

"Okay. I'm really sorry; I'm blown away by the dealer calling the cops. Why would he do that?"

Dani explained the shakedown theory and the gravity of being caught with drugs on a yacht in most of the island countries.

"Liz told me about that last night. I had no idea they were more strict than the U.S., or that I could get you guys in trouble. But this sucks. It's my own fault, but I'm going to be in so much trouble with my father. I mean, like, I already am. I — "

"I shared that with Dani," Liz interrupted.

"We may have a problem keeping him out of this," Dani said. "It depends on how we come out with the authorities."

"You mean you might not tell him?" Cynthia said, her voice softening as she raised her eyebrows.

"Only if we have to," Dani said. "It sounds like you're in enough trouble already."

"Oh! Thank you," the girl said, jumping to her feet and wrapping Dani in a hug. "Thank you, thank you."

Dani extricated herself from the hug and said, "No promises, Cynthia. Like I said, it depends on how we come out. We need to get this sorted out in a hurry if we're going to get back to Bequia and pick up your father this evening. Otherwise, he's probably going to have to know."

"So you think you can fix this with the cops?"

"I grew up in the islands; I have lots of friends in different places. That's how I got tipped off last night."

"I thought you were American. How'd you come to grow up down here?"

"Well," Dani said, "the short version is that my mother's American and my father's French. From Martinique, originally, but he lives in Paris now. When I was a little younger than you are, they split up. I ended up farmed out to some of my father's friends and relatives down here in the summers. He was still living in Martinique then, but he traveled all the time on business."

"That's so cool," Cynthia said, her face bright. "Did you spend — "

Her question was interrupted by the ringing of the satellite phone.

"Excuse me," Dani said, as she picked up the phone and looked at the screen.

"Hi, Phillip," she said.

FESTUS FORCED his face into a calm mask; he wouldn't reveal his anxiety to the Dragon Lady. Her dwarf bodyguard, Li Wong, had picked Festus up from the bar where he spent his idle time. Wong was a sneaky bastard. Festus hadn't known he was there until Wong nudged his elbow, making him spill beer down the front of his shirt.

He had jumped to his feet, ready for a brawl, and looked down to see the little shit grinning up at him, a straight razor poised against the inside of Festus's thigh. He had seen Wong kill a man that way once, the victim bleeding out, dying almost before he knew the dwarf had cut his artery.

"What?" Festus had growled.

Wong folded the razor and gestured with his head for Festus to follow him. Now Wong was behind him as Festus sat in front of the Dragon Lady's desk. Festus wasn't sure which made him more nervous: the woman's reptilian gaze, or the dwarf's silent presence, looming close but out of sight.

"You are an embarrassment," the woman said.

Festus waited, silent.

"Are you not going to attempt some explanation?" she asked, hissing as she emphasized 'some,' the sibilance reinforcing her snake-like image.

"What you want me to 'splain, ma'am?"

"You wasted my time, and the time of my minions."

"I'm sorry, ma'am. I don't know what 'minions' is."

"The police officers who are in my pay, you buffoon."

"Ma'am, I still don't know how I've upset you." He flinched as he felt the icy edge of the razor come to rest, touching the crease where his right ear met the side of his head.

She shifted her gaze, looking over his shoulder, and smiled as she shook her head. "Not yet, little one. But soon, perhaps. I think not his ear, though. Maybe something more personal, something that won't be visible in public."

He felt the razor lift and heard a snort of laughter from Wong. "I just passed along what I saw," Festus said.

"You really don't know, do you?" She shook her head again, her face a smooth mask. "I won't let Wong cut you until you understand how you have failed. Tell him, Wong."

"There was no such yacht," Wong said, his voice a high-pitched snarl in Festus's ear. Those were the first words Wong had spoken during the entire encounter.

"But I saw it, ma'am. I followed the girl on the ferry after I — "

Pain exploded in his head and he fell from the chair, rolling onto his side as the dwarf kicked him again and again. Before he lost consciousness, he wondered how the little devil had kicked him in the head while he was sitting in the chair. Could the bastard fly?

"Take him away," Chen said, smiling at the pleasure on Wong's scrunched-up face as he panted from his exertion. "But keep him alive. Find out who told him about the girl. Take that person as well. Keep them separated, and don't mess them up. We may need to use them before this is over."

Li Wong nodded and began to drag the heavier man from her office.

"And Wong?"

He stopped and turned to face her, bowing slightly and waiting.

"Come back when you are finished. I want you."

She smiled at his effort to suppress his grin until he was out of her office. She always wanted him after she saw him hurt some-one; it never failed to excite her.

Cynthia sat in a corner of the cockpit, listening without comment as Dani told Liz about Phillip's conversation with the Chief Superintendent of St. Vincent's police force. When Dani had finished summarizing what he had said, Cynthia cleared her throat. Dani looked her in the eye, smiled, and nodded her head.

"Is this Phillip a lawyer of some kind?" she asked.

Liz grinned as Dani stifled a laugh.

"Sorry, Cynthia," Dani said. "That's a reasonable question, but the idea of Phillip as a lawyer just hit my funny bone. I can't imagine a less likely person as a lawyer."

"That's true," Liz added, "but I can't think of anybody I'd rather have on my side in a confrontation with the police anywhere down here."

Cynthia's brow wrinkled in a puzzled frown.

"He's a former business partner of my father's," Dani said. "He's been down in the islands forever. Before he went in business with Papa, he was some kind of agent for the U.S. government. He was an Army officer, too. He knows everybody in law enforcement and the military in the islands and Central America."

"Quite a few people in South America, too," Liz added.

"He's like my older brother," Dani said. "He's the one that I always went to when I was a kid and needed advice and couldn't ask my parents."

"And he thinks this is going to be okay?" Cynthia asked.

"He got a positive reaction from the Chief Superintendent of St. Vincent's police force; they've known one another for a long time. We'll know more once the Chief has had time to do a little checking. We aren't in the clear just yet, though."

"Is Phillip in St. Vincent?" Cynthia asked.

"He lives in Martinique. If we go there, you'll probably meet him. He often invites our guests to dinner at his house," Dani said.

"His wife's a first-rate French chef," Liz added. "She's from one of the old French families in Martinique, like Dani's father, and they like to entertain."

"So is Martinique, like, a French colony or something?"

"It's actually a department of France," Dani said. "Guadeloupe is, too. They're the biggest and the richest islands in the Eastern

Caribbean. The people are French citizens; they speak French and vote in the French elections. Their currency is the euro."

"That's really cool," Cynthia said. "I didn't know that. Are we going to head back to Bequia now?"

"Not just yet. Phillip thought we should hang around out here until he heard back from the Chief. If we get the all-clear, it'll only take us a couple of hours to get back. We've been edging back to the east since sunrise, but I want to stay in international waters for now."

"So what do you think will happen? Are they going to arrest the crooked cop? And Wilbur?"

"It's hard to say. Things like this often don't move in a straight line in this part of the world. St. Vincent's a sovereign nation, but it's not any bigger than a small town in the states. Everybody knows everybody else's business; there are lots of family relationships and confusing political alliances," Liz said.

"Who's Wilbur?" Dani asked.

"Oh. He's the taxi driver I bought the weed from."

"I see," Dani said. "Well, I don't know. I'd be surprised if the police didn't want a statement from you, but we'll just have to wait and see. There's a range of possibilities. The whole problem could just disappear like it never happened, or there could be some kind of major scandal. We'll know more in a little bit. Just hope for the best," Dani said.

5

"WE HAVE AN APPOINTMENT WITH SOMEONE FROM THE OFFICE OF
the Chief Superintendent of the Royal St. Vincent and the
Grenadines Police Force," Dani said, addressing the man behind
the counter in Bequia's government building.

The man looked down at a sheet of paper on the counter.
"Would you be Ms. Berger?"

"Yes, I am."

"And the other ladies? They are Ms. Chirac and Ms. Savage?"

"That's right," Dani said.

The man stepped to his right and opened a door into the
lobby. Motioning for them to come behind the counter, he said,
"Follow me, please."

He led them down a short hallway to a closed door marked
"Boardroom," and knocked.

"Come in," they heard. The voice was deep and well-
modulated.

Their guide opened the door and stepped aside, gesturing
for them to enter. A tall, handsome man in his middle years
stood behind a massive table, smiling as he studied them. Dani
took in the well-tailored, dark blue suit, his blue-black skin tone,

and his immaculate grooming as she made room for Liz and Cynthia.

"Please, ladies, be seated. May I offer you refreshments?"

"Nothing for me, thank you," Dani said, realizing from his appearance that this must be the Chief Superintendent. Although she'd never met him, she was relieved by his personal involvement. She knew from Phillip and her father that he was an honest and reasonable man.

"No, thanks," Liz and Cynthia said, in chorus.

"That will be all, Penford," their host said, and their escort left, closing the door.

"Thank you for coming. I'm Rupert Mason, the Chief Superintendent of the Royal St. Vincent and the Grenadines Police Force. Ms. Berger, I recognize you; you very much resemble your father, at least as he looked before you were born. It's been too long since I've had the pleasure of his company. Would you other ladies be kind enough to tell me your names?"

Once Liz and Cynthia had introduced themselves, Mason sat down across the conference table from the three of them.

"As you might imagine, this is a somewhat sensitive situation. I'm assuming Phillip Davis has filled you in?"

"Yes," Dani said. "He told us what he knew."

Mason folded his hands on the table and gazed out the window for a moment. "We haven't been able to find the commander of the drug interdiction unit. We had not yet discovered that he was absent when I last spoke with Mr. Davis. He did sign out a patrol boat last night, and the crew took him and two of his men to Bequia. They returned to Kingstown after they were unable to find your yacht. There are some irregularities. To begin with, there was no warrant issued to authorize the boarding and search of your yacht. In fact, there was no paperwork of any kind. He told the crew of the patrol boat that he had a tip from a well-known drug dealer, a man called Festus Jacobs."

He let the silence hang for a moment, staring at Cynthia. "Ms.

Savage, do you recognize that name?"

"No. I'm sorry, but I don't."

"You ladies understand that this is all off the record?" Mason asked.

Liz, Dani, and Cynthia nodded.

"Ms. Savage, we know that you were in possession of a sizeable amount of marijuana when you left the ferry yesterday afternoon. That is a very serious offense. You could be sentenced to several years in prison. Do you understand this?"

Cynthia swallowed. "Y-yes," she said.

"And you know that you could have cost Ms. Berger and Ms. Chirac their yacht, and possibly caused them to be sentenced to prison as well?"

"Yes, sir. I thought — "

"Because of my long relationship with Ms. Berger's father and Phillip Davis, I'm taking their word that you made a mistake; that you were misled by this taxi driver, who told you that marijuana was not illegal in our country. I need to hear you say that you've learned your lesson from this unfortunate experience."

"Oh, yes, sir. I definitely have."

"Good. Then there will be no repercussions for any of you, as long as you're willing to cooperate in our investigation."

"Thank you," Dani said.

"Yes, thanks," Cynthia said.

"Did you get the name of the taxi driver, Ms. Savage?"

"Wilbur is his first name. That's all I know."

"We booked the pickup with Joe's Taxi and Tours," Liz added.

"Thank you. That will help."

"Will I have to go to court?" Cynthia asked. "I'm only here for — "

Mason raised a big, manicured hand, interrupting her. "I don't think so. We understand that you're only here for a short visit, and we have ample evidence to proceed against these men without your testimony. However, I have had a statement drawn up for your signature. It's a mere formality, but I need it in my file to support opening an investigation into this matter. I believe it's accurate based on what Mr. Davis told me, but I want you to read it carefully. If there's anything in it that's not correct, please mark it up and initial the changes, and I'll do the same. Ms. Berger and Ms. Chirac, I'll ask that you sign as witnesses to Ms. Savage's signature — not to the accuracy of the contents."

He took an envelope from the inside pocket of his jacket and withdrew a single, typewritten sheet. He passed it to Cynthia, waiting in silence as she read it. When she looked up, he asked, "Did I get it right?"

"Yes, sir," Cynthia said.

He handed her a heavy, gold pen, and she and Dani and Liz signed the statement.

"Thank you, ladies," he said, folding the sheet back into the envelope and returning it and the pen to his inside pocket. "It was a pleasure to meet you, though I regret the circumstances. Ms. Berger, please tell your father hello. I hope that someday we'll meet again; he's a true gentleman."

"Thank you, Mr. Mason. I'll do that."

"Ms. Savage?"

"Yes, sir?"

"You're a lucky young woman. Don't step out of line again; you may not be so fortunate next time you run afoul of the law."

"Y-yes. Thank you, Mr. Mason."

"You should be careful for the next few days, until we have these men in custody. I don't think you're in danger, but this is a small country, and they may worry that you can identify them, Ms. Savage."

"We'll keep our guard up," Dani said. "Thanks again, Mr. Mason."

"My pleasure. Please remember to pass on my greetings to your father."

"I certainly will."

"Good day, ladies. Enjoy the rest of your time in St. Vincent and the Grenadines."

———————

"Back to the boat?" Liz asked, as they stepped out of the government building into the midday sun. "It's past lunch time."

"How about lunch at Mrs. Walker's?" Dani asked. "My treat. That'll keep you out of the galley, Liz, and then we can crash until time to meet your father, Cynthia."

"Good idea," Liz said.

"Fine with me," Cynthia said. "Is Mrs. Walker's a restaurant?"

Dani smiled, and Liz said, "Among other things. She has a little store that sells groceries and liquor, and a funky little dining room that serves some of the best local dishes I've ever eaten."

"Her late husband was another of my father's associates," Dani said. "When I was little, I used to stay with her a lot while they were working."

"What did your father do?" Cynthia asked, as they walked along the tree-shaded lane that served as Bequia's main street.

"Oh, he's in the import/export business; he trades mostly in heavy machinery. Back when he was starting out, he spent a lot of time courting government officials."

"Hey, Dani!" Sam, the model boat builder, called, interrupting their conversation.

Dani stopped at his folding table, glancing at his wares as she said, "Good morning, Sam. Thanks for the tip last night."

"Everyt'ing good?" he asked.

"Ev'y li'l t'ing gonna be a'right," Dani said, picking up one of his models and turning it in her hands.

"You like it?" he asked, grinning, winking at Liz and Cynthia.

"Yes, I do." She handed the carved, painted model to Liz. "What do you think?"

"It looks like *Vengeance*," Cynthia said, "but not exactly."

"You got a good eye, missy," Sam said.

"Sam, meet Cynthia Savage," Dani said. "Cynthia and her father are our guests for a while."

"Welcome to Bequia," Sam said.

"Thank you," Cynthia said. "That's a beautiful model."

Sam smiled. "*Vengeance* is a beautiful yacht. I make some of the details different on the model, 'cause t'ings don' always look right when you make 'em so small, see?"

"Yes, I do see. I'm studying art, and I'm learning about that sort of thing; it's true in drawing and painting, as well. You have to try to capture the effect that the subject has on the eye, rather than just scaling it down."

"Tha's a ver' good way to say it, I t'ink. Liz call it artistic license, mebbe, or perspective. Right, Liz?"

"Right. I didn't know you were an artist, Cynthia."

"Liz paint pictures," Sam said. "They look like photographs, only more real. Make you want to touch t'ings."

"I'd like to see some of your paintings, Liz. That sounds really cool."

"Most of the paintings aboard *Vengeance* are Liz's," Dani said.

"Do you paint, Cynthia?" Liz asked.

"I'm learning, but I'm not very good."

"Me, too. We all get better with every brush stroke, right, Sam?"

"Yes, but you ver' good, jus' the same."

"Did you bring your stuff, Cynthia?" Liz asked.

"No, just a sketch book."

"Well, if you have the urge, you're welcome to use mine. Just let me know. I'd love to see your work."

"Let's get lunch, you two," Dani said. "If I weren't starving, I'd fall asleep on my feet. I like the model, Sam. Let me know when you're satisfied enough with it to sell it."

"I will, Dani. Soon come. Stay safe; I'm glad t'ings come out okay las' night."

6

"Hi, Dad! Over here," Cynthia called, waving, as Ed Savage made his way through the crowd disembarking from the ferry.

"Hello, Cyn," he said, with a curt nod, as his eyes swept over Liz and stopped on Dani.

"Welcome to Bequia, Mr. Savage," Dani said, reaching for his carry-on bag.

"Thanks, I've got it," he said, shifting the bag to his left hand and grasping her extended right hand in his own.

He held her small, callused hand for a beat too long, looking into her eyes until she blinked and withdrew her hand. "You must be Dani."

"Yes," she said, "and this is Liz Chirac." She inclined her head in Liz's direction.

He barely glanced at Liz, fixing his eyes on Dani again. "Your picture in the brochure's attractive, but it doesn't do justice to your eyes. They're a blue like I've never seen before, like the ocean."

Out of the corner of her eye, Dani saw Liz and Cynthia exchange glances. Cynthia rolled her eyes and Liz smirked.

"You must be tired, Mr. Savage," Liz said. "Let's get you settled on *Vengeance* with something cold to drink in your hand while I cook your 'welcome aboard' dinner. We waited for you, instead of having it last night."

"Great. Thanks," he said, still looking at Dani and grinning. "Oh, and please call me Ed. I left Mr. Savage back in the office."

Liz and Cynthia led the way to the dinghy dock, Dani and Ed trailing behind them.

"Cynthia told me you're a lawyer," Dani said, sneaking a look at Ed's chiseled profile as they picked their way across the sandy lot between the ferry dock and the dinghy dock. "What sort of law do you practice?"

"I'm a trial lawyer — civil litigation. Mostly, I represent plaintiffs in product liability cases."

"I see. And your office is in Atlanta, I believe?"

"That's right."

"Are you in a big firm?"

"No. I don't like partners."

"No wonder your vacation got delayed, then. It must be hard to get away if you're solo."

"Well, I do have a bunch of lawyers working for me. I just like to call all the shots."

"I can understand that. I was never any good at being a 'team player,' as they called it. That's how I ended up doing this."

"What did you do before?" Ed asked.

"My mother's family's in the investment banking business. I spent a couple of years not fitting in and finally decided to follow my passion."

"Always a good choice. How did you find a passion for the sea?"

"My father. He's always been a yachtsman."

"Is he in the investment banking business, too?"

"No. He's in international trade, but he has several big yachts in charter in the Med. It's a sideline for him. He passed on his love of sailing to me."

"Do your parents live in New York? I think of New York when I hear 'investment banking,' I guess."

"My mother does. You're right about the bank being there. My parents split up long ago, though. My father's French, from Martinique, originally, but he lives in Paris, now."

"Oops," he said, putting a hand on her shoulder and directing her attention to the dinghy dock. "Guess we'd better catch up."

Dani looked around, stunned to discover that the two of them had stopped in the little park while they were talking. Liz and Cynthia were standing on the dinghy dock, chatting as they waited.

"I SHOULD WARN HER," Cynthia said to Liz as they watched Dani and Ed.

"About your father?"

"Yeah. He's smooth with the ladies. It's like a game with him."

"She's a big girl," Liz said. "I don't think he'll get very far with her."

"I hope not, for her sake. He's a real shit where women are concerned. I mean, he's nice to them, but he's like a tomcat; he can't keep it in his pants."

"Cynthia! You're talking about your father," Liz said, blushing.

"Well, it's true. He breaks the heart of every woman he takes a fancy to. It's embarrassing to be around him."

"At least he's not berating you for sneaking off with your boyfriend," Liz said.

"Oh, he'll get there once we're alone. And he doesn't know for sure where I was. Only that I wasn't with my girlfriend. It's just that he's got his eye on Dani right now. It's a question of priorities for him. He needs to line up his entertainment. Watch yourself; you'll probably be next."

As DANI and Ed walked onto the dinghy dock, she saw a man scramble up from a go-fast boat that had pulled in next to where Liz and Cynthia were standing. When he shoved Liz aside and grabbed Cynthia, Dani charged forward. He was pushing the struggling girl toward the waiting boat when Dani brought her fist down on the top of his spine in a hammer blow.

Stunned, he released Cynthia and whirled to confront Dani, swinging his right fist in a powerful round-house punch. She lurched toward him, stepping inside the punch and trapping his right arm with her left as she drove her right elbow into his throat with enough force to collapse his windpipe. She followed through with a knee to his groin. He gagged and fell backward into the waiting boat, both hands pressed to his throat as he tried to breathe. The boat roared away into the gathering darkness.

Dani turned to see Liz and Ed helping Cynthia to her feet. "You okay?" she asked.

"Yes," Cynthia said.

"Liz?" Dani looked at her friend.

"I'm fine. He took me by surprise."

"He won't be grabbing anybody else for a while," Dani said.

"Thanks to you," Ed said.

Dani noticed that he was looking at her with a mix of awe and fear, eyes wide and face white. She was disappointed; she realized she'd been enjoying his attention earlier. She knew that most men were put off by women who kicked male ass. "It was just instinct," she said, annoyed to hear an apologetic tone in her voice.

"I don't think so. You've honed those moves; I've seen boxers that weren't that fast."

"You box?" Dani asked.

"I tried, when I was in college, but I didn't have the killer instinct, according to my coach. I got tired of getting my ass kicked in the ring, so I decided to take out my aggression in court."

Dani nodded.

"What did they want with Cynthia?" Ed asked, after a moment.

Dani saw a look of panic flash across the girl's face at his question. She winked at Cynthia and shrugged. "Hard to say. Unprovoked personal attacks are almost unheard of down here. He must have been high on something, or maybe he mistook her for someone else."

"Shouldn't we call the cops?" Ed asked.

"Those guys are long-gone. The cops will just tie us up filling out reports and nothing will come of it, but if you want to, we can," she said.

Ed thought about that for a few seconds and looked at Cynthia, raising his eyebrows.

"Let's just forget it, Dad. No harm done."

7

"WANT A NIGHTCAP?" LIZ ASKED DANI, AS SHE HUNG THE DISH
towel in its place. Their guests had retired to their cabins half an
hour earlier. "I'm not sleepy yet, after that nap this afternoon."

"I'm not, either," Dani said. "Do we have any of that shrub
left?"

"Sure," Liz said, putting two glasses on a tray. She reached into
their liquor locker and extracted a half-empty bottle of
Martinique's signature liqueur. Pouring two fingers into each
glass, she handed Dani the tray. "I'll join you in the cockpit in a
second. I just want to set out the coffee stuff for tomorrow
morning."

Dani was no sooner seated than Liz sat down across from her.
She handed Liz a glass and raised her own, extending it toward
her friend.

"Cheers," Liz said, touching her glass to Dani's. She took a sip
of the shrub and said, "How are you feeling about our guests,
now."

"He's really handsome, with those dark eyes and the black,
curly hair," Dani said.

Liz hid her smile behind her glass. It was a rare thing for Dani to be so unguarded.

"His skin's so smooth," Dani continued.

"Cynthia wanted to warn you about him," Liz said.

"Why?"

"She makes him out to be something of a heartbreaker," Liz said, amused to see the flush rise on Dani's cheeks in the moonlight.

"Um ... why should I care about that? Silly girl; I told you she'd have excess hormones."

"You're her new role model," Liz said. "She thinks you hung the moon, as the saying goes."

"She's a nice kid; I didn't expect to like her, but you were right. She's fun to have around. I hope Ed gives her a break on this boyfriend thing."

"Careful. She pointed out to me that all he really knows for sure is that she wasn't with her girlfriend. Don't slip up and betray her confidence."

"She's pretty shrewd. I'm not sure I'd have been that self-possessed at her age."

Liz burst into laughter at that.

"What?" Dani asked frowning.

"You, the one who spent her 16th summer as a mercenary in Nicaragua."

"Don't tell her about that, Liz."

"Okay, but why not? She'd like that."

"It might get back to Ed."

Liz took a sip of her drink and began coughing to cover her laughter. Regaining her composure after a few seconds, she asked, "Now that we have some privacy, what do you really think those two men at the dinghy dock were up to?"

"I think the Chief Super was right; somebody must be worried about what Cynthia might know," Dani said. "I'll feel better about that once we're somewhere else. We need to talk Ed and Cynthia into getting under way tomorrow, if we can."

"But the only people she could identify are the taxi driver and the bartender on the ferry," Liz said. "I can't imagine that they're important enough to warrant attacking her. By the way, while Ed was preoccupied with you, I did ask if she recognized either of them. She didn't."

"What do you mean by that?" Dani asked.

Liz looked puzzled. "She didn't remember seeing either — "

"Not that. What you said about Ed. You think he's preoccupied with me?"

Liz paused before she answered. Could Dani not have noticed? Deciding that her friend's finely honed perception didn't always extend to social encounters, she said, "Yes. He seems smitten by you."

"Oh," Dani said, a faraway look coming over her face. "Think I'll turn in, now," she said, draining her glass as she stood up.

"KILL HIM," the Dragon Lady said, upon learning of Festus Jacob's failed attempt to kidnap the girl.

Li Wong nodded, hiding his relief. He had not told her that Jacobs had died on their way back from Bequia, suffocating slowly from the crushed larynx he'd suffered. Wong had ordered the other man with him to dispose of the body, weighting it and dumping it in the deep water off the west coast of St. Vincent.

"The taxi driver, too," she said

"Do you wish me to make examples of them?" he asked.

"No. The one example will be enough; he's the one who could do the most damage, too. Have you found him yet?"

"Not yet. No one has seen him since the failed raid the other night. The police are looking, too. The Chief Superintendent has already appointed an interim replacement to run the drug squad."

"Who is it? One of ours?"

"No, unfortunately. A man called Dawson. Harry Dawson. He's as straight as they come."

"Find some leverage, Wong. Or we'll have to take him out, somehow."

Wong nodded. "What about the girl?"

"What about her?" the Dragon Lady asked.

"Do you still want her?"

"Why would I have changed my mind?"

"Jacobs and the taxi driver are the only ones she can identify," Wong said.

"What about the bartender from the ferry?" she asked.

"Williams," Wong said. "Joseph Williams."

"She saw him, didn't she?" she asked.

"I assume she did. He — "

"Kill him."

"Then she won't be able to identify anyone connected to us," Wong said.

"And your point is?"

"She will be no threat to us," Wong said.

The Dragon Lady paused for a moment, as she thought about letting Wong in on her grand plan. She decided to keep it from him. He would serve her needs well enough if he thought this were a simple kidnapping for ransom. If he fell into Gregorio's hands at some point, Wong might be made to talk. It would be best if he didn't know her ultimate goal.

"Fool. We don't know how much the taxi driver told her. He's got a reputation for trying to impress the girls, remember. He almost got us in trouble once before. We should have cut our losses then instead of listening to Jacobs. Besides, it's not just that she's a threat. Her father is wealthy; he'll pay to get her back.

These people have cost me a great deal of lost business, not to mention the loss of our key contact in the police."

"But once she's ransomed, she might still lead them to us," Wong said.

She shook her head, clicking her tongue. "Sometimes you are thick-headed, my little one. Once we have the money, you can make her disappear ... any way that you choose."

She laughed as his face flushed. "You think I don't know about your peculiar appetites, my little pervert?"

JAMES CHELMSFORD CONGRATULATED himself on his foresight. He had known when he started taking payoffs from the Dragon Lady that the sweet arrangement couldn't last. Foresight or not, he had been surprised that his career had ended on such a trivial note. He had expected that he would be discovered in one of the endless investigations that the U.S. DEA precipitated in the islands. Instead, he was a victim of simple miscommunication. In some ways, though, it was a relief that he was finished with the duplicity.

He had plenty of money in his numbered accounts; he was set for life. He just couldn't live in St. Vincent and the Grenadines any longer, but that was all right, too. Once he got clear of the islands and established a false trail with an interim identity, he thought he'd spend a few months in New York.

Then there was his place in Rio; he'd set that up years ago. In the longer term, that's where he planned to retire. His immediate problem was to get to Miami and assume his new identity.

He'd had a bad feeling about this latest venture when he couldn't find that yacht in Admiralty Bay. To a suspicious man like him, that smacked of a setup. When he had called his office yesterday morning at eight o'clock and learned that Rupert Mason had already been through the files on his desk, he had hung up the telephone and grabbed the boogie bag that he kept in the hidden compartment in his closet.

He'd left his villa by the back door, not even pausing to lock up. He wouldn't be back. He worked his way through the cane fields to the little overgrown bay on the west coast of St. Vincent where he kept his speedboat, tossing his bag aboard as he cut the mooring lines. He fired up the three 300-horsepower outboard engines and roared away, leaving St. Vincent and his troubles in a cloud of spray.

In a few hours, he tied the boat up to the dock outside the villa that he leased in Antigua. He had spent the rest of the day making reservations under his interim identity, the one supported by the passport and credit cards that he kept in a hidden safe in the villa. Tomorrow, he would enter the U.S. at the airport in San Juan, and from there, he'd fly to Miami, where he would change identities again.

He would enjoy a few days at South Beach and check out the women at the clubs for a night or two. Then he'd be off to New York. Life wasn't too bad on the run — not if you were prepared, he thought, smiling, as he set the alarm for six a.m. He didn't want to miss his flight.

8

MARISSA CHEN SAT BEHIND THE CARVED TEAK DESK IN HER DIMLY lit office contemplating the recent setbacks to her business. She fingered a favorite bas-relief dragon on the front of the center drawer. She'd brought the desk with her from Hong Kong when the British had allowed their colony to revert to mainland China.

She had preferred colonial rule; the colonial officials tended to be less committed to enforcing the laws than the Chinese bureaucrats. When her shipments had been seized a second time and she hadn't been able to find anyone to bribe, she had paused her trading while she considered where to relocate. On balance, she was happy with her choice of St. Vincent, another former British colony that was unencumbered by communist zealots and small enough that finding the right officials to bribe was simple.

In her 15 years here, she had diversified. She ran a vertically integrated business now, growing her own product and controlling its distribution. In the Caribbean countries, she had her own retail distribution channels, although she still depended on the mob for distribution in her largest market, the U.S.

While that cut into her profit margins now, she had plans to take over the mob's role in the U.S. market soon. In the meantime, her mob connections offered other benefits. A short phone call to one of her contacts in Miami had yielded a lengthy dossier on this lawyer, Edward Savage. Marissa didn't expect to gain any new information on Savage, but she wanted Jimmy Gregorio, the mob boss in Miami, to know she was asking. She was betting that Gregorio would wonder why, and that would lead him into the trap that she was setting.

Savage was a multimillionaire, although he lived a modest enough life. Marissa admired that; she abhorred the frivolous display of wealth. It wasn't the way of her people. Money should be invested to make more money; it shouldn't be frittered away on foolish luxuries. Savage's wealth was liquid; most of his millions were in brokerage accounts. He would have no problem raising the money to ransom his daughter.

She had been relieved to learn that unlike a lot of the lawyers she had encountered, Savage had no underworld connections. His clients were legitimate businesses, publicly traded corporations for the most part, so he wouldn't be able to mobilize a counterattack. His only options would be to pay the ransom or go to the authorities. She smiled at the thought of his going to the authorities in this part of the world. The ones who weren't on her payroll were too disorganized to be a threat to her.

Her biggest concern was how much ransom she should demand. Savage was a playboy; that was his one weakness. He spent his spare time chasing women. While he didn't neglect his daughter, he didn't appear to be a doting father, either. The Dragon Lady had been surprised over the years at the way some parents reacted to ransom demands, but she thought he would want his daughter back intact. She knew better than to ask too much; protracted haggling could ensue, and that afforded time for things to go wrong. In her grand scheme, the ransom wasn't important except as window dressing.

She was impatient for Wong to get back from his mission to Antigua so that they could move on the girl.

LI WONG WAITED in the cramped cabin of the go-fast boat. He knew he would miss the fun when the two crooked Antigua cops rousted James Chelmsford, but his appearance was too distinctive for him to risk being seen by people in the neighboring villas.

There would be ample time for him to enjoy himself at Chelmsford's expense while they were *en route* to St. Vincent. The Dragon Lady had left him plenty of leeway in dealing with their former associate. Her only requirement was that he be found dead in Bequia, with the requisite maiming that would make his death a warning to others.

Wong had been with Marissa Chen for a long time; he had worked for her father in Hong Kong for years before she took over the family business. He found her much more fun to work with than her father had been. Only part of that was due to her penchant for kinky sex.

She had a better head for business than her father, and a better appreciation of the value of periodically making an example of some hapless member of her organization. Wong had become her weapon of choice when she had discovered his talents. For his part, he was devoted to her because she let him live out his darker fantasies, often with her participation.

He had been a bit surprised that she didn't want to be part of this evening's activities. He would miss watching her exercise her skills with Chelmsford, but her absence freed him to do those things that she forbade him to do in her presence. He had not yet learned how she discovered his deepest depravities, but it amused him that she liked for him to tell her about the things he did, so long as she didn't have to watch.

He felt the boat shift as the two men bundled Chelmsford into the cockpit. He stayed in the cabin until the boat accelerated to cruising speed. He knew then that they were in the ocean, and that no one would hear Chelmsford. He opened the door and found himself face to face with his victim, who began to scream as soon as he saw Wong.

"MORE COFFEE, ANYONE?" Liz asked, coming up the companionway ladder with a thermal carafe.

Dani and their guests were finishing breakfast at the foldaway table in the cockpit and watching the early morning activity in Admiralty Bay.

"Yes, please," Ed said, holding his mug out toward her.

"No, thanks," Cynthia said.

"I'll get some once we're underway," Dani said. "Ed and Cynthia want to see the Tobago Cays."

"Great," Liz said. "Are we leaving soon?"

"May as well," Ed said, taking a sip of his coffee.

"I'll just — " Dani was interrupted as a small, local boat drew alongside.

"Good morning, *Vengeance.*"

"Morning, John," Liz said. "Do you have any of that banana bread today?"

"Still hot, Liz," the man said, holding up a loaf in a plastic bag. "How many you want?"

"Oh, give us four," Liz said, noticing that the inside of the bag was beaded with moisture from the warm bread. "We're going down to the Cays for a while. Might as well stock up."

"You hear the news?" he asked, as Liz pressed some bills into his hand.

She shook her head. "What's happening?"

"Willis was goin' out for lobster early this mornin'. Found a body in the park. Turns out it's a p'liceman."

"Oh," Liz said.

"Yes. The man who was in charge of the drug squad."

"What happened to him?" Dani asked, standing up and moving toward the spot where John held on to *Vengeance*.

He shook his head. "Bad, ver' bad." He looked down at the water for a moment. "You know 'bout the *loup garou*?"

Dani nodded.

"I don' believe in *loup garou*, me," he said. "But tha's what mos' people t'ink got him. He t'roat all torn and bloody. Bite marks all over he — he not wearin' no clothes, see." He shook his head. "Awful."

"Could it have been dogs?" Liz asked.

"Dogs?" he asked. "I don' t'ink so. No dogs on Bequia like that. I s'pose some dogs mebbe do that to a man, but not the dogs we got here, I don' t'ink. Good that you leave. No tellin' wha's goin' on here, but I t'ink it was the drug people did it. He tongue was taken, see. They do that, means they t'ink he tellin' stuff to people he shouldn't tell."

"Was he taking money from the drug dealers?" Dani asked.

"I don' know. Mus' not speak ill of the dead, but he was one rich man. Mos' only one way p'lice get rich." He nodded his head. "I bes' go to the other yachts while the bread still warm. You folks enjoy the Tobago Cays. Be safe down there. *Loup garou* don' s'pose to go where no animals, I t'ink." He bent down and started his outboard engine, waving as he made his way to the next boat in the anchorage.

"*Loup garou*?" Cynthia asked. "Like a werewolf?"

"That's what *loup garou* means," Ed said. "I'm surprised they'd have a superstition like that down here. There aren't any wolves here, are there?"

"No," Dani said, "but Voodoo borrows freely, and there's a big French influence, because of Haiti. You can't tell exactly what they mean by *loup garou* down here. It's loosely an evil spirit that's taken over the body of a person. Sometimes it includes shape shifting, sometimes not. The local version of the *loup garou* is supposed to prey on children, mostly. I guess the damage to the body is why they think that."

Cynthia shuddered. "Can we go now?"

"Of course," Liz said, gathering up the remains of their breakfast. "Give me a couple of minutes to get stuff put away, Dani, and I'll be back up to raise the anchor."

9

"Now that you've taken care of Chelmsford, it's time for you to focus on that girl."

Wong sat at the corner of the Dragon Lady's desk, sipping from a cup of tea. He'd been describing what he had just done to the former chief of the drug squad, watching her as she became aroused while he drew out the most titillating part of the killing.

"Yes," he said.

"Who will you use?" she asked, putting her hands on the desktop, watching his eyes follow her movements.

He thought for a moment. "I think the two men from Trinidad; they want a chance to prove themselves."

"Are you sure they're up to the job?"

"Kidnapping is the national pastime in Trinidad. They've done this before. Besides, I don't think her father's likely to give them much trouble; he didn't figure out what was going on the other night until it was all over. It was just the one woman that surprised Jacobs. She's not very big, and we know to keep an eye on her this time."

"You, of all people, should not underestimate a small person,

Wong." The Dragon Lady grinned at the flush that crept up from his neck.

"But she's just a girl," he said.

"Like me?"

"Ah ... " Wong's face paled.

The Dragon Lady laughed at his discomfort. "Well?" She prodded his thigh with the pointed toe of her red, high-heeled pump.

"She got lucky, that's all," he said.

"Like me?" she asked, moving one hand to her breast, teasing him. "Am I going to get lucky? Or are you the one who's going to get lucky, my little devil?"

"REST your hand lightly on the helm," Dani said, watching Cynthia as she steered *Vengeance*. They were plowing through the moderately rough seas that often formed just south of Bequia, spray flying as the yacht plunged along at almost ten knots on a beam reach in the 15-to-20-knot breeze. "She's balanced; she'll mostly steer herself. You can feel a bit of pressure in the helm from time to time when she changes her angle to the wind. Just think of matching the pressure that you feel; don't think of it as turning the helm, or you'll over-steer."

Cynthia nodded. "This is so cool. How long ago did you learn to sail?"

"Longer ago than I can remember; I grew up sailing with my father."

"So he has a yacht?"

"Oh, he's always had boats. He owns several big charter yachts in the Med; it's a sideline business for him."

"Bigger than *Vengeance*?"

"Yes. Much bigger. When I was your age, I worked as deck crew on them on my vacations from school."

"Wow! What fun!"

Dani smiled. "Not really. I was the one that got all the scut work. We're talking about boats that had crews of maybe 15 people."

"How many guests, then?" Ed asked. He had just joined them in the cockpit.

"Oh, it varied. Sometimes just one or two, sometimes an extended family." She turned to face him, taking in his bare, muscular torso. "Careful of the sun," she said. "It will burn you much more quickly down here in the tropics; there's less UV attenuation because of the short path through the atmosphere."

"Just trying to catch up with you; I couldn't help admiring your tan," he said.

Dani noticed Liz looking up through the portlight from the galley, a smirk on her face. "You're doing well with the steering, Cynthia," Dani said, slipping from behind the helm where she had been sitting next to the girl. "Think you can handle her for a couple of minutes?" she asked, standing up and stretching her back.

"Sure, I think so. Why?"

"I need to go below for a minute. I'll be right back. Excuse me, Ed," she said, letting her hand linger on his shoulder as she squeezed by him.

"What's up?" Liz asked, as Dani came below.

"Oh, I just thought I'd work on my tan," Dani said, going into the cabin that they shared and closing the door.

"Whoa," Liz said, grinning, as Dani emerged from the cabin a minute later in a skimpy, black, crocheted string bikini. "Did you buy that from the place in Bequia?"

"Yes. Years ago."

"What are you — "

"Stow it, Liz," Dani said, spraying herself with sunblock from an aerosol can and mounting the companionway ladder.

Liz stifled a laugh as she turned away, hiding her grin. She'd never known Dani to wear a bathing suit except to swim, and then she favored tank suits.

"ANYBODY WANT SOME JUICE OR COFFEE?" Liz called from the galley as she looked out the portlight into the cockpit.

"I'll take some juice, thanks," Cynthia said. "I think Dad and Dani probably just want us to leave them alone."

"Oh?" Liz said, as she brought two glasses of cold passion fruit juice up to the cockpit.

"Yeah. He's disgusting. Tell her not to encourage him; he's bad enough without her leading him on."

"Leading him on?" Liz asked, handing Cynthia a glass and taking a seat beside her. "Where'd they go?"

"Behind that little sail up front. The staysail, I think Dani called it."

Liz rose to a crouch so that she could see under the sail. Dani was stretched out on the foredeck, facedown, sunning herself. Liz giggled when she saw that the tie was undone on Dani's top. She watched with interest as Dani handed Ed a tube of sunblock. As he began to rub it into her back, Liz said, "I can't believe it. She really is leading him on."

"Well, maybe she just doesn't know his type," Cynthia said, "but she's playing into his hands — no pun intended."

"Or vice versa," Liz said, a grin spreading across her face.

"What do you mean?" Cynthia asked.

"She put on sunscreen before she came on deck."

"Oh," Cynthia said, a fleeting look of disappointment on her face. "She didn't seem like that type."

"She's not," Liz said. "I don't know what's going on, but she just came back from a long weekend in Brazil with the only guy who's ever held her interest."

"Did he dump her, or something?" Cynthia asked.

"I don't know. She never talks about her love life. Except for the guy in Brazil, she's brushed off every man I've ever seen make a move on her — until now."

"Well, this isn't likely to end well for her," Cynthia said. "I really like her, too. Any chance you can intervene?"

"I told her what you said last night. That's the best I can do; she's likely to punch me out if I say any more."

Cynthia shook her head and took a sip of juice. "Well, I'll ask him for some father-daughter time tomorrow. You said there's some good snorkeling on the reef in the Tobago Cays?"

"The best," Liz said.

"I'll ask him to take me, just the two of us. I'll tell him I need some advice about a boy; that'll get him, for sure. Then you can at least maybe get her to talk to you about this before she gets hurt."

"Sounds good to me," Liz said. "You hungry for lunch yet?"

"Getting there. That's a good excuse to break up their little tête-à-tête, huh?"

"We'll see," Liz said.

10

"You seem to know a lot about Voodoo, Dani," Cynthia said, as they were eating dinner. They had been discussing the bread vendor's mention of the *loup garou.*

"Not a lot," Dani said, "but you can't grow up in the islands without learning something about it."

"Did you know people who believed in it?" Ed asked.

Dani studied his face for a moment before she said, "Yes. I have a distant cousin in Martinique who's a *mambo,* a high priestess."

"That's really cool," Cynthia said. "Did you ever go to, like, any of the ceremonies, or anything?"

"No," Dani said, with a smile, "but we had some charter guests once, academics, who were studying Voodoo."

"That seems odd," Ed said. "What kind of academics would study Voodoo?"

"Cultural anthropologists," Liz said. "And they knew all about Dani's cousin. She's actually one of the foremost practitioners of Voodoo."

"No offense, Dani," Ed said, "but I always thought Voodoo was bogus, like witchcraft, or something."

"I'm not offended, but it's no more bogus than any other religion. I'm not a believer, but I respect the people who are. At least, I respect the ones who are sincere. It's a force for good, like most religions."

"I thought the islands were predominantly Christian," he said.

"Voodoo isn't at odds with Christianity," Liz said, "at least from the Voodoo perspective. Some Christians see it differently."

They were quiet for a moment, addressing themselves to the curried fish that Liz had served. Cynthia broke the silence.

"Dad, Liz was telling me about the fringing reef out there, earlier." She gestured to the east, where the swells rolled in and broke over the shallow barrier of coral.

"Yes? What about it?"

"Because the Tobago Cays are a marine preserve, the reef is one of the best snorkeling spots in the Caribbean," Liz said. She caught Dani's eye and said, "I thought while Dani and I scraped the barnacles off *Vengeance's* bottom in the morning, you and Cynthia could take the dinghy over there and scope it out." As Dani started to object at the mention of scraping barnacles, Liz nudged her leg under the table. She'd explain her subterfuge about the imaginary barnacles later.

"Please, Dad?" Cynthia asked. "I need to talk with you about, um ... well, I could use your advice about something personal."

"How can I refuse?" Ed asked, with a grin.

"WHERE ARE ED AND CYNTHIA?" Liz asked, rinsing a plate and passing it to Dani to dry.

"Sitting up on the foredeck, looking at the stars," Dani said, wiping the dish and putting it aside. "Why?"

"Just curious. She was hoping for some time alone with him. She wanted to talk with him about boy trouble."

A distant look came over Dani's face. "Boy trouble? Think he's any good at advice to the lovelorn?"

"How would I know? You're the one who's been spending time with him."

Dani put down the dish towel and turned to face Liz. "What do you mean by that?"

"Just an observation."

"He's our guest. I was just keeping him company."

"In a bikini? I've never seen you wear a bikini when there were other people around."

Dani's face flushed and she clenched her teeth. Liz took a step back, alarmed, but then she saw her friend's chin tremble. She stepped forward and put her arms around Dani's wiry shoulders.

She felt Dani relax. "Want to talk?"

Dani nodded and Liz released her. She rubbed at her eyes with the back of her hand. "Yes, maybe so. I don't have much experience with men."

"What's going on, Dani? You haven't been yourself since you got back from Brazil."

"That whole thing with Ralph," Dani said, "it wasn't what I thought."

"It rarely is, at least in my experience," Liz said. "Want to tell me what happened that upset you so? Sometimes it helps to talk it over with someone."

"I don't know where to start, Liz. I haven't a clue what happened. When he invited me to visit, I thought he wanted to ... well, you know."

"Mm-hmm," Liz said. "And?"

"And I was just ... I felt ... " she shook her head. "I don't even know where to begin."

"Start with getting off the plane in São Paolo, maybe."

"He met me in the arrivals area with a dozen roses," Dani sniffed.

"That's a good start, anyway," Liz said. "What did you do?"

"I thanked him and shook his hand."

"You shook his hand? No hug? Or kiss?"

"We were in public, Liz!"

"I see. Then what?"

"He drove me to his villa. It's huge — in a walled compound with security guards."

"Uh-huh," Liz said. "And?"

"He showed me to my room. Well, a suite, really. I put the flowers in the refrigerator and — "

"The refrigerator? You put them in the refrigerator?"

"What was I supposed to do? I knew they'd wilt if I didn't do something."

"Okay." Liz shrugged. "And then?"

"He said cocktails and dinner would be in an hour, if I wanted to freshen up. I thanked him and said I'd see him then."

"So how did you dress for cocktails and dinner?"

"My little black dress with the strappy sandals you let me borrow, and my pearls."

"Good. And how was dinner?"

"That's when it got really weird. Remember Carlotta Solanó?"

"The woman who killed Angela Cappelletti's father a few months ago in Miami?"

"Right."

"Yes. What about her?" Liz said.

"She was there, dressed like a hooker. She acted like one, too."

"What did she do?"

"Gave me a big hug and one of those kissy things like they do in the movies. Then she held me at arm's length, staring into my eyes, and told me how excited she was that I might join her and Ralph."

"Uh-oh," Liz said, shaking her head. "I think I see where they were going. What happened next?"

"It's not what you think — not what I thought, either. The whole thing was a damned job interview."

"Job interview? They wanted to hire you?"

"Not exactly. They were looking for another partner."

"Yuck," Liz said. "He never struck me that way, from what you told me about him."

"Me either," Dani said. "I thought he was a solo operator."

"I'm lost, Dani. What do you mean, solo operator?"

"I didn't think he'd be part of a big organization, even if he and Carlotta run it."

"What organization?"

"They call it S and S Security Service. They wanted to recruit me to run operations in the Eastern Caribbean."

"What kind of operations?"

"All kinds of cloak and dagger stuff, for anybody who'll pay. He excused himself and left me with her to talk about the details."

"What did you say?"

"I told her I was confused, that I thought he wanted a more, um ... personal relationship with me."

"How did she respond to that?"

"She laughed and said he was afraid of women like me — her, too — that we were too intimidating for most men, him included. I shook my head and said that all that time, I thought Ralph was flirting with me."

"What did she say to that?"

"She said, 'When was that?' and I told her about going up to his room in St. Lucia a couple of years ago. Then she said, 'You don't know, do you? He never told you?' and I said, 'What don't I know?' She got this really serious look on her face and told me that Ralph's married. He got married when he finished his assignment in St. Lucia, and his father-in-law is bankrolling this whole business. Ralph's been on the straight and narrow with women ever since."

"Oh, Dani! I'm so sorry. I can imagine what a shock that was."

"I still can't believe it. I'm intimidating to men? I don't get it.

Why would he be scared of me? I wouldn't hurt him. I mean, sure, I could kick his ass, but I wouldn't. I liked him, Liz. I mean, okay, he's married. I didn't want to get married, so it wouldn't have worked anyway, but why am I intimidating?"

"Maybe he just — "

"He's not the first one. I've heard that before, every time I got serious about some jerk."

"Well, a lot of men are a little put off by strong, self-assured women. Especially when they see you break somebody's arm, or something worse."

"So what am I supposed to do? Be a candy-ass?"

"All you can do is be yourself, Dani. The right guy won't be put off by you."

"I'm 26 years old, Liz. I haven't met him yet. Maybe you could teach me to act like a girl instead of one of the guys, okay?"

"I'll do my best, Dani, but you need to be comfortable with the way you are. It'll work out."

"Just try, please, Liz."

"Okay. But don't overdo it with Ed. I don't think he's your type. Besides, from what Cynthia says, he's not worth your trouble."

"I need to start somewhere. He's handy, and he's hot."

"Shh, Dani. He and Cynthia are coming aft."

WONG SAT in the visitor's chair in the Dragon Lady's office, her telephone pressed to his ear. He tried to ignore what she was doing to him and concentrate on what the man from Trinidad was saying.

"Excuse me," he said, putting his hand over the mouthpiece. He turned to face her. "I can't focus if you keep doing that," he said.

"Mm," she moaned. "Neither can I. Call them back later."

"I need to talk with him now, while they have cell service, if you want the girl taken tomorrow."

She pouted and pushed her swivel chair away from him, turning her back.

Taking his hand from the mouthpiece, he said, "Okay, I'm back."

He listened for a moment. Then he said, "Take her tomorrow, but do it carefully. Avoid attracting the attention of people on the other yachts, and whatever you do, don't kill the father or the two women. You must not do anything that will get the police involved."

He listened again. "Tell the father that he will hear from us within 24 hours regarding ransom, and if he calls the authorities, we will sell his daughter to the Arabs. He'll never see her again unless he follows our instructions."

After listening for another few seconds, he said, "That sounds good, if you can do it that way. Call my cell phone when you have her in the clear. I'll tell you where to bring her then. And don't molest her, or I'll kill you both, slowly." He hung up the phone.

"Where are they?" the Dragon Lady asked.

"The Tobago Cays. They said most of the people on the other boats snorkeled on the reef during the middle of the day; they plan to take the girl while she and the others are swimming, if they snorkel the reef in the morning. If not, they will approach the boat pretending to be fishermen with fresh fish to sell, and hold the people at gunpoint while they take her."

"A good plan," she said, rolling the chair toward him. "If the phone rings again, don't answer." She licked her lips as she reached for him.

11

"COME UP ON DECK WITH ME FOR A MINUTE, DAD." CYNTHIA STOOD and walked toward the companionway.

Ed got up to follow her and Dani said, "I'll — "

"Excuse me, Dani. Could you give me a hand with the breakfast dishes?" Liz asked.

Dani glared at her, but she nodded in agreement.

"She wanted a few minutes alone with her dad," Liz said, after their guests were on deck.

"Oh," Dani said. "Okay."

"And I need to talk to you, too," Liz said.

"Yes?" Dani said. "About what?"

Liz looked away.

"What Liz? Tell me!"

"While you and Ed were up in the cockpit before breakfast, Cynthia and I had a little chat."

"And? What was on her mind?" Dani asked.

"You ... and her dad."

Dani grinned. "What about us?" she asked, a dreamy look on her face.

"Sure you want to hear this?"

"Don't tell me he's intimidated." Dani frowned. "Did he — "

"Maybe a little bit, but you need to try playing hard to get."

"Wait. I need to what?"

"That's what Cynthia said, Dani. He's accustomed to making the moves. Sexually aggressive women scare him."

"Sexually aggressive? Me?"

"He saw through your little ploy with the sunscreen yesterday."

"Ploy?"

"Don't feign innocence with me. I saw the whole thing."

"But how did he — "

"You smelled like a boatload of freshly grated coconut after you sprayed yourself, Dani."

Dani's face fell. "Oh." She was quiet for a minute, a gamut of emotions playing over her face. "What a chickenshit," she growled.

"Chickenshit?" Liz asked.

"Gutless bastard. It's okay for him to put the make on me, but I'm not allowed to take the initiative?"

"A lot of men have this double standard, Dani. It's not — "

"Well, screw him!"

"Not likely. Not the way you're going about it."

Dani's face flushed. "No way, Liz. Not if he were the last man alive."

"Just back off a little bit. He'll come around. Trust me."

Dani studied her friend for a minute. "You think so?"

Liz shrugged. "What can it hurt?"

"Nothing, I guess," Dani said, after a moment's reflection. "But I was going to snorkel the reef with him this morning. How should I — "

"Remember, I made an excuse for us to stay back. We have to scrape the barnacles off the bottom. Tell them you may be able to join them this afternoon. Besides, Cynthia really does want some time alone with him to try to persuade him that this boy she's seeing is worthy; she'll thank you for it."

"But the bottom's clean, Liz. We just had it painted."

"They don't know that. When they come back we'll just tell them how surprised we were at how few barnacles we had."

"Okay. Will you check them out on the dinghy and show them where to find the dinghy moorings? I'm going to our cabin. Make some excuse for me. I can't face him right now. Buy me a little time to get my temper under control; I'll be okay when they get back."

"Sure. Sounds good to me. And you cheer up. You'll find somebody, if Ed doesn't come around. Don't be too hasty to jump the first guy you see just because of the Ralph thing. That kind of rebound romance never ends well."

"Thanks, Liz."

"No problem. Now get out of sight. I'll get the snorkel gear out and get them on their way."

"THEY ARE GETTING IN THE DINGHY," the man said, resting his elbows on the gunwale of the speedboat to steady the binoculars.

"All of them?" his companion asked.

"No. Only the man and the girl. The women who run the yacht are still aboard. One of them's showing the man how to start the outboard, and the other one is below deck."

"Good. Did you see if they had masks and flippers?"

"Yeah, they did. Looks like we got her."

"Good. Let's wait until they're in the water."

"Right. Damn!"

"What's the matter?"

"The woman on deck."

"So?"

"She's got binoculars. She's checking out the other boats," the man with the binoculars said.

"Easy, mon. We are invisible," his companion said. "We look jus' like the other local boats. She's not going to notice us."

"Maybe not. She just set the binoculars down. She's drinking some coffee now. How are we going to do this, mon?"

"Once they're in the water, we cut the dinghy loose from the mooring so he can't get back to the yacht to call for help. Then just run the boat between the girl and the mon. You hit him with the fish billy if he gives us any trouble, and I grab the girl, pull her in the boat. Then we run like hell through the reef channel and out to sea. Simple."

"Okay, mon."

"COME BACK UP and let's finish the coffee," Liz called down the companionway.

"Are they gone?" Dani asked.

"They picked up the dive mooring at the reef a couple of minutes ago. They're in the water now," Liz said, as Dani came up into the cockpit.

She took the mug of steaming coffee that Liz handed her and held it under her nose for a moment, inhaling the aroma. "Ah," she sighed, and took a sip.

"How do you want to spend our free morning?" Liz asked.

"Doing nothing sounds good. I haven't recovered from our lost sleep the other night."

"Neither have I," Liz said.

They each swung their legs onto the cockpit seats, leaning back against the coachroof and stretching out.

"Maybe I'll nap," Liz said.

"Sounds good to me," Dani said. "Hey, wait!" she yelped, a few seconds later.

Liz opened her eyes. "What?"

Dani got to her feet and grabbed the binoculars from the rack at the helm. Lifting them to her eyes, she said, "That's our dinghy."

"Of course," Liz said. "They left it on that dive mooring by the break in the reef. What are you — "

"It's adrift, Liz."

"Adrift? Are you sure?"

"Quick!" Dani said, putting the binoculars back in their place and reaching down to start the diesel. "Man the windlass. Let's get the anchor up and catch it before it drifts out of sight. Idiots must not have tied it to the mooring."

Liz set her coffee in the corner of the cockpit and scrambled to the foredeck. A few minutes later, Dani maneuvered *Vengeance* alongside the dinghy as Liz picked up the dinghy's painter with a boat hook.

"The painter was cut, Dani," Liz called, as she walked the dinghy back along *Vengeance's* side. She tied what was left of the painter to a cleat at the stern and said, "Let's get *Vengeance* anchored and go see where Ed and Cynthia are."

With the dinghy in tow, they returned to the spot where they had been anchored overnight and dropped the hook.

"I think I see Ed," Dani said, reaching for the binoculars as Liz returned from the foredeck to the cockpit. She focused on the man swimming frantically toward them. "Let's go," she said, jumping into the dinghy and starting the outboard.

Liz joined her and untied the painter. They raced toward the swimmer, who began to tread water as they approached.

Dani cut the throttle a few yards from him and called, "Ed?"

"They took Cynthia," he yelled, panting, "and the dinghy was gone."

"Who took her?" Dani asked, as she and Liz helped him slither over the side into the dinghy.

"Two men in a yellow speedboat. They cut between us and stopped. One of them said, 'If you ever want to see her again, wait for our instructions or we'll sell her to the Arabs.' Just that quick, they took off again, and she was gone."

"Which way?" Liz asked.

"Through the reef," he said, still gasping from his exertion.

"No sign of them now," Dani said, standing up in the dinghy to scan the horizon.

"How can that be?" Ed asked. "It was only a few minutes ago."

"A small, fast boat. They probably turned to put one of the little islands between them and us," Dani said.

"Let's call the cops," Ed said.

"That's up to you," Dani said, "but maybe you should give it a few hours and see if you hear from them. The cops down here aren't what you're used to at home."

"What do you mean?"

"At best, they aren't set up to deal with a kidnapping like this. At worst, they could be part of it."

"I can't just do nothing," Ed said, a quaver in his voice.

"I'm not suggesting that, Ed," Dani said.

"Let's get you back to *Vengeance* where you can call your office and alert them in case they get a ransom call."

"My office? Why my office? I don't — "

"The kidnappers know you aren't at home, and it's unlikely that they'd take a chance on cell service. It's too unreliable out here in the fringe areas. They must have done a little research on you before they decided Cynthia was a good target."

Ed studied her for a moment before he nodded. "Good points," he said.

"Liz can help you with the satellite phone if you don't have cell service. I'm going to take the dinghy and talk to all the local vendors."

"I thought the Cays were uninhabited," Ed said, as Dani steered the dingy back to *Vengeance*.

"They are, but a lot of people come out here from Union Island and Mayreau every day to sell stuff to the yachts. One of them might have noticed a strange boat hanging out here. They all know one another."

12

"YOU WERE GONE LONG ENOUGH. ANY NEWS?" ED ASKED FROM THE
cockpit as Dani tied the dinghy alongside *Vengeance*.

"Yes," she said, stepping onto the side deck, "but first, did you
get in touch with your office?"

"Yes. They haven't heard anything."

Dani nodded. "Too soon. They'll want you to sweat for a
while. You leave the satellite phone number with your secretary?"

"Yes," Ed said. "What did you learn?"

"Several people noticed the yellow boat with two men in it. It's
not from around here." Dani sat down across from him and
poured a cup of coffee from the carafe sitting on the cockpit table.

"Any idea where it's from, then?"

"It had a Trinidad and Tobago registration number."

Ed wrinkled his brow for a moment. "Tobago? But you said it
wasn't from around here."

"Trinidad and Tobago's a separate country — two
islands — one named Trinidad and one named Tobago. It's just a
coincidence that the Cays here share the name."

"How far is it to Trinidad and Tobago?"

"A bit over a hundred miles," Liz said.

"How long would it take them?"

"Depends on the boat and the sea state," Dani said, "but maybe from two to four hours, if they were pushing it."

"Can we get a fast boat and chase them down?" Ed asked.

"We don't know that they're going back to Trinidad," Dani said. "They could be anywhere. To me, it seems unlikely that they'd spend the time to take her that far."

"But I've always heard that kidnapping's a problem in Trinidad," Ed said. "Wouldn't they want to get her back there? Where they presumably have some connections to hide her while I ... wait ... " he shook his head, looking down at his half-empty coffee mug.

"They'd want to get her out of sight as soon as they could, I think," Dani said. "Somebody might notice two local fishermen with a young, blonde girl in their boat. From what I heard, the boat's completely open; nowhere to hide her."

"Then why would they come from Trinidad all the way up here to kidnap someone?" Ed asked.

"Kidnapping is a major industry in Trinidad," Liz said, "but it's usually wealthy locals that are the targets."

"What are you getting at, Liz?" he asked, his brow creased again.

"Unless you have some connection to Trinidad and Tobago, it's not likely that anyone from there would target Cynthia," Liz said, exchanging glances with Dani.

"She's right," Dani said. "Any of your clients or adversaries come to mind?"

"As having a Trinidad connection?" Ed asked.

Dani and Liz both nodded.

"No," he said, drawing out the word and shaking his head. "Nobody I know. So where does that leave us?"

"Hired muscle," Dani said. "It has to be somebody in this area that's behind it. Any thoughts? You asked us to pick you up in Bequia. How'd you hear about it?"

Ed looked at her, frowning, not saying anything.

"Anybody you know have ties here that might attract attention to you? Any cases that might lead someone to take her for leverage?"

"You mean, like a setup by someone back in the States?"

"Yes, maybe," Dani said.

"Not that I can think of. I picked Bequia because of an article I read in some in-flight magazine. Can't even remember which one. We're wasting time. We can't just wait for a ransom call. What are we going to do? I think the cops should — "

"I'll call a friend who has solid connections to senior law enforcement people down here," Dani said. "I just wanted to know if you had any thoughts as to who might be behind this."

"How's your friend going to get anything done? Is he a cop?"

"He's retired," Dani said. "He was a partner of my father's. They did a lot of business with the governments down here, and he still lives in the islands."

"But where will they even start?" Ed asked. "You said the guys who took her could be anywhere."

"Yes, but my friend has contacts he can trust everywhere, and we have the registration number of the boat. We'll start by finding the two guys."

"But what if they've already hidden her somewhere? They aren't going to tell the cops anything; they'll lawyer up, and then what?"

"It doesn't work like that here, unless you let the police get to them first," Dani said.

"What? You've lost me."

"That's okay. We have some resources and latitude that the police don't have."

"You're starting to scare me," Ed said.

Liz saw the muscles in Dani's jaw twitch. "We'll find her, Ed," Liz said. "This is Dani's home turf. Trust her."

"THEY HAVE HER," Li Wong said. "They're headed for Hillsborough, Carriacou."

"Why there?" the Dragon Lady asked, her cold gaze fixed on the bridge of Wong's nose as she inhaled cigarette smoke.

"*Lotus Blossom* is there," he said, his fingers twitching as he picked at the legs of his trousers.

"Not there. I don't like it."

"But they need to — "

"They need to do as I say," she said, removing the six-inch-long cigarette holder from her lips and tapping the ash in the carved jade bowl on her desk. "And so do you, my little one." She gave him a smile that didn't reach her eyes.

"Of course, madame," he said, bowing his head. "I only wanted — "

"Call them immediately. Have them make the handoff inside the reef at Petite Martinique, well away from the town. *Lotus Blossom* must not anchor; as soon as she is aboard, have them put out to sea. They should take up a position 15 miles to the west, over the horizon."

"Yes, Madame. I'll call them immediately," Wong said, rising to his feet.

"Wong?"

"Yes, Madame?"

"I want you aboard *Lotus Blossom* as soon as possible. I'd prefer that you were there for the handoff. One of the men can run you down to Hillsborough in the Donzi. Order *Lotus Blossom* to wait for you. They are not to make the rendezvous without you. Do you understand?"

"Yes, Madame."

"I'm holding you personally responsible for the girl. She is not to be touched without my order. Do not disappoint me."

He chewed the inside of his cheek as he waited to see if she was finished. When she raised the cigarette holder to her carefully made-up lips and nodded at the door, he gave a slight bow and scurried away.

CYNTHIA HAD MANAGED to roll onto her side and push herself up against a portable ice chest to keep her face out of the foul-smelling water that sloshed in the bilge of the wooden speedboat. She could feel the bruises on her hip and shoulder from the pounding of the boat as it raced over the choppy water.

The smaller, more light-skinned of her captors had zip-tied her wrists behind her and then zip-tied her ankles before forcing her into a face-down position, all while his partner drove the boat at breakneck speed. Her skin crawled at the recollection of his callused hands stroking her thighs and buttocks as he cackled.

She shivered at the thought of what they might do to her. She kept her eyes half-closed against the blazing sunlight and studied the two men. Both were rough-looking, but the driver was the more muscular of the two.

The smaller man, the one who had tied her up and fondled her, was wiry. His muscles didn't bulge, but they moved like pieces of rope beneath his smooth, bronze skin. From his straight, dark hair, oiled and pulled back in a short ponytail, and his chiseled features, she thought he was of East Indian extraction.

The driver was several shades darker, but he too, looked to be of Indian descent. She guessed he weighed half again as much as the smaller man, but from their faces, they could be brothers. It alarmed her that they made no effort to keep her from seeing their faces. She'd read enough crime books to know what that meant.

She saw the smaller man turn toward her. Seeing that she had moved, he nudged her with a foot to her thigh and caught her eye. He made a kissing movement with his well-shaped lips and grinned at her, running his tongue over his lips as he swept his eyes over her exposed body. She cursed the skimpy bikini that she wore, wishing that she had worn a one-piece bathing suit.

The small man nudged the driver and said something to him. The big man looked back at her and grinned, nodding. He said something to his companion, but she couldn't hear the comment over the roar of the two big outboards. They both laughed, and the smaller one reached into the cooler at her back and took out two cans of beer. He leered at her again before he popped the tops and handed one to the driver.

While they were occupied with their beers and whatever conversation they were having, she felt behind her. She was able to move her hands and fingers enough to find a sharp edge on the piece of scrap metal that she thought must serve as an anchor, based on the glimpse she caught as they pushed her down into the bilge earlier. She twisted her body until she was able to press the zip-tie around her wrists against the edge. She worked it up and down with a sawing motion, feeling the plastic tie begin to loosen.

13

BEFORE SHE CALLED PHILLIP, DANI CONSIDERED HOW TO MANAGE the conversation to keep Ed from learning of Cynthia's drug purchase. It was a trivial issue, but her instincts told her the less Ed knew about it, the better. She made the call, and when Phillip answered, she said, "One of our charter guests has been kidnapped, Phillip," in a soft tone, the phone held close to her lips.

"The girl? Or her father?" Phillip asked, remembering their earlier conversation.

"The guests are a single father and his 16-year-old daughter," she said, hoping he would get the idea that she couldn't speak freely.

"You told me that yesterday," Phillip said. "Who got kidnapped?"

"No," she said, persisting, "I really have no idea why, but two men ran a speedboat between them while they were snorkeling on Horseshoe Reef, here in the Tobago Cays. They pulled her into the boat and told her father to wait for a call. They said, 'If you ever want to see her again, wait for our instructions or we'll sell her to the Arabs,' and then they took off through the cut in the reef. They cut the dinghy adrift to keep him from getting back to *Vengeance*."

"Probably the drug dealers," Phillip said.

"I'm not sure what you mean by drug dealers," Dani said.

"Is the father listening to you?" Phillip asked, finally realizing that she was trying to hide something.

"Yes."

"Have you told him about the girl buying drugs?" Phillip asked.

"No. I *need to know* something Phillip."

"Need to know? You mean he doesn't need to know? You don't want to tell him about the drugs?"

"Right."

"Okay. Got it. Go ahead."

"The father, that's Ed Savage, wants to involve the police. I've explained why that might be dangerous to the girl, given that we don't know who to trust. I thought maybe you'd let the Chief Super know what's happening, if you think that's okay."

"Let me think about that. Are you thinking of handling this without the police?"

"I thought that might be a good idea," Dani said.

"Yes, probably so," Phillip said. "Any idea on where to start?"

"I asked around among the vendors in the Cays. They saw the boat. It's a yellow 24-footer with two 250-horsepower Yamahas. Registration on the bow was *TFT 4868*."

"Trinidad," Phillip muttered.

"Yes. Anything we can learn about it might help."

"I'll see what Sandrine can find out through the customs channels, but the quickest way to find them is probably to sic Sharktooth on it. Want me to call him?"

"Yes, please. Fill him in on what you know, and ask him to call me."

"You want me to tell him the whole story?"

"Please."

"Got it. I'll get him to give you a call ASAP."

"Thanks, Phillip. I'll wait for his call. Tell Sandrine hello from both of us." She listened to Phillip's goodbye and disconnected the phone.

"What did he say?" Ed asked, as Dani put the satellite phone on the cockpit seat beside her.

"He's going to call a friend of his who's the Chief Superintendent of the police force here," Dani said, casting a warning glance in Liz's direction.

"That's a relief," Ed said. "I'll feel better with the cops working this."

"Well, he's going to cover us with the police, but he thinks we'll be better off on our own."

"I don't get it," Ed said, frowning. "If he thinks they're part of it, why would he call this guy?"

"He knows the Chief's not part of it, but remember, in a fast boat, you can slip from country to country in a few minutes down here. Corruption is everywhere, and even the honest police can get all tangled up in politics when they go outside their own country."

Ed caught his lower lip between his teeth and looked down into the footwell of the cockpit for a moment. Looking up at Dani, he shook his head and said, "I gather someone's going to call you. Is that this Chief Superintendent?"

"No. Another friend who has an informal network of people all through the islands."

"What kind of network?"

"One that operates on personal loyalty instead of politics."

"That's pretty damned vague, Dani. How's that going to get Cynthia back?"

"First, we'll find those two guys with the boat, wherever they are."

"Okay, I can see where that might happen, but then what?"

"Then we'll — " She was interrupted by the ringing of the satellite phone. "Excuse me," she said, picking it up and looking at the display.

"Good morning, Sharktooth," she said, as she lifted the phone to her ear.

CYNTHIA FELT the boat slowing down as the roar of the big outboards decreased. She had managed to free her hands by cutting the zip-ties at her wrists. She had kept them behind her lest her captors notice, so her ankles were still bound. She was sunburned to the point of pain, and her spine tingled with anxiety about what might happen when the boat stopped. Her thoughts were interrupted when the slight man crouched beside her, grinning.

She flinched as he cupped the back of her head in his left hand; he laughed and pried her jaw open, shoving a wad of dirty rags into her mouth. He wrapped a strip of cloth around her head and tied it in place to hold the gag.

Her eyes wide now, she braced herself. She had just decided to claw his face when he rose from his crouch and covered her with a heavy canvas tarp. The fabric abraded her sunburned skin as he pulled it over her, cutting off her view. The tarp was coarse and stiff, crusted with filth and reeking of dead fish.

The boat slowed to an idle, and she felt it bump to a stop against something solid. She heard a voice that didn't sound like either of her captors ask, "Gasoline?"

"Yeah, mon," the larger of her captors answered.

She felt the boat shift as one of the men climbed out of it. Something was dragged across the canvas tarp over her torso, coming to rest on her shoulder. She heard a gurgling sound and smelled gasoline.

She thought about removing her gag, uncovering herself, and yelling for help, but before she could act, she heard the pump cut off. What she now realized was the fuel hose was lifted from the tarp across her shoulder. Careful not to move the tarp, she brought her right hand up to the gag and began to work at the knot. Then the boat shifted again.

"We're going to go get some food," the larger man said, from several feet above her. She surmised that he was on the dock. "You want us to move the boat?"

"How long you t'ink you be?" the unfamiliar voice asked.

"Maybe one hour," the smaller man's voice said, from the boat.

"No longer than that," the larger of her captors agreed.

"Jus' leave it here, then. Nobody gon' want fuel fo' several hours, 'til the fishermen come in," the unfamiliar voice said.

The boat shifted again as the smaller man climbed out. Cynthia listened to the creaking of boards, picturing the men walking away along a dock of some kind as the sound of their voices faded. She forced herself to wait, counting off what she thought was five minutes while she untied the gag.

She dug the rags out of her mouth and restrained her urge to vomit as she shifted her position so that she could push the zip-tie around her ankles against the makeshift anchor. With one solid thrust with her leg muscles, she freed herself.

Poking her head out from under the tarp, she peered around. Satisfied that she was unobserved, she slithered out from under the tarp and rose to a crouch in the boat. As she had thought, the boat was tied alongside a fuel dock. The dock was a prominent feature of the waterfront in a small town, from what she could see.

A hundred yards from the dock, there was a white sand beach. Above the high-water mark, children in uniforms played kickball in a fenced schoolyard. Two nuns supervised the children.

She could see a structure where the dock reached the shore, and from the beer posters on the wall facing her, she guessed that it might be a bar, perhaps a restaurant. She didn't dare walk down the dock past it for fear that her captors were having lunch there. She slipped over the side of the boat into the water and swam to the beach, deciding to approach the nuns and ask for their help.

An unnerving silence settled over the children on the playground as she approached, self-conscious about her skimpy bikini. Ignoring the glare from the older of the two nuns, she approached the younger one. The children drew back, hiding behind the older nun.

"Good afternoon, sister," she said.

The woman nodded slightly, holding her gaze.

"I'm in trouble; I need your help."

The nun's eyes dropped briefly as she studied Cynthia. After a moment, she nodded.

"Come," the nun said. "First, you must cover yourself. Then we can talk." She turned and began to walk toward a breezeway that connected the schoolhouse to a smaller structure. She opened a door and stood back, gesturing for Cynthia to enter.

Cynthia stepped through the door into a small, clean room with a table and four chairs. She took in the crucifix on the whitewashed wall as her hostess opened a roughly built, unpainted cabinet. The nun turned, a folded garment of white cotton in her hands.

"Put this on for now; we'll find something else in a bit."

Cynthia unfolded the soft, worn cloth to find that it was a spotless, simple shift, several sizes too large for her. Grateful, she slipped it over her head. "Thank you, sister," she said.

"You're welcome," the nun said, her face softening into a smile. "What's wrong?"

Frankie Chaterji was about to order another round of beer
when his cell phone vibrated against his thigh. He and his cousin
Kumar were almost finished with their lunch of curried mutton;
he thought about ignoring the call. Glancing at the clock on the
wall of the ramshackle snack bar, he realized that this call might
be Li Wong, ready to take the girl off their hands.

He slipped the phone from the pocket of his ratty jeans. A
look at the screen confirmed his suspicion. "Yeah?" he said,
touching the connect icon.

"Frankie?"

"Yeah, Wong. Where are you, mon?"

"*Lotus Blossom* is just inside the reef. Bring her to me, now."

Frankie, annoyed that Wong hung up after issuing the abrupt
order, put the phone back in his pocket and took a last sip of his
beer. "Damn freak," he muttered.

"What did he want?" Kumar asked.

"Bring him the girl. They are out in the harbor at Carriacou."

"Let's go, then. He gonna pay us now?"

"He damn well better, or we'll keep her and have a little fun,"
Frankie said.

Kumar stood up, grinning at that thought, and put a 50-dollar
E.C. note on the table. He headed back down the dock to their
boat, Frankie on his heels, mumbling under his breath.

"Shit!" Kumar said, seeing their empty boat. "Little bitch is
gone."

"She cannot be too far," Frankie said. "Small island."

"What the hell are we going to do?" Kumar asked.

"We must find her, mon. I will call Wong, buy us some time."
Frankie extracted his phone and called Wong back.

"The girl got away while we were eating lunch," he said when
Wong answered. "Give us a few — " He listened for a moment,
looked down at the phone, and put it in his pocket.

"What did he say?" Kumar asked.

"He said we are to come get him; he bitched about how we are good for nothing. He will fix it himself."

Kumar frowned. "Best we go get him, I think." He stepped down into the boat and began untying the dock lines as Frankie clambered aboard.

14

"How long ago did this happen?" the priest asked, sitting across the table from Cynthia in the whitewashed room with the crucifix on the wall. The young nun put a mug of tea in front of each of them and sat down in one of the unoccupied chairs.

"It was this morning, after we had breakfast. It couldn't have been much later than 8:30, Father," Cynthia said.

The priest glanced at his watch. "It's 1:30," he said. "Your father saw this happen?"

"Yes," Cynthia said. "Like I said, we were — "

"I'm sorry. You did say the two of you were swimming together, but how close were you to him? Would he have noticed immediately?"

"I'm sure he would have, Father. We were a few yards apart, if that. They drove the boat between us. He would have had to notice right then."

"Yes, I see. So he must have raised the alarm by now. Do you know if the yacht was in cell phone range? Could he have called the police?"

"They have a satellite phone; it works everywhere, Dani told me."

"Dani?"

"The captain."

"And these two men who kidnapped you, are they still on the island?"

"I don't know, Father. They were going to get lunch, I think. That's when I escaped. That was only a few minutes ago, so they probably are. Why?" Cynthia asked, frowning.

"I'm worried that they may be looking for you. I'm trying to think of how to keep you safe."

"What about the police?" Cynthia asked.

The priest and the nun looked at one another for a moment.

"You have no idea why they took you?" the priest asked, breaking a silence of half a minute.

Cynthia shook her head, becoming exasperated. "No, but why would that matter?"

"Have you been involved with any locals?" he asked, then, seeing the flush rise on Cynthia's cheeks, he continued. "I don't mean in a personal way, my child."

"I don't understand, Father."

"Did you get involved with any of the drug people, Cynthia?" the young nun asked.

"N-no," Cynthia said, clenching her fists under the table.

"We aren't judging you, child," the priest said in a soft tone. "It's just that sometimes the police aren't, um ... "

"You think they may be crooked?" she asked.

"That's another judgment we shouldn't make. Things can be difficult in a poor country, though. Their ability to protect you from certain types of people may be compromised."

"Well," Cynthia said, "I have to do something. If I just hide here, they'll find me. My father's a lawyer. I'm sure by now he will have gone to the authorities. That's the way his mind works."

The priest nodded, stroking his chin with his hand. After a moment, he said, "Okay, then. If he's raised the alarm, the police almost have to react appropriately, I think. There would be too much scrutiny otherwise. Sister, why don't you call Constable Jones, while Cynthia and I drink our tea?"

The young nun rose from her chair and nodded, leaving the room.

"WHO IS THIS 'SHARKTOOTH' character?" Ed asked, when Dani disconnected the call and returned the phone to the cockpit seat.

"He's a character, all right," Liz said.

"You'll meet him, soon enough," Dani said. "He'll be here in 45 minutes or so."

"That fast?" Liz asked, eyebrows raised.

"He was in St. Lucia when he called. Visiting some relatives, I guess," Dani said.

"That's a long way, isn't it?" Ed asked.

"Maybe 70 miles," Dani said, "depending on where exactly he was, but he'd already started this way before he called."

"Is he a private pilot or something?" Ed asked "How can he get here that quickly?"

"No," Dani said. "He doesn't like airplanes, but he's got an extra-fast boat."

"He must. You're talking about nearly a hundred miles per hour."

Dani grinned. "Oh, it's faster than that. It's a Cigarette Marauder, with over three thousand horsepower."

"Does he race it or something?"

"Or something. It's better not to ask him too many questions about it."

"What does he do? Why's he coming?"

"He's coming to help us find the two guys from Trinidad. He's another of my father's partners. He's already put out the word on those two to his network. I'd be surprised if he hasn't located them by the time he gets here."

"What does your father do?"

"He's in the import/export business. He brokers all kinds of deals, mostly for heavy equipment, government projects, that kind of thing."

Ed studied her for a moment, maintaining eye contact as he waited. When she didn't say anything else after a full minute, he looked away. "What happens when he gets here?" he asked, after another long silence.

"We'll take *Lightning Bolt* to wherever those two jerks are and ask them a few questions," Dani said.

"We?" Ed asked.

"Sharktooth and I," Dani said. "You and Liz can stay here in case they call."

He shook his head. "I'm coming," he said.

"You're out of your depth. At best, you'd be in the way, and at worst, you could get hurt."

His face flushed and he jumped to his feet, towering over her as she sat on the cockpit seat.

"Now you listen to me, young woman."

With no apparent effort and little motion, Dani hooked a foot behind his ankle and raised her right hand, pushing stiffened fingers into his solar plexus. He gasped and sat down, hard.

"Don't try to throw your weight around, Ed. I'm on your side, but your boxing coach was right. You don't have the killer instinct."

He glared at her for a moment. "And you and this Sharktooth guy do, I guess?"

"We've — "

Liz stepped between them. "Everybody's upset. Let's remember who the bad guys are. We're going to get Cynthia back. That's what matters."

"What if they don't have her any longer? How will you get them to talk?"

"Sharktooth is a persuasive man," Liz said. "Trust us. They'll tell him everything they know. Wait until you see him. Then if you don't think you're in good hands, we'll talk some more."

CYNTHIA and the priest sat next to one another in a small conference room at the police station, a young-looking constable in an immaculate, heavily starched uniform on the other side of the table.

She had just finished explaining what had happened to her. The policeman had listened without saying anything, making notes on a pad of ruled paper.

"Have you found the men in the yellow boat, constable?" the priest asked.

"No. They were eating lunch at the snackette at the fuel dock, as Miss Savage surmised. They got a phone call as they were finishing, and they left in a hurry. This would have been just a few minutes before Sister DeMontfort called me."

He flipped back through a couple of pages, read and underlined something, and looked up. "I'm very sorry this has happened to you, Miss Savage. It is an embarrassment to my country. I think the firs' thing we mus' do is get in touch with your father."

Cynthia's eager look reflected her relief. "Yes, please," she said.

"Do you know if this yacht, *Vengeance*, has a satellite phone?"

"Yes, they do."

"And would you have the number?"

"No. Only my father's cell phone number."

"Mm," he said. "Cell phones don't usually work out there in the Cays. I'm puzzled about one thing, though."

"What's that, constable," the priest asked.

"When Sister DeMontfort called, the firs' t'ing I did was to check wit' St. Vincent to see if your father had made a report. I thought surely he would have; it had already been some hours.

When I found that he had not, I thought they mus' not have a satellite phone. Even so, they could have used the VHF radio."

"What are you getting at, Constable?" the priest asked, reaching out to pat Cynthia's hand as she fidgeted.

"I don't know; I am some confused about how to reach the yacht. I have — "

He was interrupted by a knock on the door. A questioning look on his face, he stood and turned, opening the door.

"Good day, Constable Jones."

"Good day, Mr. Wong. Excuse me sir, but I am — "

"Yes, yes, I know. I just spoke with Sister DeMontfort. Perhaps I can help. May I join you?"

"Yes, of course. Please come in," the constable said, ushering a dwarf with Oriental features into the room and holding the fourth chair for him to sit down.

"Good day, Mr. Wong," the priest said.

"Thank you, Father, and the same to you."

"Miss Savage," the priest said, turning in his chair, "allow me to introduce our good friend, Mr. Li Wong."

"Hello, Mr. Wong," Cynthia said.

"A pleasure to meet you, Miss Savage."

"Mr. Wong and his employer, Madame Chen, have been most generous in their support of our poor parish, Cynthia," the priest said. "Without their contributions, I'm not sure we could keep the school open, let alone provide books and supplies for the pupils."

"It's our privilege to support you in your work, Father," Wong said. "*Lotus Blossom* is anchored in the harbor at Hillsborough. I'm on the way back to St. Vincent from Grenada, and I came over to Petite Martinique in the tender to call at the convent while the crew took care of some minor engine maintenance. Sister DeMontfort told me about what happened. I wanted to offer Miss Savage the use of *Lotus Blossom* to return to her father and the yacht, *Vengeance*, I think it is."

"That's most kind of you Mr. Wong," Cynthia said.

"What a fortunate t'ing," the constable said. "We were just trying to find a way to get in touch with the yacht."

"The Lord works in mysterious ways," the priest said, crossing himself.

"When can we leave, Mr. Wong?" Cynthia asked.

"The tender is waiting to pick us up at the fuel dock and take us to *Lotus Blossom*."

15

DANI TURNED HER HEAD TO THE SIDE, CUPPING A HAND BEHIND HER right ear. "I think that's *Lightning Bolt*, running with open exhausts."

On her cue, the others heard a low-pitched whine that increased to a throaty roar in a matter of seconds. As Liz pointed at a plume of spray on the horizon to the north, it vanished and the sound abated.

"He just throttled back and cut in the mufflers," Dani said, getting up to rig fenders along the port side of *Vengeance* as a long, low, speedboat threaded its way through the anchorage.

Ed watched as a giant Rasta man brought the boat alongside, letting it coast to a stop as it kissed the fenders. He handed Dani a bow line and vaulted over *Vengeance's* lifelines to make the stern of his boat fast. Once he cleated the line, he rose to his full height of almost seven feet and wrapped Dani in a hug that all but hid her from view as he lifted her from the deck.

"Been way too long, ladies," he said, in a rumbling bass voice. He set Dani on her feet and turned to embrace Liz. "You got some food for me, Liz?"

"Of course," Liz laughed. "Let me warm up some curried fish while you get acquainted with Ed."

"Okay, but I eat it on the way. Those bad boys from Trinidad, they in Petite Martinique. We need to move quick."

Dani said, "Ed Savage, meet our friend, Sharktooth."

Ed got to his feet and reached out to shake hands. He flinched as his hand disappeared into Sharktooth's baseball-glove-sized paw, then grinned at the big man's gentle touch.

"Pleased to meet you, Mr. Savage," Sharktooth said, withdrawing his typically limp, island handshake.

"Ed will do just fine, but could you tell me your real name?"

"People say Sharktooth, an' I answer. That's all a name good for." He locked eyes with Ed until the lawyer nodded and looked away.

"Fair enough," Ed said. "Where is this Petite Martinique place?"

"Petite Martinique," Liz said, handing Sharktooth a frosted glass of passion fruit juice through the companionway. "Curry will be just a minute."

"Thank you," Sharktooth said.

"How far is that?" Ed asked.

"Jus' a few minutes," Sharktooth said.

"I'm coming with you," Ed said.

Sharktooth glanced at Dani. Seeing the look in her eyes, he turned back to Ed and shook his head. "No," he said.

"I can't just sit back here and wait."

Sharktooth studied him for a moment. "I see you worry 'bout your daughter. Bes' way you can help is stay here an' take the call from the bad people. Mebbe we find her in Petite Martinique, but mebbe not. Mus' cover all the possibilities."

"But if she's in Petite Martinique — "

Sharktooth held up his oversized hand, stopping Ed. "The two men were eating lunch at a snackette on the fuel dock. Their boat was tied up there, but nobody saw Cynthia. Cynthia? Right?"

"Yes. Cynthia," Ed said. "But she must be there if they're there."

"Mos' likely, they hide her somewhere before they go to Petite Martinique. Mebbe another islan', mebbe a boat. Petite Martinique a ver' small place. Bes' if you here to take that call. Nothin' you can do that me an' Dani can't do better by ourselves. We used to workin' together, you see. You don' wan' to slow us down some, do you?"

"No, certainly not, but I — "

"I can only imagine how you must feel, Ed," Dani said. "Believe me, we'll call you the minute we learn anything, okay?"

Ed's lips pulled into a tight line, like a twisted scar across his lower face. He said, "Okay, but if they call ... "

"Let us know. Sharktooth's satellite phone number is in our directory. Listen to what they have to say and focus on making a deal with them. Make them believe that's your only hope, okay?" Dani waited for him to speak, but he just nodded his agreement, his shoulders slumped.

Liz handed Sharktooth a one-quart plastic container filled with steaming curry, a fork sticking out. "Let's go, Dani," he said, cradling the hot food in his hand as he rose to his feet.

ED WATCHED as Dani and Sharktooth untied *Lightning Bolt* and jumped down into the boat, their movements coordinated like dance steps. Liz retrieved the fenders and stowed them.

"Can I get you anything? Coffee? Juice?" she asked, pausing before she settled onto the cockpit seat across the table from him.

"No, thanks. I'm okay for now," he said, his eyes following Sharktooth and Dani as the boat threaded its way through the anchorage and disappeared behind an island. "She's amazing," he said, a dreamy look on his face.

Liz looked at him, wondering at the change in his attitude over the short time since Dani had knocked him back to his seat.

"A beautiful woman, and so sure of herself," he said, smiling. "How long have you known her?"

"We met a little over two years ago," Liz said.

"I thought you'd probably known one another much longer, like since you were in college."

"No. We met in Antigua, just a few weeks before we decided to buy *Vengeance*. I was on a sort of sabbatical, and Dani was between crew assignments."

"Sabbatical? From work?"

"Yes."

"You have an English accent."

"I got my secondary education at a girl's school in the U.K. I'm from Belgium, originally."

"I see. And Dani's American?"

"When it suits her," Liz said, smiling at the transparency of his questions.

"What's that mean?"

"Sometimes she doesn't want to be American. Mostly, she uses her U.S. citizenship because it allows us to have *Vengeance* flagged in the U.S."

"Does she have a foreign passport, too?"

Liz laughed. "Only an American would look at it as having a *foreign* passport. She's a French citizen, too, through her father."

"Interesting. She told me she spent her summers in the islands, until she was old enough to crew on his charter yachts in the Mediterranean."

Liz nodded and smiled.

"So, I can't help but wonder," he said, getting to his point at last. "Are she and Sharktooth, uh ... "

Liz chuckled, her suspicions about where his questions were leading confirmed. "Hardly," she said. "She's known him since she was a child; his wife used to take care of her sometimes when Sharktooth and her father were working together."

"Oh, I see. Silly of me, but they just seemed so relaxed with one another, I ... well ... "

Liz smiled. "I understand."

"I don't mean to be nosy, but is there a man in her life? I mean ... "

"She keeps that part of her life private, Ed."

"Even from you? You seem like best friends."

"Even from me."

"I'm becoming quite fond of her, Liz, but she's hard to read sometimes."

"She certainly can be," Liz agreed.

"I don't want to push myself on her if she's ... um ... well, you see, I realize it could be awkward for her, me being a paying guest, and all. I just wanted a little guidance, so I wouldn't put her on the spot."

Liz laughed. "Sorry, Ed. I'm not laughing at you; that's quite considerate of you. The irony of the situation tickled me."

"Irony?"

Liz thought for a moment, and then shook her head. "Your sensitivity is commendable, but it's unnecessary. Dani doesn't hold back; she'll let you know if you're out of line. The fact that you're paying the bills won't keep her from speaking her mind. I'm really not comfortable pursuing this topic further, if you don't mind."

"I understand. I'm sorry if I've made you uncomfortable, and I appreciate your candor. You must think I'm a jerk, worrying about that kind of thing when my daughter's been kidnapped."

"It's not my nature to make judgments like that, Ed. We all deal with stress differently. Agonizing over something you can't control never makes things better, and right now, all you can do is wait. I'm sure any distraction is better than dwelling on your anxiety."

"THIS IS AWESOME, MR. WONG," Cynthia said, as one of the uniformed crew members helped her aboard *Lotus Blossom* from the tender. "I've never been on a yacht like this." She ran her right index finger along the gleaming varnish on the teak rail and looked aft. "Is that a British flag?"

Wong smiled and bowed slightly. "My employer believes in maintaining tradition. This yacht belonged to her father, back in the days when Hong Kong was a British Colony."

"Does she still live there?"

He shook his head. "No. She found doing business under the communists too difficult. She has been in St. Vincent for many years now."

"What kind of business is she in?" Cynthia asked as Wong led her through a corridor paneled with deeply polished rosewood.

"She's into many different businesses."

"Is she aboard? Will I meet her?"

He looked back over his shoulder and smiled up at her. "She's not aboard at the moment, but it's possible that you'll meet her. She's quite interested in you."

"She's interested in me?"

"And she knows your father must be anxious to be reunited with you." He had stopped in front of a cabin door; he stood looking up at her, studying her face for a moment. "You look perplexed."

"How does she know about me? Or my father?"

"Ah, yes. Of course, I see now why you are puzzled. I called her before I volunteered the use of *Lotus Blossom* to reunite you and your father, to be sure that the delay wouldn't be a problem to her."

He opened the door and gestured for her to enter. Cynthia paused in the doorway as she took in the grandeur of the stateroom.

"Oh!" she said. "It's gorgeous. This is bigger than my room at home; I had no idea that yachts were like this."

Wong smiled at her. "Please," he said. "Make yourself comfortable. This is Madame Chen's cabin; she suggested that you use it as your own. You may wish to shower and freshen up." He sniffed, wrinkling his nose, and ran his eyes over the white cotton shift. "There will be a selection of toiletries in the head, and I'll have a stewardess lay out some clean clothing on the bed for you."

"That would be great, Mr. Wong. I don't know how to thank you."

"Perhaps someday you'll be in a position to pass on the favor, Miss Savage. If you need anything, just use the bell-pull beside the bed to call the stewardess."

He bowed slightly and backed out of the room, closing the door behind him with a soft click.

Cynthia went into the bath and turned on the shower, stripping off the shift and her foul-smelling bikini as she waited for the water to heat up.

16

"WHAT DID YOU DO WITH THEM?" WONG ASKED ERIC SCHMIDT, THE captain of *Lotus Blossom.*

"They're tied up in one of the storage lockers next to the engine room."

"Ah," Wong said. "And their boat?"

"In the garage, where the tender you were using goes. I wanted to get that yellow boat out of sight as quickly as I could."

"Yes, that's good," Wong said. "Once we're over the horizon, you can dispose of them."

"Do you wish them to be found? We could — "

"No, I don't think so. Just make them disappear in deep water. The boat, too. There will be fewer questions that way."

"As you wish, Mr. Wong. We can tow the tender until then and bring it aboard once their boat's no longer in the way."

"Actually, Eric, I need the tender again, and probably Riley. We have to lay a false trail. Everyone on the island knows by now that I brought the girl aboard, thanks to those two morons."

"Why Riley? He's my pick to handle the disposal. Couldn't one of the other men — "

"There will be some theatrics required, and Riley enjoys certain things that the others might find perverse."

"I see," the captain said, going pale beneath his tan. "Will I need to bleach the teak deck again?"

"No. Riley and I will confine our activity to the tender. You can just hose it out when we're done."

"I should probably have someone rig the steam-cleaning equipment to get rid of the trace evidence," the captain said.

"Not necessary, in this case. Riley and I will both appear to be victims, so the trace evidence will only serve to corroborate our story, if it comes to that." Wong grinned at the captain's discomfort.

"Don't look so queasy, Eric. Riley enjoys this kind of thing as much as I do. Summon him, please."

"What about the girl?"

"What about her?"

"Will we keep her aboard?"

"Only for a little while. When Riley and I get back, I'll arrange for a transfer. Then you will need to remove any trace evidence that would indicate her presence aboard *Lotus Blossom*."

"Yes, I understand, Mr. Wong. Let me get Riley for you."

"Just have him meet me in the tender, please. We need to hurry. As soon as we leave, you get under way. Head due west until you're over the radar horizon from the islands. You understand?"

The captain nodded, reaching for an intercom handset.

"And Eric?"

"Yes, sir?"

"Treat the girl as a guest; make sure nothing happens to her, and give her anything she wants, but don't allow her out of Madame Chen's stateroom."

Cynthia made the most of the steaming shower; she'd found the shower on *Vengeance* to be adequate, but this one was luxurious. She lathered and rinsed her hair twice, then applied some of the conditioner that she found on the shelf.

She contemplated filling the tub and enjoying a bubble bath, but decided that she might not have time. She settled for the delicately perfumed, hard-milled French soap instead, scrubbing herself thoroughly with the loofah and then standing under the near-scalding water as long as she could stand it.

Turning off the water, she wound an oversized bath sheet around herself and stepped to the vanity to blow dry her hair. She considered using some of the makeup that she found on the vanity, but decided against it; she'd be back aboard *Vengeance* soon, and then she'd just need sunscreen.

She opened the head door a crack and peeked into the stateroom. There was no one in the room, and as Wong had promised, there were clothes laid out on the bed. She walked to the bed and dropped the bath sheet, running her hand over the cream-colored silk lounging pajamas that had been left for her.

The silk was heavy, soft and rich to her touch. She eagerly stepped into the pants and tied the drawstring, relishing the way the fabric caressed her sunburned thighs. She picked up the top, pausing for a moment as she held it to her chest, enjoying the feel of the raw silk on her tender skin.

With a sigh, she put the top on and walked toward the door, thinking she would find Mr. Wong and thank him. She was surprised to find that the door to the stateroom was locked. She looked down, studying the knob, searching for a latch of some kind, but none was there.

She knocked on the door, tentatively at first, then with increasing force, but there was no answer. She remembered that Mr. Wong had mentioned the bell-pull by the bed. Walking to the bed, she realized the yacht was moving. Feeling disoriented by the increasing acceleration, she sat down on the bed.

There was a curtained window along the side of the bed. She shifted her position to where she could push the curtain aside, but she could see nothing except pristine blue water and an impossibly beautiful sky. The few clouds were so well defined that she wondered for a moment if they were real or some image on the glass. She couldn't guess where they were headed, but judging from the surface of the water, they were moving at a high speed, much faster than *Vengeance* had gone.

She thought again about the bell-pull, but she felt a tremor of fear at the thought of the locked door. She decided to examine the stateroom before she summoned anyone, to see if she might find some hidden mechanism to open the door.

Cynthia was a veteran of several years of weekly visits to a shrink as a result of her difficulty dealing with her mother's death. She recognized that she was engaging in what her counselor called avoidance behavior; she might still be a prisoner, but she didn't want to confirm it just yet. She let herself escape into imagining the reunion with her father and Dani and Liz.

WONG AND THE FIRST MATE, Riley, stood facing one another in the tender as it bobbed in the remains of *Lotus Blossom's* wake. The yacht was rapidly diminishing in size as it streaked toward the horizon.

"Ready?" Wong asked.

The burly first mate grinned. "Yeah, Mr. Wong."

"You go first, Riley. Make it count; don't hold anything back." Wong braced himself as Riley set his feet and launched a hard, scarred fist.

Wong enjoyed the explosion of pain from his forehead as his vision went red. He wiped the blood from his eyes, grinning at the muscle-bound first mate. "Good one. Again, Riley. More blood, this time. Go for the — "

Wong blacked out momentarily when Riley's fist split his nose like a piece of ripe fruit. He shook his head, wiping his eyes again.

"Okay?" Riley asked.

"Fine, Riley."

"Again, Mr. Wong?"

"What do you think? Do I look like I've been beaten senseless yet?"

"Where you want it, then," Riley asked.

"Bust my lips; careful of the teeth, though."

Riley delivered a vicious backhand blow that split both of the little man's lips. "Ain't nothin' left to bleed, Mr. Wong. Your turn, boss."

Wong had been braced against the steering console, the better to stand up to Riley's punches. He nodded and stepped forward. "Ready?"

Riley dropped into a boxer's stance and grinned. "Yes, sir."

Wong shifted slightly, and Riley saw that he held his straight razor down next to his own thigh, where Riley couldn't reach it.

"Go ahead, Boss," Riley said. "Make me bleed, too."

Wong laughed. "If I cut you again, you'll bleed to death before we get there." He reached in a locker and passed the big man a towel. "Wrap your forearms up before you go into shock."

Riley reached for the towel and caught a glimpse of the blood coursing from the gashes on both forearms. As the first mate's knees went weak, Wong pushed him back against the pneumatic tube on the port side of the tender and wrapped the towel around one of his forearms. Grabbing another towel, he wrapped the other arm.

"Hold those in place. I'll get us to the fuel dock. Don't forget; two East Indians in a yellow speed boat. Knocked me out, cut you up, and snatched the girl."

The mate, his skin gone pale beneath his tan, mumbled his

understanding as Wong started the engine and slipped behind the helm.

17

"I DON'T SEE ANY BOATS LIKE THE ONE ED DESCRIBED," DANI SAID, lowering the binoculars as she and Sharktooth idled through the anchorage off Petite Martinique in *Lightning Bolt*.

"Wait," Sharktooth said, edging closer to the fuel dock. "That RIB got blood all over it." He pointed to a large, inboard-powered rigid inflatable boat of the sort used as tenders on large yachts. It was tied to the fuel dock with no one around it.

He pulled in behind the RIB and shut off his engines as Dani tied bow and stern lines to the pilings.

"The attendant's not around," she said. "Let's check at the office."

"Mm-hmm," Sharktooth said.

They climbed up onto the dock and walked toward the shore. Dani pointed out the trail of blood drops on the weathered boards under their feet. No one was in the office, but there was a woman behind the counter in the snackette at the head of the dock. She was talking softly on a cell phone when they walked in.

She finished her call and said, "Good afternoon. Welcome."

"Good afternoon," Sharktooth said.

"You can sit anywhere you like," she said, waving at the empty tables.

"Actually, we were looking for the fuel dock attendant," Dani said.

The woman shook her head, a solemn look on her face. "He gone. Took them po' men to the clinic."

"From that yacht tender?" Dani asked.

"Mm-hmm, yes," the woman nodded. "Terrible."

"There was a lot of blood in the tender," Dani said. "What happened?"

"Them two men from Trinidad," the woman said shaking her head and clicking her tongue in disapproval. "Knew they was evil soon as they come in here. Sometimes, you can jus' tell when Satan done put the touch on a body."

"They in a yellow boat, with two big outboards?" Sharktooth asked.

"Mm-hmm. They do sump'n to you folks, too?"

Dani and Sharktooth exchanged quick looks. She nodded, and he said, "They kidnapped a guest from our charter yacht up in the Cays."

The woman nodded. "We 'spected it was sump'n like that. She done got away from 'em, praise be to Jesus."

"She escaped?" Dani asked.

"Mm-hmm. Went to the church. Father Daniel was helpin' her. He took her to the p'lice, an' while they was figgerin' out how to get her back to her father on that yacht, Mr. Wong come along an' say he give her a ride back to the yacht she on."

"Mr. Wong?" Dani prompted.

"Mm-hmm. He on Madame Chen's yacht, *Lotus Blossom.* He been doin' some bidness dungda Grenada, an' he come by heah to bring somethin' to Father Daniel, I t'ink. Sister DeMontfort, she tell him 'bout this po' girl, an' he go to the p'lice an' say he take her back to the yacht, 'cause he goin' thataway anyhow."

"Uh-huh," Sharktooth said. "Tha's ver' nice of him. So he take her back up to the Cays?"

"Well, not 'zackly, see. Them two devil men, they musta see the girl get in the tender goin' out to *Lotus Blossom*. They stop the tender an' take the girl back. Beat up Mr. Wong real bad, an' cut the man wit' him. Tha's where Walter gone."

"Walter?" Dani asked.

"Mm-hmm. Walter work on the fuel dock. He take 'em to the clinic. They in bad shape."

"They say which way the men in the yellow boat went?" Sharktooth asked.

The woman shrugged. "Reckon mebbe they hurt too bad to see."

Dani looked at Sharktooth for a moment and then turned back to the woman. "Thanks for your help. Could you ask Mr. Wong to give me a call when he's able?" Dani handed the woman a business card. "I'm the captain of the yacht the girl was taken from. Her father's beside himself with worry. I'm sure he'd like to speak to Mr. Wong and thank him for his help."

"No problem. Mr. Wong, he in much bettah shape than the other fella. Reckon they figured he couldn't do them much harm, little dwarf fella like him. Jus' hit him a few times." She shook her head. "Other fella big an' strong. They cut him up bad."

"Thank you," Sharktooth said. He and Dani walked back down the dock to *Lightning Bolt*. "What now?" he asked, once Dani had untied the dock lines.

"Back to *Vengeance*, I think."

"You don't want to try to talk to this Wong?" Sharktooth asked.

"Not just yet. Let's see if he calls. While we're waiting, we can see what we can find out about him and this Madame Chen."

"I'll put the word out again 'bout the yellow boat, too," Sharktooth said, reaching for his satellite phone.

"GOOD AFTERNOON. This is the yacht, *Vengeance*," Liz said, answering the satellite phone. The display showed 'calling number blocked.'

"Give me Edward Savage," the caller said, the voice warbling.

"Just one second." Liz put her hand over the mouthpiece.

"Ed, this is probably the kidnappers. The voice is electronically disguised." She handed him the phone, switching it to speakerphone mode.

"This is Ed Savage."

"Liquidate your brokerage accounts," the voice gargled. "You need to wire us $10 million in the next 48 hours if you want to see your daughter again."

"I want to talk to — "

The warbling voice cut him off. "Follow our instructions, or else we'll sell her to the highest bidder. Right now, you need to be raising the cash. We'll be in touch." The connection was broken.

"Shit," Ed said, giving the phone back to Liz and hiding his face in his hands.

She put the phone on the seat beside her and laid a soothing hand on his forearm, patting him. "It's progress."

"Yeah, I suppose. I'd like to know she's okay, though."

"That's understandable. They'll probably let her talk to you at some point. One thing about kidnappers in Trinidad is that they're professionals; they're just in it for the money."

"Do they usually release their victims?"

"Yes. It's a business to them. They have to maintain a certain level of credibility, or they couldn't operate effectively. It could be worse."

"Why do you guys seem to know so much about this kind of thing?"

"Dani and I both have some personal experience with kidnapping."

"How's that?"

"We've both been kidnapped."

"Both of you?"

"At different times."

"For ransom?"

"Y-yes."

"What was the hesitation for?"

"There was more to it than just ransom. We'd gotten crossways with some drug runners who dabbled in human trafficking. There was an element of payback."

"But you both survived," Ed said.

"That's the important thing," Liz said, nodding.

"Were you running drugs or something?"

"No, of course not. We were just in the wrong place at the wrong time."

"And the kidnappers?"

"They aren't around anymore."

"In prison?"

"No."

"You mean they got away?"

"No. Dani and her friends prefer their own form of closure, and as the song says, the sea never gives up her dead."

"You mean — " He stopped talking when Liz jumped up and pointed at the rooster tail on the horizon to the south.

"*Lightning Bolt*," she said, pointing. "They're back."

"WHERE IS THE GIRL?" Marissa Chen asked, the telephone handset wedged between her left shoulder and her head as she worked her way through the stack of documents on her desk, signing in the places that had been marked with tags by her attorney.

"Ah, we have her; she is secured," Wong said, standing on the bridge of *Lotus Blossom* as he watched Eric Schmidt directing the crewmen down on the foredeck. They had hoisted the tender aboard and were scrubbing the bloodstains away.

"Answer me, my little one," the Dragon Lady said, her tone betraying her impatience.

"She's here aboard *Lotus Blossom*, but — "

"You fool! Aboard *Lotus Blossom*! I'll — "

"Please, Madame, it's only temporary. She escaped."

"Escaped?! What are you saying, Wong? Escaped from where?"

"From the men who took her, but it's under control, now."

"Not if she's on my yacht, it isn't. Where are those two buffoons? You said they could pull this off."

"We're going to handle them; we're under way, and as soon as we're out of radar range of the islands, we'll dump them."

"There must be no trace of them, Wong. Nothing to connect them to us."

"I understand, Madame. They and their boat will never be seen again."

"Where were they when the girl escaped?"

"Having lunch on the fuel dock in Petite Martinique. They left her tied up under a tarp in their boat."

"What happened?"

Wong described the events that led to his 'rescue' of the girl from the police station.

"Imbecile!" she hissed. "Now she was last seen in your company, bound for my yacht."

"I've taken care of that, Madame." He went on to explain the ruse he had employed. "So for now, everyone thinks the two men from Trinidad recaptured her."

"And you got to indulge in your favorite pastime, you little pervert."

"I only did what was necessary."

"Will Riley recover the full use of his arms?"

"He should, Madame, with time."

"Meanwhile, he's useless to us."

"With respect, Madame, he corroborates the illusion."

"Who knows besides the people on Petite Martinique?"

"Ah, the woman who runs that yacht, *Vengeance*. She came looking for the girl."

"She what? How did she track the girl to Petite Martinique?"

"I don't know, yet, Madame, but I — "

"Don't know yet? Did you talk to her?"

"Not yet. She talked with Irene at the snackette. She left a business card, and asked for me to call her."

"You will not do that. Do you understand?"

"Yes, Madame, as you wish, but — "

"I will deal with her directly. Who is she?"

"Danielle Berger."

"And her telephone number?"

Wong read off the digits to her.

"Was she alone? How did she arrive in Petite Martinique?"

"She was in a parasailing boat, driven by a big, bald-headed Rasta man."

"Bald? Why does Irene think he's a Rasta then?"

"She said he was a giant; maybe 7 feet tall, and dreadlocks to his waist, but bald on top."

"Hmph. Must be one of the boat boys that hangs out in the Cays, looking for parasailing business. Check him out, but stay out of sight."

"Yes, Madame."

"And get the girl on the *Lion of Judah* immediately."

"Yes, Madame. They're on the way to our rendezvous as we speak."

"Good. Once that's done and all traces of her presence are removed, bring *Lotus Blossom* to Wallilabou. Make sure to clean up the evidence of the two fools you hired, too."

"As you wish."

"And, Wong?"

"Madame?"

"Is your face damaged?"

"I have stitches, but — "

"Where?"

"My right eyebrow, my nose, and my upper and lower lips."

"Hurry with your tasks. I want you."

"Of course, Madame." Wong grinned, enjoying the way the stitches pulled at his flesh.

ED PACED on the side deck as *Lightning Bolt* drew close to *Vengeance*. "Did you find them?" he yelled, as soon as they were within hailing distance.

Dani shook her head. "We just missed them," she said, handing the bow line up to Liz, who crouched on the deck forward of Ed.

Dani scrambled up and tied the stern line, and Sharktooth followed close behind her. Dani put a hand on Ed's shoulder. "She almost managed to get away from them," she said.

"She what? How?"

"We don't know the details," she said, "but she escaped while the two men were eating lunch. She went to the parish priest for help, and he took her to the police station."

"Well, where is she, then?" Ed asked, his hands grasping Dani's shoulders as he stared into her eyes.

"A man that the locals all knew and thought well of came along while they were wondering how to proceed and offered to bring her here on his yacht."

"Okay," Ed said. "So?"

"So they were in the tender, going out to the yacht, when the two men caught up with them. They beat up her rescuer and seriously wounded the man driving the tender. They took her away."

"Shit! That's awful. I was excited there for a minute, but this has to be worse than before, now, doesn't it?"

"That's hard to say," Dani said.

"How could it not be worse? They'll be angry with her now," Ed said.

"Remember what we were talking about a few minutes ago, Ed," Liz said. "This is business for them. Sure, they'll be upset with her, but she's still valuable to them. They'll just be more cautious with her now."

He shook his head, dropping his hands from Dani's shoulders.

"Ed, she's clearly got a survivor's attitude," Dani said. "For her to escape, that means she's got her wits about her. She's going to be okay; attitude is 90 percent of getting through this kind of thing."

"Let me make us some lunch," Liz said. "Ed, why don't you tell Dani and Sharktooth about your phone call?"

Liz went below into the galley, and the other three settled in the shade of the cockpit awning. Ed recounted the brief call from the kidnappers.

"Did Liz call Phillip?" Dani asked.

"Haven't had a chance, yet," Liz called up from below. "We got the call right before I spotted you returning."

Dani picked up the satellite phone and scrolled through the menu. Before she placed the call, Ed asked, "What can he do?"

"See if we can get any information on who made the call," Dani said, pressing the connect icon.

"But it said 'calling number blocked,'" Ed said.

Dani nodded, but proceeded to give Phillip the technical details on their phone. She disconnected and turned to Ed. "He has some contacts that can sometimes work past that. It has to do with correlating data from a bunch of different places. No guarantees, but it's worth a try."

"That sounds like some kind of NSA spook stuff," Ed said.

"I don't know." Dani shrugged. "Have you done anything about raising the money?"

"Not yet. Why?"

"Because they may be tracking your account activity to see if you're working on it."

"How could they do that?"

"Ed, I have no idea. I only know that there's no privacy when it comes to that kind of data anymore — not from anyone who's determined and unconstrained by rules."

"Shit. That's scary."

"Get over it. Can you raise that kind of money in 48 hours?"

"Yes. That's just about the extent of my liquid assets, though. I'm lucky they didn't ask for more; I probably couldn't raise it. Not fast, anyway."

"See what I mean? They probably know all about your finances. They knew exactly where to draw the line on the ransom, didn't they?"

He nodded, a chastened look on his face. "Can I use that phone?"

"Sure." She handed it to him, and he keyed in a number without needing to look it up.

18

Sharktooth joined them in the cockpit. He had been up on the foredeck, speaking on his own satellite phone in soft tones.

"Anything new?" Dani asked, as he sat down next to her.

He held a hand out flat, palm down, and rocked it side to side. "Some. Not much."

"What?" Ed asked, disconnecting from his call and handing the phone back to Dani.

"The fellas from Trinidad, they bad people. Hired muscle, like you guess, Dani. Been in so much trouble, don't nobody in Trinidad want to use 'em anymore. Police watchin' everyt'ing they do."

Ed's face fell. "That's not good."

Sharktooth shrugged. "Jus' mean they can't get work in Trinidad. Word is, they hook up with somebody in St. Vincent."

"Do they have a history of kidnapping?"

"Mm-hmm. Every bad boy in Trinidad have a history of kidnapping. Kidnapping the national sport."

"Anything else?" Dani asked.

"What that lady at the snackette tol' us," Sharktooth paused until Dani nodded. "It all check out right. I called Father Daniel. He tol' me same t'ing she say."

"Who's Father Daniel?" Ed asked.

"He my mother's stepfather's uncle's grandson. My cousin, I t'ink."

"The parish priest in Petite Martinique who helped Cynthia," Dani added. "Did he tell you any more about this Mr. Wong?"

She saw Ed's eyebrows twitch and said, "Mr. Wong was the man who offered to bring Cynthia here on his yacht."

"Mm-hmm. Mr. Wong work for a lady in St. Vincent name Marissa Chen. They in the spice trade, come from Hong Kong after the Chinese took it back from the British. She rich lady, give lotsa money to Father Daniel for the school. An' not jus' that. She give money to all kindsa charity in the islands."

"What's Wong's relationship to her?" Dani asked.

"He the right-hand man. Run t'ings, day to day, from what Father Daniel say. He a dwarf; work for the Chen family from when the lady's father run the business. They bust he face up pretty good, what Father Daniel say. Mebbe 20 or 30 stitches."

"That woman said they cut the other guy," Dani said.

"Mm-hmm. Both arm; cut up bad. Mebbe not be able to use hands right."

"God help Cynthia," Ed mumbled, sniffing back tears.

Sharktooth laid a big hand on his shoulder and looked him in the eye. "They most likely won't hurt her. Not as long as you do what they say. It's business; if they hurt their hostages, people won't trust them."

"Trust them? They're kidnappers," Ed said.

"But if they don't deliver the victim when the ransom's paid, they won't be able to make a deal on their next job. That's the way it works, at least down here." Sharktooth dropped his island accent as he tried to soothe Ed.

"I've always heard about them sending a finger, or an ear, or something like that," Ed said.

"Mm-hmm. Mostly, they only do that if you don't follow their instructions."

"So you're saying I should just meekly pay the $10 million dollars and not try to find them?"

"You should follow their instructions to the letter until we find them," Sharktooth said.

"And then what?"

"And then we put them out of business. Kidnapping ver' bad t'ing. Mos' people in the islan', they happy to see kidnapper disappear." He grinned as he shifted back to his local language.

Ed stared at Sharktooth for a moment, then turned his gaze to Dani's icy blue eyes. He swallowed hard and looked away just as Liz passed a platter of sandwiches up through the companionway.

HAVING CURLED into a fetal position on the queen-sized bed as she fought her anxiety, Cynthia jerked to a sitting position when she heard the latch on the door snap open. She rose to her feet as the door swung back, stifling a scream when she saw Wong's bloody face. He cackled with laughter and stepped into the cabin, followed by two uniformed crewmen that she hadn't seen before.

"What happened to you?" she asked.

He grinned, stretching the stitches in his lower lip. Drops of blood beaded around the stitches and began to run down his chin. "Just a little diversion."

"Why did you lock me in?"

The men with him laughed. Wong went into the head, emerging with her bikini and the cotton shift. He tossed them at her. "Put these on."

"What? Why?"

"Change of plans. You won't need silk pajamas where you're going."

"Where I'm going? I thought — "

"Enough. I don't have time for you right now. Strip off those pajamas."

Frightened, she took a step toward the head. One of the crewmen moved between her and the door, grinning as he ran his eyes over her body.

"Now," Wong said, raising his voice, "or I'll let them help you change clothes."

"Can't I have privacy?"

Wong sighed. "You two, turn around."

The crewmen did as ordered. "I'll close my eyes and give you ten seconds, starting NOW."

Cynthia stripped and put on the bikini, still damp from when she had rinsed it. As she dropped the shift over her head, Wong said, "Okay, take her to the dinghy."

"Am I — " she asked, doubling over with a gasp as Wong drove his fist into her stomach.

The crewmen grabbed her arms and frog-marched her through the passageway to the stern platform where the tender was waiting, its engine idling. They shoved her toward the RIB. As she stumbled forward, one of the people in the RIB, a woman, caught her and helped her aboard. Wong scrambled after her.

"Let's go," he ordered, and the RIB surged forward, swerving toward a rusty little freighter that rolled in the swell a few hundred yards away, black smoke belching from its stack in irregular bursts.

Cynthia made out the crudely painted name on the rounded stern as they approached. *Lion of Judah*, the vessel was named, and the hailing port was Port-au-Prince, Haiti.

"Where are you — " Her question was cut off by the vicious slap that Wong delivered to the side of her head. She blinked, dazed by the blow.

"Shut up," he ordered. "Do as you're told, and maybe your father will pay your ransom."

She caught herself as she started to speak, closing her mouth on her next question.

"Good girl," Wong said. "You're learning. Perhaps I'll have time to teach you more, before this is over."

She stroked her cheek, feeling the swelling which had already begun. Wong laughed at that. The RIB bumped to a stop against a small platform that marked the end of a ramp that led up to the deck of the battered little ship. Two men in ragged clothes stood on the platform, leering at her.

Wong jerked her to her feet and pushed her forward. One of the men grabbed her by her upper arm and dragged her onto the platform as she stumbled to keep her footing.

"Keep her safe," Wong said.

The man, who still held her arm in a painful grip, laughed.

"I'll be back," Wong said. "I'd better not find that you've touched her. Do you understand?"

Cynthia saw a flash of movement, and the leg of the laughing man's pants fell open from his crotch to his ankle, cut cleanly by the razor that Wong folded and put away as if nothing had happened.

The man's face went pale as his laughter stopped. "Yes, Mr. Wong," he said in a sober voice.

"And keep her by herself. Don't put her in with the others."

"Just as you say, Mr. Wong," the man said. He tugged Cynthia's arm, turning her toward the ramp, and pushed her forward. She heard the RIB leave. As she and her two escorts stepped onto the flaking paint of the freighter's deck, two more men hoisted the ramp.

The man holding her arm barked something in a guttural voice. Cynthia couldn't understand the language, though she recognized a word or two of French. The other man who had been on the platform grabbed her other arm as the one who had spoken released his grip.

The man who had spoken shifted his hand to her chin and

turned her head, forcing her to look at him. "You go him, bitch. You make trouble, I cut you bad so even Wong no want you." He spat in her face and jerked her head to the side as he let her go. He gave another order in the language that Cynthia thought must be pidgin French of some kind. So frightened she almost couldn't remain standing, she let the other man lead her below deck.

MARISSA CHEN STUDIED the email from the private investigator to whom she had been referred by her mob contact. The Dragon Lady believed in knowing all she could learn about any potential adversary, and at the moment, that was how she classified Danielle Berger. Wong hadn't been able to explain how the Berger woman tracked Cynthia Savage to Petite Martinique. Berger must have connections somewhere; there were too many islands too close to the Tobago Cays for her to have ended up at Petite Martinique by chance.

She skimmed Berger's biographical data, seeing nothing there that would explain her appearance in Petite Martinique. Berger and her partner Liesbet Chirac both had backgrounds in financial management prior to buying their yacht. Berger had worked for her family's investment bank in New York, while Chirac had worked in Brussels for the E.U. They had owned the yacht for about three years, and had bought it in Antigua, although it was U.S. flagged. Chen made a note on a legal pad to find out how the two met.

There was no information on Chirac save her education and her employment by the E.U. Berger, on the other hand, had worked as hired crew on several yachts during her time in university, and had left the family banking business a year before she and Chirac bought *Vengeance*. During that year, she had been employed as crew on a British yacht, the *Ramblin' Gal*.

She had abandoned that job without notice, disappearing

from the yacht while it was in Mayreau, part of St. Vincent and the Grenadines. Her unexplained absence had caused some difficulty for the yacht's owner when he had tried to clear out for Antigua. The email offered no explanation for how that had been resolved, nor any accounting for Berger's activity during the period between her disappearance and her purchase of *Vengeance*.

Chen made another note to herself. She would follow up with her local contacts. There would be some record; the immigration people were tenacious in their pursuit of crewmembers who jumped ship in their country.

She read on, finding nothing else of interest in the investigator's report. Tearing off the page of notes she had made, she opened the manila folder that held the rest of her scribbled notes on the operation. She inserted the new sheet in the front, noticing as she did that the satellite phone number that Wong had given her from Berger's business card was the same as the number that her minions had obtained from Ed Savage's office.

That was no surprise, but it did cause her to make another note to herself to find out if Berger had a personal cell phone number. Cell phones were less secure than satellite phones, especially in the islands. She might be able to track the woman, or even have her calls monitored. She closed the folder and dropped it in the file drawer of her desk, thinking that she would have a cup of tea before she called her contacts in immigration to ask about Berger.

The intercom line on her desk phone chimed before she picked up the handset. Pressing down the key, she said, "Yes? What is it, Veralyn?"

"Mr. Wong is here, Madame Chen."

"Ah, thank you, Veralyn. Send him right in. And, Veralyn?"

"Yes, Madame?"

"Cancel my appointments for this afternoon, and hold my calls. I do not wish to be disturbed while Mr. Wong is here."

19

"HE'S FALLEN FOR YOU, BIG-TIME," LIZ SAID, GRINNING AT DANI AS she poured her another cup of herbal tea.

They sat in the shadows in the cockpit. Ed was below in his stateroom, trying to sleep. He had excused himself after dinner, saying he wanted to take a prescription tranquilizer and try to get his blood pressure under control. Sharktooth was on the foredeck with his satellite phone, speaking softly in patois.

"What?" Dani asked, looking distracted. "Who's done what?"

"Ed," Liz said. "He was like a teenager. Thought he was being really clever."

"What are you talking about?"

"It's working," Liz said.

"Sorry to be dense, Liz, but I have no idea what you're talking about. What's working?"

"Playing hard to get. You're driving him crazy."

Dani smacked her forehead with the heel of her hand. "That jerk."

Liz frowned. "But I thought you wanted — "

"I can't believe it. His daughter's been kidnapped, and he's still acting like a, a ... " her face turned red.

"You're blushing," Liz said.

"Blushing? I'm trying to restrain my impulse to kick his sorry ass. I can't believe he's got sex on his mind when his daughter's in trouble."

"Well, since you quit fawning over him, he's really taken the bait."

"I don't have time for that. To hell with him and his flirting. We need to find Cynthia before something bad happens to her."

"You don't believe the line we've been feeding Ed? About professional kidnappers?"

Dani shook her head. "No. The coincidence with this drug business argues against that. Let him believe it; no need to alarm him, but my bet is that the ransom demand is an afterthought. I think they want her silenced."

"But who could she identify that she hasn't already told the police about?"

Dani shrugged. "Good question, but we can't ask her now. When I talked to Phillip a few minutes ago, he said the Chief Super had told him that the taxi driver had gone missing. So has the bartender from the ferry. They're looking for a guy who was a known associate of both of them. He hasn't been seen for a couple of days, either."

"Wow! Guess somebody's nervous, then. What could she know?"

"She must have stumbled over something without realizing it, or at least they think she did, which is just as bad. Oh, and that guy they're still looking for?"

"What about him?"

"He matches the description of the guy I knocked off the dinghy dock the night we picked Ed up."

"Oh," Liz said. "You think he was trying to snatch her then?"

"It looked that way."

"Yes, it did. That does reinforce the connection between her drug buy and her kidnapping, doesn't it?"

"It does."

"Did Phillip have anything else to offer?"

"Nothing except what Sharktooth already told us. I did ask him to check up on this Chen woman, though."

"From what the priest told Sharktooth, she and Wong are do-gooders. Why do you want him to check them out?"

"Coincidence? My suspicious nature? The whole thing just feels wrong."

Liz nodded.

"And I can't believe that shithead has time to think about sex when Cynthia's ... " Dani shook her head and took a sip of coffee. "What did he say, anyway?"

"Well, he tried to be subtle, but it was easy enough to see what he was up to. The clincher was when he asked if you and Shark-tooth were a couple."

Dani laughed at that. "There'd be no competition from Ed if we were; that's for sure."

"He was also fishing for whether you'd said anything to me about his attention. He didn't want to press on if it was making you uncomfortable."

"Uncomfortable? What was he thinking?"

"Well, he thought that since he was a paying guest, you might feel some obligation to go along with his advances."

"What a piece of shit. How can he have sex on his mind at a time like this?"

"Some men react to stress that way, Dani."

"Maybe so, but this comes across as too calculated to be that kind of thing. I'm irritated with myself that I even thought about getting involved with him, now."

"Don't be too quick to judge him. He's still a hunk."

"He's all yours; I'm busy."

Liz's face flushed. "That's not why I told you. I just — "

"It's okay, Liz," Dani said, laughing. "Thanks for passing it along."

CYNTHIA SAT ON THE SOUR-SMELLING, stained mattress in the dark, cramped cabin. Her head ached from the racket of the engine on the other side of the steel bulkhead. The heat was oppressive, and the air stank of diesel fuel and stale tobacco smoke, but the dominant odor was the one that wafted from the filthy bedding.

She had first tried sitting down on the deck, leaning her back against the bulkhead between her and the engine room, but then the vessel had accelerated, and the vibration and noise had driven her across the cabin to lean against the door.

She found that the deck in front of the door was sticky with some unidentified substance. Repulsed, she retreated to the relative comfort of the bunk that was wedged into the opposite corner; there was no other space large enough to afford her a seat.

She was startled by a loud squeak. Peering through the gloom, she saw the hand wheel in the middle of the watertight door turning. Someone was coming into the cabin, and she had no means to defend herself, nowhere to hide. The door banged open and she screamed when she saw the two men who had brought her aboard silhouetted in the light from the corridor. One of the men carried two dented buckets, one in each hand. He set them on the deck and reached to the side, fumbling with something on the bulkhead outside the door. There was a loud snapping sound, and the room was bathed in sickly yellow light from a single bulb in a wire cage above the door.

He leered at her and licked his lips, laughing as she wedged herself farther into the corner. He picked up the two buckets and set them on the deck inside the door. He turned and took a heavy bowl from the other man.

She saw that a spoon protruded from the bowl and felt her stomach growl. She was astonished to discover that she was hungry. The man set the bowl beside the two buckets and backed through the doorway. The other man swung the door shut, and the wheel in the center spun again.

She got up and went to where the bowl and the buckets were sitting against the bulkhead. One bucket was empty; the other was about two-thirds filled with dirty-looking water. She picked up the bowl and sniffed at the contents. To her surprise, the aroma made her mouth water.

She stirred the food with the spoon and saw that it was a watery, gray stew of some kind. Rice, tomatoes, and gristly looking bits of meat were the only identifiable ingredients.

Raising the spoon to her mouth, she took a tiny taste. A myriad of flavors exploded in her mouth, foreign to her, but nonetheless appetizing. She took the bowl back to the bunk and sat on the edge, cradling it in her lap as she began to devour the stew. Before she was sated, the bowl was empty. She wiped a finger through the bowl, collecting the greasy remnants, and licked up the last drop. She set the bowl on the floor by her feet, and lay down, feeling sleepy. As drowsiness overcame her, she wondered what was in the stew that made it taste so much better than it looked. She decided she'd rather not know, and drifted into a fitful sleep.

"THE CALL CAME from a satellite phone stolen from a yacht up in Chateaubelair a few weeks ago," Phillip said.

"Did they get a location?" Dani asked.

"No, only the usual satellite footprint — not much good to us."

"No," Dani said, "but odds are if it was stolen on the island, it's still in the neighborhood."

"That's a leap, Dani. There's no way to prove it."

"Strong suspicion's good enough for me. I don't need proof. You learn any more about Chen and Wong?"

"The Chief Super confirmed what Sharktooth got from the

priest. He knows them by reputation. Didn't even need to check and call me back."

"So he thinks they're above suspicion?"

"Come on, Dani. He's too good a cop for that. Nobody's above suspicion, but Madame Chen's not the kind of person whose feathers you want to ruffle without hard proof. She hosts the Prime Minister and his wife on that yacht you mentioned."

"*Lotus Blossom*," she said. "Anything of interest there?"

"Registered in Bikini to a shell corporation. No luck trying to figure out who's behind the corporation, but it's no secret that the yacht's hers. The corporate ownership's probably just for tax purposes, and maybe to dodge any nuisance liability suits. The boat's a classic; built in the '50s by Feadship for her grandfather."

"Any interesting pattern to where she keeps it, what she does with it?"

"Not really. It shows up from time to time in all the usual places, but it sounds like she mostly keeps it down in the Grenadines. She spends quite a bit of time aboard, entertaining local politicians up and down the island chain."

"What about her, personally?"

"Single, never been married. Some speculation that she and this Wong have an off and on thing. The Chief says she's an attractive woman."

"And Wong? What about him?"

"He's a family retainer from back when the Chens were in Hong Kong. When the colony reverted to China in '97, Marissa Chen left and moved her whole operation to St. Vincent. There wasn't much to move, at least as far as the business was concerned. They're spice traders, brokers, according to the Chief, so they don't carry inventory. No warehouses or equipment of their own. Just money and contacts."

"So she brought him with her? He must be important to her."

"Wong was practically adopted by her grandfather and was several years younger than her father. Her father put him to work in the business when he took over from the grandfather. Marissa took over from her father several years before '97; he died from a heart problem while he was still a young man. She brought Wong with her, but her other employees are locals."

"The Chief knew all that background from Hong Kong?"

"No. I have a friend who was tight with the colonial police in Hong Kong."

"Why would he know so much about spice traders?"

"They kept a close watch on most of the people who were moving spices. Smuggling spice and smuggling other things weren't that different."

"The Chens smuggled spices?"

"Some of the countries where they sourced their goods might have seen it that way. My friend said nothing ever stuck to the Chens."

"Damning with faint praise," Dani said. "The woman we talked to in Petite Martinique referred to Wong as a 'little dwarf fella,' when she told us about him getting beat up."

"Right. The Chief said he's a dwarf, and kind of squirrelly."

"Squirrelly? How?"

"Chip on his shoulder about his size. He's a tough little bugger — been in more than his share of barroom scrapes. Usually comes out on top. He's hurt some big guys, and Chen buys him out of whatever trouble he gets himself into. The Chief says he doesn't start the fights, but he seems to be a magnet for bullies."

"Okay," Dani said. "Anything else?"

"Not yet. Sharktooth get any word on the boys from Trinidad?" Phillip asked.

"Nothing. Vanished into thin air."

"Any gut instincts?"

"Yes," Dani said. "There are too many coincidences."

"For instance?"

"The guy the police are still looking for ... "

"Festus Jacobs," Phillip said.

"Right. His description matches the guy who tried to pull Cynthia into that boat night before last."

"So?"

"He was a known associate of the two men she bought the ganja from."

"And?"

"That makes me think her kidnapping's related to her purchase."

"But why would they try to snatch her? The men she could identify are out of the picture."

"We don't know the timing. They may have disappeared or been killed because Jacobs failed to capture her."

"That's a stretch, but go ahead. More coincidence?"

"Yes. This whole thing with Wong showing up just when Cynthia needed a ride home stinks."

"But the guys in the yellow boat did Wong and the other man some serious damage."

"Maybe. But their spotting the girl with Wong is another big coincidence."

"Not so big. Surely they were looking for her, and Petite Martinique's a small place."

"Yes, that's true. So why didn't anybody see those two between the time they finished lunch and the time they attacked Wong? If they were searching for the girl, somebody should have noticed, but the constable couldn't find them when he called around."

"When was that?" Phillip asked.

"Between the time the nun called him and the time the priest took Cynthia to the police station."

"Where'd you get that?"

"Sharktooth."

"Anything else?"

"Not yet, but he's checking with his contact in customs in Grenada."

"For what?"

"Wong and *Lotus Blossom* were supposedly on their way back from Grenada when he stopped at Petite Martinique."

"Hm. Let me know what you find out."

"I'll do that."

"Need anything else?"

"Not that I can think of. I'll be in touch when we hear back, though. Thanks, Phillip."

"No problem."

Dani disconnected the call and went below to talk to Liz and Sharktooth, who were discussing a painting that Liz was working on.

20

"WE SEE THAT YOU'VE ISSUED SELL ORDERS TO RAISE $10 MILLION. That's good. You'll find a reward at http://youtu.be/htY7GnFITOo. Check it out." The warbling voice was further distorted by the tiny speaker of the satellite phone as it sat in the middle of *Vengeance's* dining table.

"It takes four days for settlement before I'll have the cash," Ed said.

"Too bad. You have 40 hours left. Don't make your beautiful, sexy daughter pay."

"Please don't hurt her. I'm — "

"Hurt her? She looks like she'll enjoy it. Check out that video link." There was a soft click as the connection was broken.

Ed slumped against the table. "How far is the nearest Internet cafe?"

"We've got Internet access via satellite," Dani said. "Give us a couple of minutes to get the equipment fired up."

Liz moved to the chart table and began flipping switches. As she waited for the system to lock on to the satellite, she said, "You can probably get an advance against the proceeds of the trade, under the circumstances, Ed."

"How would I do that?"

"You'd need to talk to somebody higher in the food chain at the brokerage, and it'll cost you some money, but they'll probably work with you."

"Thanks, Liz. They're closed by now, but I'll get on it first thing in the morning."

"If they can't help you, talk to your banker about a short-term loan until the trades clear," Liz said. "What was that web address?"

"Http://youtu.be/htY7GnFITOo," Dani said, reading from the notepad on the table in front of her.

Liz keyed the address into the web browser on their laptop and picked it up, taking it to the table. She put it in front of Ed, angled so that she and Dani and Sharktooth could see it as well. She clicked the return key, and they watched as a full screen video loaded and began to play.

There was disco music playing, and raucous laughter, with what sounded like catcalls in pidgin French. Cynthia, clad only in her skimpy bikini, danced listlessly to the music, a blank, frightened look on her face. The camera zoomed out and swung to show several men leering and clapping as they yelled at her. The lighting was dim; no details of the men or their surroundings were visible. The camera swung back to Cynthia and zoomed in, showing her face and chest. A blurred hand reached into the frame from the side and cupped her breast, squeezing. She winced, and the hand jerked. Part of the back of a man's head showed as he leaned in to whisper in her ear. She nodded, tears in her eyes, and looked straight into the camera, saying, "Please, Daddy do what they — "

The screen went black, and Ed put his face in his hands.

"I DON'T UNDERSTAND how Berger tracked the girl to Petite Martinique so quickly," the Dragon Lady said. She glared at

Wong for a moment, but he said nothing. "Did you find out about that parasailing boat?"

He inclined his head in a brief nod. "Yes. It is registered in St. Lucia. It is kept in a small, shallow cove near Marigot."

"And who owns it?"

"I don't know, yet, Madame. It's registered to a company there. The agent is an attorney. Different people are seen using the boat; one matches the description of the big Rasta, but there are others."

"Who is the big Rasta, Wong?"

"My source doesn't know his name, but he is not from St. Lucia. They think maybe from Dominica."

"And the other men who use it?"

"They come from Martinique; they speak French. Sometimes the big man is with them, sometimes not. He speaks French with the other men when he's there, but my source says their use of the boat is strange."

"Strange in what way?"

"They often take it out at night. Sometimes they go out for several days. The locals think this is odd, for a parasailing boat."

"Yes, I see. Have they seen Berger around the boat?"

"No. Nobody recognized her name, either."

She studied one of the Japanese watercolors that hung on the wall.

"Did you learn anything about her from the people in Miami?" Wong asked, after a protracted silence.

She blinked and shook herself, turning to look at him. "Sorry. I was thinking. You asked me something?"

"I didn't mean to interrupt your thoughts, Madame. I wondered if the people in Miami had any information on Berger."

"Some, but nothing useful. Her mother's family owns an investment bank. She worked there for a while before she got into the yachting business."

"Are her parents still active in the banking business?"

"Her mother is. Why?"

"No particular reason. I thought it might help to look at the information differently, that's all. And what about her father?"

"There was no mention of her father; I assume he's dead, or of little importance."

"It would be interesting to know more about him. It's odd that they would have no information on him."

The Dragon Lady made a note on her pad. "An excellent point. I'll ask. Meanwhile, see if you can find out anything about the big man from Dominica."

"Yes, Madame."

"Is the girl aboard *Lion of Judah* now?"

"Yes."

"And is she segregated from the others?"

"Yes, but may I ask why?"

"A whim. If I decide to sell her, the less she knows about us the better. Those animals we're keeping there know too well what their fate is. She doesn't need to know about our sex trafficking."

Wong frowned.

"What's wrong?" the Dragon Lady asked.

"I thought I was going to dispose of her once we got the ransom."

"I did mention that possibility, didn't I?" She smiled at him.

"Yes."

"I may change my mind. I realized that I could do both."

"Both, Madame?"

"Collect the ransom from her father and sell her to the Arabs. Don't worry; we'll find another plaything for you, my little fiend."

"It's not that, Madame."

"What, then?"

"I understood that she wouldn't leave our care alive."

"So what if she does?"

"She knows who we are."

"What do you mean, knows who we are? Has she seen you?"

"Yes, Madame, of course. It was necessary to recapture her after those fools allowed her to escape. Remember, I spirited her away from the police."

"So she saw you. And she knows your name."

"Yes, Madame. She also saw *Lotus Blossom*, and the priest and the policeman both mentioned you by name in her presence."

The Dragon Lady's lips compressed into a thin line as she digested what he had said. As she started to speak, the intercom buzzed. Annoyed, she pressed down on the key and barked, "I said I wasn't to be interrupted, Veralyn."

"It's that man from Miami; you told me to always — "

"Did he say what he wanted?"

"No, Madame. Only that it's important and it has to do with some lawyer's daughter. He said you'd know."

"Leave me, Wong. Find out about the Rasta and get back as soon as you can. I have to take this call."

She keyed the intercom. "Put him through, Veralyn."

"I DON'T KNOW who was behind it," Sharktooth said, "but they asked about *Lightning Bolt* and they asked about you."

"By name?" Dani asked. She and Sharktooth stood on *Vengeance's* foredeck, gazing at the other yachts anchored between *Vengeance* and Baradel, the easternmost of the Tobago Cays.

"Mm-hmm. You an' some big Rasta." He grinned. "But they don' have his name. Jus' yours."

"It has to be Wong or Chen, then," Dani said.

"Mm-hmm, 'cause you left the business card for Wong," Sharktooth said.

"I can't think of any good reason for them to be asking about us," Dani said.

"No," Sharktooth said. "Ver' suspicious they do that."

"Any specifics on what they asked?"

"First they ask about the boat, and did you have any connection to it. Lomax tell them he don't know Danielle Berger. Then they ask did anybody see a lady look like you aroun' the boat, an' then they ask 'bout the big Rasta."

"What did Lomax tell them?"

"That the boat stay there sometimes. That he didn't know 'bout you or the big Rasta, but sometimes French-speaking men from Martinique aroun' the boat, mostly at night."

"Was this a phone call to Lomax?"

"No. Two p'licemen he don't recognize come aroun' and ask. Say they heard boat mebbe runnin' drugs."

"So," Dani said, "if Wong and Chen were behind this, they have some pull with the police in St. Lucia."

"Tha's no surprise, Dani. Mebbe they pay some p'lice, mebbe not. I ask Lomax if he t'ink Madame Chen behind the questions, an' he say he don' see a reason why a rich lady like her be interested."

"Why'd you ask about her?"

Sharktooth grinned. "Same reason you t'ink she ask the questions. Logical, once they use your name. Probably only one place that come from."

"Why does Lomax know of her?"

Sharktooth shrugged. "Rich lady, high profile. Lomax know 'bout mos' people that spend money in St. Lucia. She probably give money to some church, mebbe, or to the school."

"Did he get their names? The policemen?"

Sharktooth grinned. "Of course. I email to Phillip already."

"That's good. I'll ask him to call that friend of his."

"Cedric," Sharktooth said, "The Deputy Commissioner. I did that, too. Asked Phillip to call us on your satellite phone later."

"Good," Dani said. "We should probably go below and give Liz a break."

"A break?"

"Yes. She's trying to keep Ed distracted and get our dinner together."

"Mm. We bes' go, is right. Don' want that mon to interfere with deenah."

21

DANI CLAMBERED DOWN THE COMPANIONWAY LADDER, SHARKTOOTH
following her as he sniffed at the distinctive aroma of West
Indian curry wafting up from the galley.

"How's dinner coming?" Dani asked. She noticed as she got far
enough below to see into the galley that Liz and Ed stood side by
side in front of the stove. Ed jumped at the sound of Dani's voice,
dropping his left arm, which had been draped casually around
Liz's waist as she moved her hip against his to the rhythm of soft
steel pan music that came from the stereo.

"Smells awesome, doesn't it," Ed asked, looking back over his
shoulder at Dani.

Liz had her strawberry blonde hair twisted up into a tight bun
on the back of her head. Dani watched, amused, as a tell-tale
flush climbed from Liz's collar to her hairline.

"Sorry," Dani said, suppressing a laugh. "Did we interrupt
something?"

"Uh," Ed said, turning and stepping away from Liz as she set
her wooden spoon in a drip tray on the counter and turned to
face her friends, blushing.

"Of course not, Dani," Liz said, a sharp tone in her voice.

Sharktooth looked back and forth from Dani to Liz, puzzled. Dani wondered whether Liz was angry or just embarrassed, and whether she was flustered by Ed's attention or by the interruption.

The ringing of the satellite phone on the chart table defused the awkward moment. Sharktooth picked it up and handed it to Dani. Glancing at the caller i.d. screen, she raised the phone to her ear.

"Hello, Phillip," she said. "Can I put you on the speaker?"

She set the phone back on the chart table and switched it to speakerphone mode. "That was quick," she said.

"What?" Phillip asked, confusion in his voice.

"Sharktooth just told me he had asked — "

"Oh. That's not why I'm calling. I haven't gotten in touch with Cedric yet."

"What's up, then?" Dani asked. She glanced at Liz and smiled when she saw that Liz still looked off balance.

"I just got a call from Rupert Mason."

"The Chief Superintendent in St. Vincent? What was on his mind?" Dani asked, amused by the way Ed was looking at Liz, who was avoiding eye contact with him.

"He learned from some kind of routine internal report that the department had received a request for information about J.-P."

"From whom?"

"He couldn't tell, for sure. It came through channels from somebody on a South Florida drug interdiction task force. The person making the request was some kind of administrative assistant and had no idea who asked, or why. Mason thought we should know."

"What did they do with the request?"

"They have no records on J.-P. in their files. But you know that."

"Did the Chief think anybody talked out of turn?"

"He said the people in records are all kids; none of them would remember J.-P., so they sent back a 'nothing to report.' You have any idea what's going on?"

"Only what Sharktooth emailed you about," Dani said. "Can you think of anything, Sharktooth?"

"No," Sharktooth said.

"Liz?"

Liz, still avoiding Ed's eye, shook her head. "No, no idea."

"Okay," Phillip said. "If you think of anything, I'll be here. I'll give you a shout as soon as I talk with Cedric."

"Right. Thanks, Phillip," Dani said, pressing the disconnect button.

"What was all that about?" Ed asked. "Who's J.-P.? And Cedric?"

"J.-P. is my father," Dani said.

"Why would this Mason think you should know someone was asking about your father? And who's Mason?"

"You don't miss much," Dani said. "Rupert Mason is the Chief Superintendent of Police in St. Vincent."

"It's my background as a trial lawyer," Ed said. "I'm conditioned to catch small irrelevancies. It's one way to trip up a hostile witness."

"I'm not hostile."

"No." He smiled. "No, I didn't mean it that way. You mentioned the Chief Super earlier, but I didn't have a name — just the title."

Dani nodded. "He and my father and Phillip go back to when I was a child. They look out for one another — always have. That was a strange request; my father wouldn't be the subject of a request from a U.S. drug interdiction task force. Why that's so doesn't matter right now, but Mason knew it. That's why he passed it on to us."

"So he thought it might have something to do with Cynthia?"

"In a situation like this, you look for any facts that touch on any of the people involved. Mr. Mason's too good a cop to jump to conclusions about what it might mean. It's just a data point he thought we should have. It may mean nothing."

"Okay, I get that. Now, back to Cedric — who's he?"

"He's the Deputy Commissioner of Police in St. Lucia; the highest ranking person who's not a political hack. He's another old friend of theirs. We need some information from him."

"What kind of information?"

"Can you bring Ed up to speed, Sharktooth? You two go up on deck and I'll give Liz a hand with some cocktails and snacks. Then we can get out of her way and let her finish cooking dinner."

"You told me your father did a lot of business in the islands, but you never really told me what he did," Ed said, settled in the cockpit with Dani and Sharktooth.

Dani passed him a rum punch from the tray that she brought from below. "No, I didn't, I guess. He and Sharktooth are partners." She took a sip from her own glass and reached for a cube of cheese and a water cracker.

Ed turned to face Sharktooth. "How about it, Sharktooth? What do you and Dani's dad do that keeps you so well connected to the governments down here?"

Sharktooth grinned and shrugged his massive shoulders. "We jus' buy an' sell stuff. Mos'ly we sell fo' mo' than we pay, see. Tha's how we make money."

Dani saw a flicker of irritation cross Ed's face. "Papa sources goods in Europe, and they sell them down here. He helps the suppliers arrange financing to make the purchases possible. A lot of the time, the governments of small countries can't afford the things they need for modernizing infrastructure."

"What kind of things do you guys sell, then, Sharktooth?"

"Jus' about whatever the customer wants," Sharktooth said, another foolish grin on his face.

Dani sent him a warning glance. In spite of his education, he could pass for an imbecile, and she knew he enjoyed doing it. She could see that Ed's patience was wearing thin; she didn't want him to provoke Sharktooth. The Rasta giant could shift his demeanor from amiable dunce to menacing lunatic in the blink of an eye. She knew he wouldn't really hurt Ed, but she didn't want him to frighten the man, either.

"Sharktooth has a number of businesses that keep him connected to the local politicians besides his trading with my father. Their partnership's only a small part of Sharktooth's activity. A lot of what he does is related to enhancing the tourist appeal of the different islands, and helping local businesses organize to take advantage of tourism. So that's why he has all the local connections."

"I see. Sounds like you're a real entrepreneur, Sharktooth."

"I try," Sharktooth said.

"But the thing I find most amazing about him is his artistic talent," Dani said, hoping Ed might pursue a less dangerous line of questioning.

"Artistic talent?" Ed asked, taking a sip of his drink and raising his eyebrows in a skeptical look. "What sort of artist are you, Sharktooth?"

The big man looked down at his hands. "Um, I, ah ... my wife and I, we have a small gallery. She runs it."

"I see. Where is it?"

"Dominica. In Portsmouth. Ver' small business."

"And do you specialize in local artists?"

"Mm-hmm."

"Paintings? Or sculpture, or what?"

"A little of everything."

"Don't be so reticent," Dani said. "Tell him. It's not something you should be ashamed of, Sharktooth."

The giant appeared to shrink several sizes. He squirmed in his seat and fingered his dreadlocks. Ed studied his evasive behavior for several seconds.

"I'm not a judgmental person, Sharktooth. Dani's right. Tell me what's going on."

"I paint a little bit," Sharktooth mumbled, giving Dani a glare that could melt ice.

"You paint? That's great! Cynthia's talented that way. What sort of painting do you do?"

"My wife an' Liz call it primitive impressionist."

"Did you study art in school?"

Sharktooth shook his head. "International finance."

"Really?" Ed studied the hulking, rough-looking man in front of him. "Where'd you go to school?"

"University of the West Indies."

"And," Dani said, kicking Sharktooth under the table. She was relieved that Ed's interest had shifted to the puzzle of Sharktooth.

"I went to graduate school in the U.S.," Sharktooth mumbled.

"Where?" Ed asked.

"Wharton," Sharktooth said, almost whispering.

Ed said, "You're the only person I've met who went to Wharton who didn't tell me about it in the first ten seconds."

"Sorry," Sharktooth said. "Not important," he added, in a soft voice.

"His doctoral dissertation dealt with a strategy for developing an economy based on ecotourism and using it as a transition to high technology manufacturing."

"How do you find time to paint?" Ed asked.

"Painting keep me from goin' crazy. I jus' smear the colors on the canvas, but Liz an' Dani see stuff in there I don' know 'bout 'til they tell me."

"Not just us, Sharktooth," Dani said. "His paintings are in juried collections in quite a few galleries, but he doesn't want his local pals to know. He's afraid they'll think he's a sissy."

"Well, I'm amazed. I'd like to see some of your work. I just found out that most of the paintings below deck are Liz's work."

"She paint like a photograph, only look more real," Sharktooth said. "Liz is the real artist, not me."

"Some of her stuff was definitely impressionism," Ed said. "There's one of a sunset over the sea that's absolutely dazzling."

"Liz didn't paint that," Dani said, watching Sharktooth cringe. "Did she claim that was hers?"

"No. I just assumed it was. Who did that?"

Sharktooth looked away and pinched Dani's leg under the table.

"I'd better go see if Liz needs a hand," Dani said.

"Sharktooth? You painted that sunset?" Ed asked, as Dani stood up.

Sharktooth dipped his head the least bit, an embarrassed look on his face. "Mm-hmm."

"You really are a man of many talents," Ed said. "That's a gift, to do that with color and light."

"But it don' look like a picture," Sharktooth said. "I can't make the paint do like Liz does."

"That's the very thing that makes it special," Ed said. "Anybody who looks at it feels like they're watching the sun go down over the water. It's way more evocative than a photographic image could ever be."

"That's what his wife and I keep telling him," Liz said, passing a steaming tray through the companionway to Dani. "While you put that on the table, I'll get the wine."

22

"Yes, that's correct," the Dragon Lady said, in response to a question from the man in Miami. "We do have his daughter. What difference does that make to our arrangement?"

"I'm not sure, just yet," the man said. "I need to talk to some people, now that I know for sure. It's possible that having the girl might put you in a position to do us a favor."

"I don't expect to hold her very long. I have my own plans — "

"Don't be hasty, Marissa," the man said.

She fought back her visceral reaction to his presumption. Nobody but her parents and her brother had ever called her by her given name without paying a severe price.

"We may have a use for her, babe. I'll have to get back to you, but in the meantime, take good care of her."

"Oh, I'll do that. Don't you worry."

"If you value our relationship, you'll keep her alive, and keep her captive until you hear from us," the man said, his tone hard. "We know about the ransom demand. We may wish to up the ante, so to speak."

"I'm not acknowledging that we're holding her for ransom," she said, glad of the encrypted satellite phones they were using.

"But if, for the sake of discussion, we were, you should be aware that there could be more at stake than just $10 million."

"I'm not sure what you mean."

"You cannot know what I mean, but understand that $10 million is just the beginning."

"As I said, Marissa, I need to talk to some people, but I think we'd be prepared to meet any price you might set. I'll have to call you back, but don't worry, we'll be ahead of your deadline for the ransom."

"Do what you wish, but do not assume that I'm amenable to letting you have her, at any price."

"Don't forget who you're dealing with, woman."

"I shan't, young fellow. Nor should you."

"I'll be in touch, hon. You'd best hope it's by telephone," the man said, disconnecting the call.

The Dragon Lady sat for a moment, thinking. She buzzed her secretary on the intercom.

"Yes, Madame?"

"Get Wong in here, right now."

"Yes, Madame."

"ARE YOU ANGRY?" Liz asked, in a whisper. She and Dani were alone at last, in the cabin they shared when guests were aboard. There was a narrow space separating their bunks, and they could hear Ed's soft snoring from the aft stateroom.

"Angry? No. Why?"

"About me and Ed?"

Dani chuckled. "No. Is it you and Ed, now?"

"Well, like a friend of mine said, 'he's hot and he's here,' so I haven't done anything to discourage him."

"Just remember Cynthia's advice," Dani said.

Liz laughed at that. "He's definitely into 'love the one you're with.'"

"No doubt about that," Dani agreed.

"You're sure you're not upset?"

"Oh, come off it, Liz. You knew from the start he wasn't my type. He's a twit."

"That's true, but he's a good-looking twit. A girl can dream."

"It looked like you were doing more than dreaming."

"Oh, I'll flirt with him, but I won't let it go too far. He's not my type, either, and it could turn awkward with all that's going on."

"Okay, but now I'm confused."

"About what?"

"Well, you know about me and men. You helped me figure out that I was on the verge of making a fool of myself with Ed because of my disappointment over Ralph."

"I didn't say that," Liz protested.

"No, and thanks for that. You didn't have to say it; you just gave me some perspective so that I could see it myself."

"I'm glad if I helped."

"You did, but I'm still puzzled."

"Ask, then. Liz-the-love-expert is waiting for your calls."

"What are you up to with Ed?"

"Oops. I guess I assumed a certain basic level of knowledge on your part. I — " Liz let out a muffled grunt as Dani's fist connected with her shoulder. "Ouch! That's your one free punch, woman. Next one will cost you."

"Any time you think you're ready to swim with the sharks, sucker."

"Quiet, or we'll wake up Ed," Liz said. "I'll kick your butt another time."

"Chicken," Dani taunted, under her breath. "Now, answer me. Why are you leading him on if you aren't interested?"

"Just to keep in practice, I guess. Besides, it's distracting him a little bit."

"More than a little bit, I'd say. How do you think you can keep him in check?"

"That's where skill and experience come into play. It's so intuitive that I'm not sure I can explain it to you, but if you watch carefully, you'll get the basics in no time."

"You're making me feel like a voyeur."

"Oh, think of it as clinical observation. You're not going to see anything that's beyond PG-13, here. Like I said, he's fun to play with, but I'm not going to let things get serious."

"You're very sure of yourself," Dani said. "I wish I had your confidence."

"You aren't lacking in confidence, Dani. You're just in unfamiliar territory, like I used to be in bar fights."

"You can hold your own pretty well these days; I can still take you, but — "

"I'm still learning from you about that," Liz interrupted. "You can learn about men from me. You've got all the basic equipment; you just need to learn to use it differently. Study my moves in this, like I've studied yours in the other."

"You think I can?"

"Of course. Just pay attention. Like you taught me, keep a broad focus so you don't miss any critical tells from the opposite side. Enough of this. Now, what's our next step to find Cynthia?"

"We're not gaining anything by sitting here in the Cays. I'm thinking it's time to get back to Bequia, where it's a little less remote."

"A little less remote?"

"This thing with Chen and Wong, for example. There's something off about the way they showed up at the critical moment, and now they're asking questions about me and Sharktooth."

"You think they may be behind the questions about J.-P., too?"

"It wouldn't surprise me. The coincidence factor says they're the ones, but I do wonder how they managed to get the questions to come from some drug squad in Miami. Sharktooth might be able to find some loose ends by poking around in Kingstown. I want to know what they do besides donate money to charity, but I'd like to know if they're connected to the cops in the States, too."

"That makes sense," Liz said. "Maybe your godfather could find out more about that."

Dani thought about that for a few seconds. "I haven't talked to Mario in way too long. I'll call him tomorrow, once we're under way. That's good thinking, Liz."

"I learned from a master — or, I should say, from a mistress."

"Yuck. I'm nobody's mistress. Shut up and go to sleep, Pollyanna. We'll rise early and sail hard."

"Do you remember Joe DiFiore's younger brother?" Marissa Chen asked.

Li Wong sat across her desk, wondering what was coming next.

"The kid he sent out from Miami to look over our operation before they decided to distribute our stuff?" Wong asked.

"Yes. That one."

Wong recalled that she had been offended by the man's crass manner and his comments on a woman's proper place. "Mike, his name is."

"Possibly. Do you know if Joe has more than one brother?"

"Only Mike," Wong said, waiting.

After thirty seconds, she said, "I want you to hurt him."

"Mike?" Wong asked, his voice rising in surprise. By now, their partnership with the mob was well-established, and Joe DiFiore was their main contact. Wong hadn't thought of Mike since his annoying visit, years ago.

"Yes. I considered Joe, but I want him intact."

"Intact?"

"I want Mike damaged permanently."

"Killed?"

"No. I want him to be a constant reminder to his brother and the rest of those pigs that I am to be accorded the respect due me."

"You realize this may escalate, Madame," Wong said.

"If you handle it properly, it certainly will. Your personal touch is unmistakable, but they will never prove we did it. All they'll have is suspicion."

"My personal touch? You want me to go to Miami?"

"Or wherever this scum is to be found. You know what to do. Bring me the evidence of your success. Preserve it in formaldehyde. I think I'll keep it on my desk."

"To be clear, Madame, you wish him to survive this, ah ... experience?"

"Yes. Paralyzed would be nice, perhaps, but he must live. I want him to be a burden to Joe DiFiore, a reminder that he should respect women."

"I'll need some assistance if he is to live after my, uh, ministrations."

"Whatever you need. Take our plane; I want this done now."

"Madame?"

"Yes?"

"He may be able to identify me."

"Of course he will. That's essential if they are to get the message."

Wong nodded, thinking.

"Are you afraid of them, my little one?"

Wong shrugged. "A man like DiFiore will seek revenge; it's a part of their culture."

"I'm counting on it, but that will bring him to us, into my web, so to speak. Don't be afraid. I'll protect you. When we're done, Joe will be gone, and there will be no one to avenge Mike."

"But what about distribution in the States, then?"

"Joe DiFiore is one man. There are many men in that organization; he isn't in charge. I'm tired of dealing with their second tier. We will change that. I want more influence over the way our products are sold, and a bigger cut."

Wong nodded. He understood her greed; it had propelled her to heights far beyond any her family had achieved before she took over.

"One day, we will move to Miami, little one. Trust in me."

"Always, Madame."

"Good. Go. You have work to do."

Wong stood and stepped toward the door of her office.

"Wong?"

He stopped, turning toward her, and bowed slightly. "Yes, Madame."

"It is to be intact — no pieces bitten off, do you hear me?"

"Yes, Madame."

23

DANI LEANED BACK AGAINST THE COCKPIT COAMING, HER ARMS stretched out to the sides. One bare foot resting on the helm, she enjoyed the feel of *Vengeance* charging through the moderate seas on a beam reach. Feeling pressure on her foot as the wind backed, she considered easing the sheets.

They'd been under sail for about twenty minutes. Liz had helped her make sail and get the boat balanced for the breeze, and then excused herself to take two mugs of coffee to the foredeck, where Ed sat on the forward end of the coachroof.

Dani had watched with interest as Liz handed him one of the mugs and sat down beside him. He had shifted a bit to make room for her, and then put his arm around her. His hand rested on her hip, and her head was on his shoulder. Dani shook her head, remembering their conversation last night. Liz might think she was the one in control, but Dani had her doubts. To her, Liz looked like the submissive one.

She raised her eyes to the wind vane at the top of the main mast, checking the angle of the apparent wind. She looked down at the compass and decided that the wind shift was cyclical. Instead of easing the sheets she relaxed her foot against the helm.

In response to the decreased pressure on the helm, the bow fell off the wind a few degrees. *Vengeance* sped up a little, and the helm felt neutral against her foot again.

She would wait a few minutes and see if the wind clocked, allowing her to bring the boat back onto her desired course without trimming the sails. She saw that Liz had shifted her position just enough so that Ed had removed his hand from her hip. She had lifted her head and turned to face him, smiling up at him as she said something Dani couldn't hear.

It occurred to Dani that Liz had controlled the physical contact with Ed with the same sort of finesse that she had just used to avoid trimming the sails. Dani thought about that; her own reaction would have been to grab his wrist and force his hand to a less intimate place, like the coachroof. Maybe she *could* learn something about men from studying Liz's moves.

Liz had broached the subject of their return to Bequia this morning while they were eating breakfast. Ed had been reluctant to leave the Cays.

"It seems like that's taking us farther away from Cynthia," he'd said.

"No," Dani had said, ready to argue the point, but Liz silenced her with a glance.

"It puts us closer to people who can help us find her," Liz had said, picking up the conversation. She had looked up at him and batted her eyelids, a somber look on her face. With wide eyes locked on his, she had continued. "We don't know that she's in the vicinity any longer, and being in the Cays restricts our communications to the satellite phone. Your cell phone will work in Bequia, in case Cynthia gets a chance to sneak a call to you. She knows your number, doesn't she?"

"Sure. She memorized it when she was a little kid. I hadn't thought of that. You think she might be able to get her hands on a cell phone?"

"I don't know, Ed, but if she does, that's the number she'll call. She won't have our satellite phone number."

"They won't let her near a phone," he had said, shaking his head. "They didn't intend to let her escape, either, but she did. Don't underestimate her just because she's your child. She's a resourceful young woman."

He had nodded. "You're right about that. She knows how to get what she wants from me, for sure."

"And you're certainly no pushover. If she can manipulate her own father, imagine what she can do if she turns her attention to those lowlifes. They aren't trial lawyers, trained to question everything. They think she's just a pretty face."

"What are we waiting for? Let's go to Bequia," Ed had said.

ED GRASPED one of the mizzen shrouds and swung himself into the cockpit. Standing on the seat, he turned and extended a hand to help Liz into the cockpit, bowing from the waist and making a sweeping gesture with his other arm. She gave him a warm smile and accepted his assistance.

"Thank you, kind sir," she said, making a curtsy as she stepped over the coaming.

Dani, suppressing a bark of laughter, coughed, gagging as she looked away to hide her reaction.

"Are you okay?" Liz asked, dropping Ed's hand and sitting down beside her friend, patting her on the back until she recovered her composure. "What happened?"

"Gagged on some gnat, or something, I guess," Dani said, glaring at her with eyes red from coughing.

"Do you need some water?"

Dani shook her head. "I'm okay. I could use a little help with the headsails, though."

"You should have called me," Liz said, rising to a crouch and turning to the port-side sheet winches.

"I didn't want ... it's okay. The wind's been cycling all morning, but it's finally backed about ten degrees in the last few minutes and seems to be holding there. Sheet them in a bit as I harden up, please."

"Can I help?" Ed asked.

"Sure," Dani said. "You sheet in the mainsail when it starts to luff."

"Luff?"

"As I turn into the wind, the main will begin to spill the air. You'll see it start to shiver along the leading edge, against the mast. That's called luffing."

"Okay," Ed said. "And then what do I do?"

Liz pointed at the mainsheet winch on the coachroof. "Watch me. I'll crank in the headsail sheets as Dani turns into the wind. When you see the main start luffing, you crank in the mainsheet with that big winch until the sail's full again."

"Got it," he said.

Dani gave the helm a slight turn to the starboard and watched as Liz and Ed trimmed the sails. She glanced down at the compass and checked her heading, adjusting the helm a bit.

"Good, Liz," she said, after studying the sails for a moment. "Ed, could you sheet in the main just a little more, please?"

He gave the winch a half a turn while watching the sail, and then looked back at Dani.

"Good," she said, nodding at him. "Thanks."

"That takes more muscle than I thought it would," he said, sitting down on the starboard side of the cockpit.

"You don't want to arm-wrestle with a grinder," Dani said.

"Grinder?" Ed looked puzzled.

"A deck ape," Dani said.

Ed shifted his gaze to Liz, raising his eyebrows.

She smiled. "Those are slang terms for the crew members

who crank the winches, like me." She balled up her fists and
flexed her arms, causing her biceps to pop up as the veins stood
out on her slender arms.

"Some deck ape you are," he said, grinning at her. "I thought
you were the chef."

"You got an appetite?" she asked, winking at him.

He grinned at her and winked back. "Mm-hmm. Lunch would
be nice, too."

Dani gave Liz a disapproving look. "I could use a break from
the helm before you get busy."

Liz looked at her for a moment. "Ed?" she said, "Could you
take the helm and let Dani come below with me for a minute?"

"Sure," he said.

Dani slid out from behind the helm and he took her place.
"Just keep her going in a straight line," she said. "You feel that
little bit of pressure from the helm?"

He nodded. "Yes."

"Maintain that. If it increases, let the bow fall off a little bit to
the port. If it decreases, bring the bow up until the pressure's
restored. The idea is to keep her at the same angle to the wind.
Got it?"

"Aye-aye, captain," he said, grinning.

She went below, Liz on her heels.

"You okay?" Liz whispered, once they were both in the
galley.

Dani nodded. "I need to go to the head."

"You look nauseated."

"From watching you two lovebirds." She stepped into the head
and closed the door.

Liz was fixing a warm seafood salad for lunch when the satellite phone rang. Wiping her hands on a dishtowel, she picked up
the phone and studied the caller i.d. screen. Not recognizing the
number, she pressed the connection icon just as Dani came out of
the head.

"Good morning," Liz said. "You've reached the yacht *Vengeance*; this is Liz Chirac. How may I help you?"

"Good morning, Ms. Chirac," a woman said. She had an English accent that matched Liz's own. "This is Marissa Chen. I wish to speak with Danielle Berger, if I may, please. Is she available?"

"One moment, please, Ms. Chen. I'll take the phone to her." Liz touched the mute icon, thinking as she did that Chen had learned English in a girl's school in Great Britain, as she herself had. To most people, Chen's diction would have sounded flawless, but Liz picked up nuances of rhythm that indicated English was a second language to her.

"For you, Dani. It's Marissa Chen," Liz said, passing the phone to her friend and returning to the galley.

CYNTHIA SAT HUDDLED in the corner of the bunk, the remains of the cotton shift wrapped around her. She barely noticed the stench, now. Breakfast had been some kind of greasy, doughy pastry, filled with a spicy paste that tasted of salt and rotten fish. As unappetizing as it was, she had eaten it, determined to keep her strength up. She'd almost escaped once. Perhaps she could do it again.

She'd had no opportunity since she'd been brought to this dirty little ship, though. After they had dragged her out of the cabin yesterday and forced her to make the video, she'd had no contact with anyone except when they brought her food.

She shivered at the memory of how frightened she'd been when they'd come for her yesterday. The man who seemed to be in charge had surprised her then, speaking English.

"Strip now, bitch," he had barked, when the door slammed open. When she raised her hands and backed away, he had nodded at the other man. The second man laughed and stepped toward her, grabbing her right upper arm in a painful grip. She had screamed, and he slapped her.

"Shut up," the first man said, and raised his right hand, grasping the neck of the cotton shift.

With a violent jerk, he ripped the flimsy fabric all the way from neck to hem. She had given an involuntary shriek of pain as the fabric abraded her sunburned skin, and he had slapped her again.

"Quiet, bitch, until I tell you to speak."

She had flinched when the man who held her moved his free hand to grasp her bikini top. Before he could rip the fabric, the first man backhanded him, splitting his lip. "No, you fool. Not yet."

With that, he had grabbed her other arm and they had frog-marched her into a dim room where several other men sat against one wall, leering and yelling at her in the language that she couldn't understand. The men holding her arms forced her back to the opposite wall.

A bright light came on, blinding her, and the man who spoke English held a newspaper up in front of her face. In the moment that it blocked the dazzling light, she saw that there was a video camera on a tripod, aimed at her. The man dropped the newspaper, and when he did, disco music blared from a loudspeaker.

"When we let you go, you will dance, bitch, or I will give you to them. Dance sexy, and I will save you from them. You understand?"

"Y-yes," she said, and he and the other man released her and backed away.

She had danced for a few seconds, and then he had squeezed her breast and whispered to her to beg her father to do what he was told. When she complied, he and the other man had grabbed her and brought her back to the little cabin, locking her in again.

She remembered seeing two frightened-looking, battered women in the corridor as they dragged her along. She thought there might have been a man with a gun, but she had been too scared to be sure what she was seeing. She had waited, terrified, for what seemed like hours. At last, the door had banged open, and the same two men had removed the two buckets, one of which she had used to relieve herself. They replaced them with two more, and left another bowl of the tasty stew.

She had thought that the bucket of water was probably for her to drink, but she hadn't been desperate enough, yet. She reasoned that the stew had enough liquid to keep her somewhat hydrated.

She had taken the cheap metal spoon and made two scratches in the scarred paint of the bulkhead beside the bunk. She couldn't see outside, so she couldn't guess the time, but she had been fed what she thought was dinner, twice, and breakfast once. She thought she must have been here two days, now. She scratched her name into the paint, as well.

She eyed the bucket of foul-looking water, thinking that soon she would have to give in and drink some. The salty filling of the pastry had given her a powerful thirst.

24

"Good morning, Madame Chen. Thank you for taking my call."

His voice was smooth, his accent cultured. The Dragon Lady had not expected that. "Good morning, Mr. Gregorio. To what do I owe this pleasure?"

"I like that, Madame — straight to business. I shouldn't have waited so long to call you. I let Joe DiFiore work with you because he was the one who first discovered the quality of your merchandise, and it just went on from there."

"Your organization is an important marketing channel for me," she said.

"And your product has come to be quite important to us. I don't intend to let personal conflicts interfere with our relationship. You and I, we are above such petty things, I think."

"I appreciate your confidence, Mr. Gregorio, but I admit to being a bit lost, here. What sort of personal conflicts?"

He chuckled. "Joe DiFiore is an animal. His brother Mike was worse. People like them have their uses, but I should never have allowed them to represent me in dealing with someone like you.

You don't have to say anything, but trust me. I've heard your complaint. You will never have to deal with them again."

"I see. And with whom will I transact business?" She made note of his use of the past tense in referring to Mike DiFiore; she wondered if Wong had gone too far.

"Oh, I think you and I should work directly with one another from now on. It's unfortunate that Mike was injured so badly in his role as messenger, but I've ensured that Joe understands. Not that I think you would worry, but rest assured that Joe will never trouble you again."

"I look forward to our relationship, Mr. Gregorio," she said, pleased to learn that Wong had left Mike DiFiore alive to serve as a reminder to these people. "I'm sure we understand one another quite clearly."

"Yes, I think we do. I do want to let you know that for the time being, I'll continue to use Joe to keep an eye on our mutual interests in South Florida, but if that bothers you, just say the word, and he'll be gone."

"I wouldn't presume to second-guess your judgment on staffing decisions, Mr. Gregorio. I know a man like Joe has his uses. I keep some dangerous pets myself."

Gregorio listened to the soft noise of the encrypted telephone connection for a few seconds. "Well, it's been a rare pleasure to chat with you. I'm sure we'll enjoy working together. It's nice to find someone with whom I can reach such a clear understanding in such a civilized manner."

"Likewise, Mr. Gregorio. If there's ever anything I can do for you, please let me know."

"Certainly, Madame Chen."

"Good day, Mr. Gregorio."

"Ah, Madame Chen?"

"Yes?"

"There is a small matter, perhaps."

"Yes? Tell me about it, please."

"There's a certain lawyer from Atlanta with whom I believe you may be doing some business."

"I think I know the man of whom you're speaking. Would that be Mr. Savage?"

"Yes, Madame."

"A fine civil litigator, I hear. I have not yet engaged his services, though he comes highly recommended," she said.

"For good reason, Madame, I assure you."

"How do you come to know of him, Mr. Gregorio?"

"He's leading a class action suit against a company in which I have an interest. A suit totally without merit, I assure you."

"I have no doubt. Lawyers are only concerned with making money. But how can I help you?"

"He's an honorable man, I believe. If you could help him see that the suit against Tequesta Recycling is without merit, he would probably withdraw as the lead counsel for the plaintiffs."

"I see. And that's all you want? For him to withdraw personally?"

"Yes. It would serve him well, and as I said, the suit is without merit. Without his participation, it will collapse. He could perhaps tell the court that some personal problem is forcing his withdrawal, so that he wouldn't have to admit that he'd been duped by his clients. We wouldn't want him to do anything that might directly prejudice the case."

"I might be able to sway him," she said, "if it's important to you."

"Oh, it's worth $50 million to me, but the important thing is his well-being and reputation, don't you agree?"

"Of course," she said. "I'm sure he and his family would suffer if he made a mistake like that. Teenaged children, especially girls, are so sensitive and vulnerable."

"I wouldn't know, Madame. But I'll trust you on that. I appreciate whatever you can do, and I'll make a deposit to the usual account in advance to defray your expenses."

"Thank you again for calling, Mr. Gregorio."

"My pleasure, Madame."

The Dragon Lady savored her victory for a moment. Then she pressed the intercom button.

"Yes, Madame?"

"Is Wong back from Florida?"

"Yes, Madame. Your plane landed about an hour ago."

"Tell him I want him."

"Yes, Madame, immediately."

"And Veralyn?"

"Yes, Madame?"

"Tell him to bring the package he brought back. He'll know what I mean. When is my appointment with the Berger woman, again?"

"Tomorrow morning, at ten. Did you want to go to Bequia on *Lotus Blossom* to meet her?"

"No. I don't have time for a boat ride. Arrange for the helicopter to take me, please. And once Wong is here, I will not want to be disturbed for the rest of the day."

"SHE WANTS TO MEET WITH YOU?" Liz asked. "In person?"

"Yes," Dani said. "Aboard her yacht, *Lotus Blossom*. She's bringing it to Bequia for the meeting."

"What could she want that would warrant that?" Liz asked.

"Who knows? She said she wanted to talk with me about one of her charities — something about mentoring teenaged girls to encourage them in entrepreneurial ventures. According to her, their opportunities are limited. All most of them think about is finding a man to take care of them and having children."

"And she's opposed to that?" Ed asked, joining them in the cockpit. He had been below, reading a case file.

"Well, I don't know that she's opposed to it. She gave me a

long spiel about wanting to see more startup ventures founded by young women — good for the economy, keeps them off drugs and out of the hands of the sex traffickers, that kind of thing."

"It's hard to argue with that. And her guy did try to help Cynthia."

Dani looked at him out of the corner of her eye.

"Well," Ed said, "he did. He got hurt for his trouble, too. I feel like I should go with you and thank her."

"Don't be so hasty, Ed," Dani said. "We still don't know how Wong came to be in the vicinity at just the right time."

"Wow! You are one suspicious lady. Glad I'm not married to you."

"Me, too," Dani said. "I don't think we'd last long as a couple."

"Well," he said, "I guess you told me. But what makes you suspicious of Ms. Chen?"

"Wong lied about why he was in Petite Martinique."

"What? But he said he was in Grenada on some kind of business for Chen. Probably to do with their spice trading — isn't Grenada a major producer?"

"Yes. It's one of the largest exporters of nutmeg in the world, and they grow a lot of other spices there, too," Liz said, as he draped an arm over her shoulders.

"So why don't you believe him, Dani?" Ed asked.

"Because he wasn't in Grenada."

"How do you know?"

"Phillip's wife checked."

"His wife? I don't — "

"She's a senior officer with French Customs in Martinique," Liz said, shifting her position slightly, forcing his arm to a less comfortable angle as she winked at Dani.

"But I thought Petite Martinique was part of Grenada," he said, removing his arm from Liz's shoulders and shifting to his right until their hips were touching. "That's confusing."

"It is part of Grenada, and yes, the name is confusing.

Remember, the British and the French traded these islands back and forth like chips in a casino back in the 18th and early 19th centuries. You can't go by the origin of names," Dani said, returning Liz's wink.

"Okay, but I'm still lost."

"She made an official request to Grenada Customs," Liz said, edging away from him on the cockpit seat, putting a few inches between them. "Sorry Ed, but I'm too hot to snuggle right now."

He grinned. "What an opening that is. But I'll let it pass. I still want to understand what Dani's thinking."

"Speaking of openings," Liz said, "don't be too sure."

"Huh?" he asked.

"About wanting to know what I'm thinking," Dani said, watching his expression turn sour. "Anyway, *Lotus Blossom* wasn't in Grenada that day. Hasn't been for several weeks, in fact. Neither was Wong."

"Could there have been a misunderstanding?" he asked.

"Possibly," Dani said. "Sharktooth's going to check."

"Yeah? I noticed his boat wasn't in the anchorage this morning. He's gone to Grenada?"

"Right. He'll check things out there and meet us in Bequia."

"How can he double check on an official inquiry?"

"He knows people," Dani said. "All kinds of people around the waterfront."

"So you'll have his information before your meeting on *Lotus Blossom*," Ed said. "Are you going to confront her about Wong?"

"I don't think so; it's better if she doesn't know how much we know."

Ed nodded. "You would have made a good lawyer."

"I guess that's a compliment, coming from you."

"You would; I'm not just saying that. You think you might learn something from her?"

"Probably. It may or may not be helpful to our immediate situation, but she'll give away something. I'll play along with her; she wanted to meet me and see if I'd fit into her mentoring program. Most likely, that'll give me the opportunity to ask her a lot of questions in return."

"And then there's *Lotus Blossom*," Liz said.

"What about *Lotus Blossom*?" Ed asked.

"She'll have to show me around the yacht when I express a professional interest. She'd be surprised if somebody like me didn't ask for the grand tour."

"How is that useful? You don't think they took Cynthia, do you? You think she might be on that boat?"

Dani and Liz traded looks of surprise.

"Well, do you?" he repeated.

"They're our best suspects," Dani said. "But no, I don't think they'd be brazen enough to invite me aboard if they were holding her there. You never know what I might see or hear down in the innards of a boat like that, though. I could pick up something that might be useful later."

"We should tell that Chief Inspector guy," Ed said. "They could — "

"They couldn't touch her," Liz interrupted. "This woman entertains the Prime Minister and his wife, remember?"

"But they could get a warrant, and — "

"You're the lawyer, Ed," Dani said. "You think there's enough to support issuing a warrant?"

He clenched his jaws and frowned for a moment. He shook his head. "Probably not, unless you had a sympathetic judge."

"Right," Dani said. "And we can guess where the judge's sympathies would be on this one."

"So I should keep working on getting the money together, huh?"

"Yes. Today's the 48-hour deadline. I'm surprised you haven't heard from them yet," Dani said.

"They're probably watching," Liz said.

"Watching?" Ed asked.

"They have some visibility into your finances, Ed. Remember, they knew you were working to raise the cash when they called yesterday about the video."

"Shit! You're right. I was so upset by the video that I forgot that. You think they're monitoring my accounts?"

"It sounds that way," Liz said.

"How can they do that?"

"Well, from a technology perspective, it's dead easy," Liz said.

"Okay, I can see that, but there are all kinds of restrictions in the way. The brokerage can't give them that kind of access without a warrant or a subpoena."

"You're thinking like a lawyer, Ed."

"Kidnappers don't bother with warrants and subpoenas. Given the amount of money that's in play, you should assume they have all of the tools that the government would have and none of the constraints," Dani said.

"I'd better go call my broker and see how we're coming. Can I use your sat phone or do you need it?"

"Sure. Sharktooth left us another one."

"Why'd he do that?"

"It's encrypted. We thought it might be good to have."

"WHILE HE'S BELOW, I'm going to call Mario and see what he can find out about who's asking questions about Papa."

"I was going to remind you."

"Thanks. I'm going to take the phone up on the foredeck. I don't feel like answering Ed's endless questions if he overhears me."

"Go. I'll keep an eye on our course." Liz slipped behind the helm.

"Good. I'll only be a minute." Dani opened the small locker beside the helm where she'd stashed the extra satellite phone.

She made her way to the forward end of the coachroof and sat down to place her call. After a few minutes, she returned to the cockpit and put the phone away. "He'll call back. It'll probably be late afternoon — maybe in the morning."

Liz nodded. "Ed's funny with his questions, isn't he?"

Dani rolled her eyes. "I have to restrain myself to keep from punching him. What a jerk. It's like this whole thing with Cynthia is some kind of academic exercise. Does he have no emotional attachment to her?"

"I think he does. He says that he compartmentalizes his emotions; it's what he has to do to be effective in court. He says all successful trial lawyers are consummate actors and storytellers," Liz said.

"Well, I'd like him a lot better if he acted like he gave a damn what happened to her. Poor kid. Who knows what she's going through? And he's all over you, now. Not that you're discouraging him."

Liz didn't say anything for a moment as she studied the sails. "Have you forgotten I'm doing this for your benefit?"

"No. I'm watching. I've seen your subtle moves. Pretty slick, actually, the way you're leading him around."

"It's kind of like dancing," Liz said.

"I wouldn't know about that."

"I could teach you."

"Another time. He's got me pissed off. Don't take me too seriously; I'm just letting off steam."

"Okay. I thought so, but I wanted to make sure."

"Aren't you tired of him trying to cop a feel?"

"I'm keeping him at arm's length without shutting him down. You said you wanted to learn the tricks."

"Better you than me. Glad he's shifted his attention to you; I only know one way to react to unwelcome touching, but I'm learning. I'm not sure I've got the self-control you have, though."

"Sure you do. You've shown it in other ways; you'll do fine."

A minute or two passed in silence while Dani thought about that. A frigate bird made a close pass, flying between the masts. It squawked and broke the spell cast by the soft sounds of the wind in the sails and the gurgle of *Vengeance's* wake.

"I agree with you, just so you know," Liz said.

"About what?"

"The way he acts. He seems to have completely forgotten that he even has a daughter."

"I was thinking that you didn't notice."

"Oh, I noticed," Liz said. "I've discussed it with him. That's when he told me about compartmentalizing his feelings. But even then, he seemed too detached. I think I'm more worried about Cynthia than he is, sometimes."

"I know what you mean. Being able to focus his attention is a commendable skill, but I think this is an inappropriate use of it."

"He's coming," Liz said, catching a flicker of motion through the companionway as he put the phone back in its place by the chart table.

25

"THANKS FOR THE SUGGESTION ABOUT GETTING AN ADVANCE ON THE
proceeds of the trades, Liz," Ed said, as he sat down beside the
companionway opening. He was facing Liz and Dani across the
length of the cockpit.

"Glad it helped," Liz said. "How's progress?"

"The money's ready, whenever they call with instructions."

"If they're monitoring your account, I'm surprised they haven't
already called," Dani said. "How long has the cash — "

She stopped to answer the new satellite phone. "Hi, Sharktooth." She listened for a few seconds. "Can I put you on the
speaker?"

She reached around the steering pedestal and set the phone
on the cockpit table.

"Mornin', mornin'." Sharktooth's voice boomed from the tiny
speaker in the odd greeting common to the English-speaking
islanders up and down the chain.

"Good morning," Liz said. "Learn anything interesting in
Grenada?"

"Sandrine's information was good; nobody saw any sign of

Lotus Blossom or Wong. Not the day Cynthia was taken, nor any time recently."

"So Wong was lying about Grenada," Ed said. "But there could be any number of reasons; I can't get past the fact that he and the other guy got hurt when she was recaptured."

"We don't know how they got hurt," Dani said. "You get anything else, Sharktooth?"

"Mebbe, mebbe not. They use a Haitian freighter to ship spices from Grenada."

"Chen does?" Dani asked.

"Mm-hmm. My frien's t'ink mebbe she charter. Use same ship many times."

"What good does that do us?" Ed asked.

"The freighter left Grenada the mornin' they take Cynthia, boun' for St. Vincent."

"So it would have been in the vicinity when she was kidnapped, then," Liz said.

"Mm-hmm. *Lion of Judah.* She hail from Port-au-Prince. Man say typical Haitian boat."

"What's that mean? Typical Haitian boat?" Ed asked.

"Old, small, rusty, poorly maintained, and dirty," Dani said. "What else, Sharktooth?"

"Rumors. Some folks t'ink *Lion of Judah* bringin' drugs."

"Into Grenada?" Liz asked. "But they grow plenty of weed there, don't they?"

"Not weed. Meth, heroin, coke. The bad stuff. An' whatever kinda pills they takin', too. Drugs like that, they don't come from the islands. Bring 'em from down south. Venezuela, mebbe."

"How come if your contacts know that, the cops in Grenada don't stop it?" Ed asked.

"Same reason the cops in the States don't stop it," Sharktooth said. "More rumors, too, 'bout *Lion of Judah.*"

"What rumors?" Liz asked, amused at the irritation on Ed's face.

"Smugglin' people, mebbe."

"Human trafficking?" Ed asked. "This Chen woman's running drugs and engaging in human trafficking?"

"Down, boy," Dani said. "We don't know what her involvement is with the *Lion of Judah*. The crews on those rust buckets free-lance all the time."

"We should call the authorities," Ed said.

"We've been over that, Ed," Liz said. "A knee-jerk reaction won't help Cynthia."

"But they said they'd sell her to the Arabs if I didn't pay the ransom, remember? It all fits. I want to — "

"Get a grip, Ed, and listen for a minute," Dani said. "Do you have any idea how ruthless human traffickers are?"

"Well, I read the news. What's your point?"

"You could get Cynthia killed. The news doesn't report what happens unless the good guys win."

"I don't understand. They stop ships like that and free the people. I — "

"How many reports have you seen where they stopped a ship on solid information and didn't find any captives?" Dani asked.

"I ... can't remember," he said, "but ... "

"But that's what happens most of the time," Sharktooth said.

"Then their information was bad," Ed said.

"Probably not," Dani said.

"Then why didn't they find the captives aboard?"

"Same reason they don't find drugs when they get a tip. The people on the ship get warned by some crooked cop, and they ditch the evidence."

"Drugs, sure. But people? Some of them would be found; they'd talk."

"But they don't," Liz said. "They're on the bottom of the ocean."

"It's as easy to ditch a person as it is to ditch drugs, or anything else," Dani said. "It takes four cable ties, a concrete block, and a couple of feet of rope per person."

Ed looked at her for a moment, frowning. "You rattled that off like most women spout off recipes."

Dani glared at him, but before she could speak, the satellite phone that was stored at the nav station rang. Liz leapt to her feet and scurried down the companionway to retrieve it. Ed was right behind her. Liz answered the call, listened for a moment, and put her hand over the mouthpiece as she handed the phone to Ed. "It's them," she said. "Repeat the instructions and I'll write them down."

Ed took the phone as she opened a drawer and took out a legal pad and a pencil. "This is Ed Savage," he said, and then listened, his face growing progressively more pale.

"What's going on?" Liz asked, a minute or two later as Ed disconnected the call and handed her the phone. "Didn't they tell you where to send the money?"

He shook his head, a faraway look on his face.

"I HAVE to get back to the States," Ed said, picking at the skin on the back of his hand as he sat at the cockpit table. Dani was still at the helm, and Liz was below preparing lunch. Dani had ended the conversation with Sharktooth while Liz and Ed were on the phone with the kidnappers.

"Tell us what they said," Liz called from below, as she made sandwiches at the galley counter.

"It's complicated," Ed said, shaking his head in dismay.

"All the more reason for you to talk it over," Dani said. "Explaining it to us may help you see your way through what's going on."

"I'm not sure how to start," he said. "I'm involved in this case, see, and they ... "

"Maybe you should just start by telling us what they said," Liz said. "I handed you the phone, and you said, 'This is Ed Savage.' Then what?"

"That electronic voice said that they knew I had the money; that I was doing well, but I had to do something else first."

"First?" Liz asked. "Before you send the money?"

"Before they tell me where to send it."

"So what do they want you to do?"

"I don't know; they didn't tell me yet. They said they'd be back in touch, but that I wouldn't be able to help Cynthia if I stayed here."

"Did they say where you should go?" Dani asked.

"They want me back in my office. I'm supposed to review the Tequesta file while I wait for their instructions."

"Any word on Cynthia?"

"Those men in the video still have her, but they said ... "

"What did they say?" Liz asked, in a soft tone.

"They have buyers coming soon to look at the 'merchandise.' My bid of $10 million might not be enough."

"They want more money?"

"That's what I asked. They laughed, and told me to get back to my office and review the Tequesta file."

"That's it? They didn't say anything else?" Dani asked.

"No. Just that the next call would be to my office, and that I'd better be there."

"What's this Tequesta file?" Liz asked.

"Tequesta Recycling is the defendant in a class action suit that I filed on behalf of about 10,000 plaintiffs."

"Tequesta Recycling? What kind of business is that?" Liz asked.

"Tequesta's a garbage collection company, basically. They've got a bunch of dumps and landfills all over the southeast. They're privately held, but their revenues are estimated at around $3 billion per year."

"That's a lot of garbage. They only work in the southeastern U.S.?" Liz asked.

"No. That's where most of their disposal sites are."

"What's the basis of the suit?" Dani asked.

"Ground water pollution from the landfill sites. The plaintiffs have suffered all sorts of bizarre medical problems as a result."

"Who owns Tequesta Recycling? You said it was privately held."

"We haven't been able to get to the bottom of that, yet. We keep running into all kinds of blind alleys — closely held offshore corporations in places that keep secrets for a fee to the government officials."

"Do you think they want you to drop the suit?" Liz asked.

Ed shrugged. "I don't know. I hope it's not that. I mean, these things take on a life of their own. I can't just drop it at this stage. I'm the lead, but there are a bunch of other lawyers with skin in the game, now. Not to mention the syndicate."

"Syndicate? You mean like the mob?" Liz asked.

"No, not that kind of syndicate. Suits like this are expensive; there's all kinds of research. Soil analysis, water analysis, geological studies, you name it. Not to mention all the medical analysis and expert testimony."

"Who pays for all of that? I thought it came out of the damage award," Dani said.

"Well, yeah, it does, if the plaintiffs prevail. But all those expenses have to be paid long before these things even get to court. It's a big gamble for the lead attorneys."

"You mean you've paid — "

"Around $35 million and counting. I don't have that kind of liquidity, so I put together a syndicate of people to fund it. They share the risk and the reward with me."

"So what kind of damages are you seeking?" Liz asked.

"A billion dollars, give or take. Maybe more. It'll gut Tequesta Recycling — no question about that."

"What else could they want?" Dani asked.

"Who knows? Inside information? A piece of the action? When there's a billion dollars in play, it could be anything."

"Have you booked flights back to the states yet?" Liz asked.

"Well, kind of. You said we'd get to Bequia a little after lunch. I've booked a charter flight to Miami and then on to Atlanta. They'll be waiting for me in St. Vincent. I told them sometime after 4 p.m., just to be safe. That still sound good?"

"Yes. We'll be dropping the anchor around 1:30 or 2:00. Sharktooth's waiting for us. He can take you to St. Vincent in *Lightning Bolt*. It's only a few minutes' run for him. You should make four o'clock with no problem," Liz said.

"Will you keep looking for Cynthia? I mean, this thing's taken on a different dimension, now. Depending on what they want me to do, I may not have a choice about the authorities, but ... "

"Yes. We'll find her. These people have started asking questions about me and my family; it's personal, now. That scares me. No way I'm backing out, whatever you decide to do. We'll keep you posted, and I trust you'll do the same?"

"If I can do it without jeopardizing Cynthia's chances."

"Believe me, we're her best shot, Ed. We're going to get her back."

"I want whoever's behind this put away."

"Me, too," Dani said. "Permanently. That's a given."

"Then you'll have to go to the authorities at some point."

"No. The authorities might get Cynthia back, but they can't handle the people behind this."

"And who do you think can, then? We don't even know who these people are, Dani."

"I only need to work my way up the chain one link at a time."

"But what do you do when you find somebody?"

"Don't ask, Ed," Liz said. "Those people have chosen to play by a different set of rules, now. They aren't accustomed to victims who understand their game."

"I don't get it, Liz."

"There are winners and losers from here on," Dani said. "Winners keep playing. Losers die. It's simple. They've made me feel threatened. I won't put up with that, and the authorities have too many limits on what they can do. Threaten my family and somebody dies."

"You're nuts," Ed said, shaking his head.

Dani grinned. "We'll see."

There was a moment of awkward silence, broken when Ed said, "Guess I'd better go pack up."

As he stood and turned to go below, the satellite phone at the helm rang. Liz picked it up, looked at the display, and said, "It's Mario," as she passed the phone to Dani. Ed disappeared down the companionway ladder, shaking his head. Liz slid behind the helm as Dani walked up to sit on the side of the coachroof with the telephone.

"ED THINKS YOU'RE BLUFFING," Liz said, when Dani came back.

"You talked to him while I was on the phone? But you were steering. I would have — "

"It wasn't an extended conversation. He just stuck his head up for a second after you went forward, and said you were 'full of shit,' to use his words."

"What did you say?"

"Nothing. He's so far out of his depth that there's no point. Poor guy."

"Poor guy, nothing. He's a jerk."

"What did Mario find out?"

"The person who sent the request through to the police in St. Vincent is suspected of being on the payroll of a local hood named Joe DiFiore. Mario says DiFiore runs drugs and prostitution for a guy named Jimmy Gregorio. Cops have been trying to nail them for years, but they've never made anything stick against DiFiore. Gregorio is so well insulated he's considered untouchable, but they're pretty sure he's the top man in the southeastern U.S."

"No thoughts as to why they're asking about J.-P.?"

"No. Mario called him before he called me back."

"J.-P.?"

"Yes. He didn't tell Papa I was involved. He didn't want to worry him unnecessarily, but he thought Papa might recognize one of the names, or have some idea why they were asking about him."

"And did he?"

"No. He didn't have a clue. That means — "

"It almost has to be related to Cynthia's kidnapping," Liz said, finishing Dani's thought.

"Yes. That's where I came out. So did Mario."

"You told him, then?"

"Yes. I didn't tell him when I called earlier; I didn't want to prejudice him with our guesswork, but at this stage, I wanted his thoughts on what could be happening."

"What did he say?"

"Mario doesn't think out loud. He absorbed it all and asked me a couple of questions. He's going to do a little checking and get back to me. I passed along what Ed told us about Tequesta, but he already knew something about that. I mean, nothing Ed didn't tell us, but apparently it's been all over the business news for a good while."

"How are you feeling about Chen, now?" Liz asked.

"Puzzled is the best description, I guess. The coincidence factor is still there. She almost has to be involved, but some things don't make sense."

"Think she might have done this under contract, or something? Or maybe she's behind Tequesta Recycling?" Liz asked.

"Either one's possible, I guess, but there's one big piece that doesn't fit into the puzzle anywhere."

"What's that?"

"The $10-million-dollar ransom demand."

Liz digested that. After 30 seconds, she said, "I see what you mean. Why ask for $10 million if what they really wanted had something to do with the lawsuit?"

"Exactly."

"What do you think?" Liz asked.

"It's making my head hurt. I'll be glad to have Ed out of our hair, though. He's a distraction we don't need."

Liz laughed. Dani looked at her in confusion for a few seconds, and then smiled. "Not that way. Not now; I've got other things on my mind."

"That's my girl," Liz said. "I'm glad he's leaving, too. Sometimes, I was tempted ... "

"Then why'd you keep dodging him? I would have looked the other way."

"I said I'd show you the ropes. I didn't think you needed lessons on how to give in. You seemed like a natural at that when — " Liz bent backward from the waist.

"Ow!" Dani grunted, as Liz slipped the punch Dani had thrown and countered with a sharp, stiff-fingered jab to Dani's kidney.

"I warned you last night, girl. Sucker punches are one to a customer." Liz said as she watched Dani gasp for breath.

"Okay, okay," Dani said, finally. "But that was vicious."

"Sorry, but I wasn't taught compassion in hand-to-hand combat. Vicious is a mild description for the woman I learned from."

26

"DID YOU GET HIM TO THE AIRPORT OKAY?" LIZ ASKED SHARKTOOTH, as Dani topped off their wineglasses.

Vengeance swung to her anchor off Princess Margaret Beach in Bequia's Admiralty Bay, with *Lightning Bolt* tied alongside.

"No problem. I took him to Young Island Cut; he took a taxi from the dinghy dock. Only a few minutes to the airport. He was earlier than he planned."

"He had a chartered plane waiting," Liz said. "That took me by surprise. It must have cost him a fortune."

"Mm-hmm. A private jet. Cessna Citation," Sharktooth said.

"He told you that?"

"No. Just that he had a chartered plane. I checked with my frien' at the airport after I dropped him off."

"I wonder why the sudden urgency," Dani said. "He's been stone cold up until now, for the most part. His reaction to the kidnapping has been really offhand, by my reckoning."

"Mebbe he know somethin' he don' tell," Sharktooth said. "How long he talk to them, that las' call?"

"Two minutes at the most," Liz said.

"How much could you overhear?" Dani asked.

"All of it. That warbling voice carries well. He gave us an accurate summary. They told him there was a change in plans — that he should keep the money ready, but they wanted him back in his office ASAP. They ordered him to study his file on Tequesta Recycling and think about what was more important — the suit, or Cynthia. They said the next call would be to his office, and that he shouldn't miss it if he wanted to see her again."

"They didn't give him a deadline to get there?" Dani asked.

"No, they didn't mention anything like that. They did say they had buyers coming to look at the merchandise, implying that Cynthia might be for sale to the highest bidder, I guess."

"Bastards," Dani said. "I wonder if he's in the habit of chartering jets."

"Mebbe. My frien' at the airport said the pilot knew him; greeted him by name, an' say it good to see him again. Pilot tol' my frien' he use the plane to travel roun' an' interview people for some big lawsuit."

"Hmm," Dani said. "But he flew down on a commercial flight. So did Cynthia."

"What are you thinking, Dani?" Liz asked.

"Trying to make sense out of it. If he had a plane at his disposal, you'd think he would have used it to get here, instead of flying all over the place making connections on puddle jumpers, like the hoi-polloi."

"Maybe he didn't want to spend the money?" Liz said.

"Then why spend it now? He hasn't seemed that worried about Cynthia, and he didn't seem any more worried about her after this last phone call, did he?"

"No," Liz said, "You're right. He seemed more worried about this lawsuit."

"Mebbe he don' pay for plane this time," Sharktooth said.

"I don't get your point, Sharktooth," Dani said.

"Who he called to arrange the flight?" Sharktooth asked.

"His secretary, I guess," Liz said. "After the call from the kidnappers, he took the phone up forward and made a call. He was only gone a couple of minutes, and then he came back and told us about it while I was fixing lunch."

"Let's check the phone and see who he called," Dani said.

Before Dani stopped talking, Liz was at the chart table. She picked up the satellite phone and scrolled through the call log. "The last call was to a number in the 703 area code," Liz said. "Is that Atlanta?"

"Virginia," Sharktooth said. "Block your caller i.d. an' call the number. We see who answer."

Liz tapped a few buttons, switched the phone to speaker mode, and set it on the bridge deck where they could all hear.

"You have reached the offices of Apex Investment Partners. We are closed for the day. Your call is important to us; please call back during our normal business hours, or leave a message. Our office is open from 9 a.m. until 5 p.m. Eastern time, Monday through Friday, or you may leave a message at the tone and we'll call you back as soon as possible."

"His broker?" Sharktooth asked.

"No. All his other calls are to the 404 area code; his office and his broker are both there."

"Tha's Atlanta," Sharktooth said.

"He mentioned a syndicate that was funding the lawsuit," Liz said.

"Yes," Dani said, "but I think those are normally other lawyers. They've got a bunch of funny constraints on who can share in that kind of thing."

"Why?" Sharktooth asked.

"Some pretense of ethics, I think. But who knows? They're all a bunch of thieves."

The encrypted satellite phone that Sharktooth had loaned them rang, interrupting their musings.

"GOOD EVENING, MY FRIENDS," Mario said, after Dani had switched the satellite phone to speaker mode.

"*Hola, Mario. Buenas tardes*," Sharktooth said.

"Hello, Sharktooth. I didn't expect to find you there, but it's nice to hear your voice. Are Dani and Liz feeding you well?"

"*Siempre. No quiero nada aquí.*"

"Ah, that is good, then. Dani, I got a call from the people who gave me the information about DiFiore."

"And?" Dani asked.

"There's something happening in the mob. Joe DiFiore's fallen from favor, it seems."

"Did they say why?" Liz asked.

"No. Nobody knows, for sure. But DiFiore's brother, Mike, was beaten and tortured."

"By the mob? Is somebody sending DiFiore a message?" Dani asked.

"Yes, it looks that way, but nobody thinks it was the mob. He was mutilated. His whole body was covered with bite marks, from his face to his toes. He was a bloody mess when the cops found him unconscious on Collins Avenue early this morning."

"Bite marks?" Dani asked.

"Yes, deep wounds, but no flesh was removed, except for his manhood, and that was cut cleanly. The wound was cauterized; someone wanted him to live."

Dani and Liz traded looks. "There was a similar incident here a couple of days ago, except the victim was found dead. He was the head of the narcotics squad in St. Vincent. The rumor is there's a *loup garou* on the loose," Dani said.

"Only in this case, the tongue was taken," Liz added.

"*Loup garou*?" Mario asked. "This was no werewolf in South Beach. The emergency room physician said the bites were inflicted by a human."

"Has Mike DiFiore recovered consciousness?" Sharktooth asked.

"Nobody knows. His brother showed up at the ER with a doctor and a lawyer and a private ambulance. The lawyer had a court order allowing Joe to take his brother. End of story, except that Joe's influence in the mob has been reduced."

"So they don't know who did it?" Sharktooth asked.

"No. The cops think it's some kind of power play in the mob, but who knows?"

"I guess nobody saw who took Mike DiFiore?" Dani said.

"That's right. He was hanging out in one of his favorite clubs, and this gal picked him up. He left with her after a couple of drinks. Bartender told the cops she wasn't anybody he'd seen before; looked like mixed blood — Black and Asian — and spoke with an island lilt. Cops can't find any sign of her, needless to say."

"Will you tell them about the case here?" Dani asked.

"You want me to?"

"What's your thought on that?"

"I wouldn't, normally. Not unless there's something to be gained from it. I can, if you wish, but I think it's your call."

"Let's keep it quiet, for now," Dani said.

"Good," Mario said. "Any progress with your hunt for the girl?"

"Not really. I've got a meeting with the Chen woman in the morning."

"Why'd you do that?"

"She called. Her story is she wants me to mentor young women, entrepreneurial types."

"Be careful, Dani."

"Have you heard anything about her?"

"Nothing specific, but I'd be surprised if she's not in the drug business. Too much similarity to the spice trade, and she's rolling in money. She's easily the richest woman in the Caribbean States. I've been hearing about her for years."

"I'm meeting her on her yacht, right here in Bequia. It's too obvious for her to be planning anything. I think she wants the same thing I do — to check out the opposition."

"Like I said, take care. You know about her boyfriend, right?"

"Boyfriend?"

"Li Wong is his name. He's a dwarf, and famously mean. The people who think she's crooked think Wong's her personal enforcer."

"Thanks. I'll keep that in mind."

"Do. And call me when you're home safe, please."

"Sure, Mario. Anything else?"

"No. You?"

"Yes. Have you ever heard of Apex Investment Partners?"

"No. Why?"

They told Mario about Ed's departure on the chartered jet and his phone call to the number in Virginia.

"Still have the number?"

Liz gave it to him, and he said goodnight, after making Dani promise again to be careful and check in with him after her meeting.

"WHAT DO you think about the DiFiore thing?" Liz asked Dani, as they sipped the last of the wine they'd had with their dinner. Sharktooth had left after the call from Mario; he had a dinner engagement with their old friend, Mrs. Walker, and would pick Dani up in the morning and take her to her meeting on *Lotus Blossom*.

"More coincidence," Dani said. "I think it's certainly the same people. You disagree?"

"No. Not at all. The similarities are too great."

"And the biting," Dani said. "That's too uncommon for them not to be connected."

"Drugs?"

"For sure," Dani said. "The cop who was killed here ran the drug squad. And Mario said the other day that Joe DiFiore ran prostitution in the southeastern U.S., as well. The people who took Cynthia are into that; I mean, they've threatened twice now to sell her if Ed doesn't do what they want."

"What did she blunder into?" Liz asked. "All she did was buy a little grass."

"Wrong place, wrong time, I guess," Dani said.

"I think there's more to it," Liz said.

"Now who's paranoid?" Dani teased. "What are you seeing that I'm not."

"Probably nothing. I'm just looking at it from a different angle."

"So, tell me."

"What if Ed's into something he hasn't told us about?"

"I'm willing to believe he's a real shit. No argument from me on that, but I'm not following you."

"I can't really connect the dots, as they say, and make a logical case. It's more like your coincidence theory, but work through this with me."

"Okay."

"He books a charter with us for a pickup in Bequia, on the advice of 'a client.' From the little he told us about this Tequesta suit, I doubt that he's got time for other clients right now. He's busy, if he's spent $35 million in prep work on that case, right?"

"Yes, that sounds right."

"So 'the client' is probably one of the plaintiffs in the Tequesta case. His daughter gets kidnapped, and — "

"Wait. She got kidnapped because she bought ganja," Dani said.

"Think about it, Dani. Neither one of us thought that made sense. Remember wondering why anyone would bother? All she could do is give up a couple of low level pushers, at most."

"But what about the shakedown?" Dani asked.

"We said it was a shakedown. What if it were not?"

"What else could it have been?"

"It could have been that the crooked cop was going to snatch her all along. Maybe whoever was paying him wanted her for leverage over Ed because of the suit."

Liz waited, letting the silence drag on while her friend thought about her hypothesis. Dani took a sip of wine and put her glass down.

"You may be onto something, Liz. But how would Chen and Wong fit in?"

"I don't have the answer to that. But I think there's a more complicated motive than just drugs and kidnapping. There has to be, now that they've dropped the lawsuit thing into the mix."

"Yes," Dani said. "And that might explain Ed's odd behavior."

"How?" Liz asked. "You don't think he's behind his own daughter's kidnapping, somehow, do you?"

"I'm not ready to go that far, but suppose he suspected all along that there was something else going on here, something besides kidnapping for ransom?"

"You mean, maybe he knew who had her?"

"Or he suspected. There's been something off about his reaction. A normal parent would have been devastated, but it was almost like he knew something was coming after the ransom demand."

"You're saying maybe he is part of the kidnapping, then. But what could he gain?"

"I don't know, Liz. I can't believe he's part of the kidnapping, but you've opened whole vistas of possibility. I think we need to put it aside and sleep on it. Not much we can do tonight, anyway."

27

"Good morning, Mario," Dani said, answering the phone as she and Liz drank coffee in the cockpit and watched the boat traffic in Admiralty Bay. She paused, then said, "No, he hasn't shown up yet. He's going to take me to my 10 o'clock meeting with Marissa Chen, so he's probably eating a huge breakfast at Mrs. Walker's."

She listened for a few seconds. "Sure. Liz should hear this. Can I put you on the speaker?"

"Good morning, Mario," Liz said, as Dani set the phone on the cockpit table between them.

"Hello, Liz. I was just telling Dani about Apex Investment Partners. My friends on the DEA task force think it's a front for the Baltimore mob. They've been watching them for a while; they think they're probably laundering drug money, but they haven't found any proof."

"Interesting," Dani said. "I wonder why Ed called them?"

"It could be innocent," Mario said. "They do have legitimate clients."

"Okay, but that was the only call he made after the kidnappers called him."

"He's raising the ransom money, maybe," Mario suggested.

"He said he already had the money from his brokerage accounts, and the kidnappers knew that. At least, that's what he told us," Liz said.

"My point was that he apparently called them, and only them, and they sent a private jet to pick him up — on a few hours' notice. I think that's a little odd," Dani said.

"Don't forget what Sharktooth told us about the plane," Liz said.

"What was that?" Mario asked.

"The pilot knew Ed well, and had been flying him around to interview people about the Tequesta suit," Liz said.

"Do you know the tail number on the plane?" Mario asked.

"No, but I'll bet Sharktooth can get it. I'm sure it got logged in at the airport, and customs, too, for that matter," Dani said. "I'll ask him to make a few calls while he's waiting to bring me back from *Lotus Blossom*."

"*Lotus Blossom*?" Mario asked.

"Chen's yacht," Dani said.

"I see. Let me know, please."

"Will do," Dani said.

"That's all I have this morning, ladies," Mario said.

"Thanks, Mario," Dani said.

"You're most welcome. Be careful, and don't forget to call when you return from your meeting."

"I will, but don't worry."

"It's my job as your godfather, Danielle. I know you can take care of yourself, but your father appointed me to worry about you before you were born."

"Thanks," Dani said, smiling. "I'll be careful, and I'll call soon."

She disconnected the call as Liz poured another cup of steaming coffee for each of them. Dani lifted her cup, holding it under her nose and inhaling the aroma.

"Nothing like fresh-ground coffee," she said, taking a sip.

"You think Ed's mixed up with the mob?" Liz asked.

Dani thought for a few seconds, and said, "It seems unlikely. He's sort of a wimp, but anything's possible with the kind of money that's tied up in that suit. And garbage disposal is a traditional mob business in the States."

"Ah, it's good to find you in your office, Mr. Savage," the electronically disguised voice warbled. "Good for Cynthia; there's a certain gentleman from the Middle East who has his eye fixed on her, hoping that you fail to follow our instructions."

"What is it that you want? I have the money."

"Yes, of course. Did you review the Tequesta file, as you were instructed?"

"Yes."

"You have the ten million, but we both know what the Tequesta suit is worth. Ten million dollars isn't significant to either of us, is it, Mr. Savage?"

Ed didn't say anything for a few seconds, and the voice resumed. "Picture your beautiful daughter in a harem, Mr. Savage. She'll be a plaything for a man who thinks even a billion-dollar lawsuit is nothing but pocket change. Do you know what I've heard he does when he tires of girls like her?" The voice paused for a second or two and resumed. "He has a string of bordellos where he sends them, until they're so used-up that he finally sells them on to someone in Bangkok. God only knows what happens there."

"What do you want?" Ed asked again.

"You should withdraw from the Tequesta suit, Mr. Savage."

"I can't just drop the suit; there are — "

"Sorry, Mr. Savage. You misunderstood. We aren't fools; we

know you can't drop the suit. We want you, personally, to with-draw as the lead attorney. Without your skills as a litigator who distorts the facts to sway a jury, we believe the suit will be less viable. Perhaps the next lead attorney will be more, ah, flexible. But that would no longer be your concern. Is that so much to ask, Mr. Savage? In exchange for your daughter? Think about it, but not for long. We'll give you until tomorrow evening to get the motion paperwork done and filed."

Ed heard a click as the call disconnected. He took deep breaths and sat back in his chair, forcing himself to relax. He had anticipated something like this after the call from the kidnappers yesterday afternoon, when they had told him to review the file. He hadn't expected that they would want him to withdraw; he'd been worried that they would want the suit dropped completely. They'd given him a more realistic alternative than he had expected. He pressed the intercom button on his phone.

"Yes, Ed?"

"Hi, Linda. Could you bring me some coffee?"

"Sure. I just made a fresh pot."

"Linda?"

"Yes?"

"And the Apex Investment Partners file, please?"

"It's in the top drawer of the first file cabinet of the Tequesta files, right in your credenza. I'll get it when I bring the coffee."

He spun his chair around and opened the drawer. "Never mind. Got it. Thanks, babe."

"BERNIE?" Ed Savage asked, barely noticing the noise added by the encryption device attached to his phone.

"Yeah, Ed. What's happening, buddy?"

Ed pictured Bernie Albertson sitting behind his massive,

gleaming desk, his manicured hands clasped behind his headful of smooth, silver hair. His feet, in the polished, handmade shoes, were no doubt resting on the side of a drawer that was pulled out for the purpose. He wondered if paper ever crossed Bernie's desk. He had speculated for years that it was a mere prop, and that Bernie was an actor of some sort, hired to project the image of old money. He was certainly no one's "buddy," especially not Ed's.

"I'm back in my office."

"I guessed that; I heard that you used one of the planes. Glad we could help you out."

"I got a call from them this morning. They've upped the stakes, just as you thought they would."

"Tell me about it, Ed. What do they want?"

"They want me to pull out."

"You mean, drop the suit?"

"No, not that. They're too smart for that. They want me to withdraw as lead counsel."

"Hmm. That would require Wilkinson's consent, wouldn't it?"

"Right. I'd have to file a petition with the court, and Judge Wilkinson would have to approve it."

"You think he would?"

"Probably, but we'd have to have somebody else ready to step in. I wanted to talk to you about that. See, I think they've got somebody in mind, from what he said. Maybe they've already got somebody lined up, one of the other lawyers in the group."

"Who would that be, Ed? You mean we have a traitor on our team?"

"Wouldn't be the first time that kind of thing has happened, Bernie. I don't have any idea who it is. Want me to ask around?"

"Nah. It was just idle curiosity."

"I think it's critical. If someone working for the other side started calling the shots — "

"Ed, Ed, Ed. It would be critical, but it's not going to happen."

"No, Bernie, you don't understand. I've got to file a petition to withdraw by tomorrow evening."

"No, Ed."

"What do you mean, 'no?' If I don't — "

"No isn't an ambiguous word, even for a lawyer, Ed. You will not withdraw."

"You don't understand, Bernie. They have Cynthia."

"I know that. I set that up, remember, and you concurred, Ed. We paid the Chen woman a fortune to make that happen; her and her crooked cop. You knew all about that."

"He's dead, Bernie. It's going all wrong."

"Who? Who's dead?"

"The cop. They found him on the waterfront a day after they took Cynthia. His tongue was cut out and the locals think a werewolf chewed him up."

"Wait a minute, Ed. Then who snatched Cynthia?"

"Two guys in a speedboat from Trinidad, but I've got no idea who they were working for."

"Chen, probably."

"I don't think so. Cynthia escaped, and two of Chen's people picked her up, pretending to be good guys. They convinced the cops that they were going to bring her back to me on that yacht with the two women."

"So, then it doesn't matter who they were working for, does it, Ed? Chen's got Cynthia, all safe and sound."

"Uh-uh, Bernie. The guys from Trinidad jumped Chen's people and took Cynthia again. I have no idea who has her. This whole thing's gone to hell. I need to do whatever it takes to get her back."

"Calm down, Ed. You knew there was some risk to Cynthia in this. We talked about that; you were comfortable with it."

"That was based on your assurance that we could trust Chen to keep her safe."

"And we could have. Nobody expected that the other side

would really take her. Makes me wonder if we were right about Gregorio."

"What do you mean, right about Gregorio, Bernie?"

"When we had him figured for the guy behind Tequesta."

"I'm confused, Bernie. You think somebody else is behind Tequesta?"

"Well, think about it, Ed. Gregorio thinks Chen's working for him, right?"

"Yes."

"So it's unlikely that he'd have Cynthia snatched away from Chen."

"I see where you're going, Bernie. Whoever took Cynthia away from Chen has to be the power behind Tequesta Recycling."

"That's right. This isn't our fault, Ed. It comes under the heading of 'shit happens,' to use the language of the unwashed."

"She's my daughter, Bernie. I can't let them sell her to some Arab who's going to put her in a whorehouse."

"That's what they're threatening?"

"Yes."

"Well, no wonder you're upset, Ed. I don't blame you."

Ed sighed, relieved. "You understand?"

"Of course I understand. I've got a daughter her age, remember."

"I know. That's why I was sure you'd agree."

"Wait a minute, Ed. Agree to what?"

"My personal withdrawal."

"Ed, I can't agree to that. Listen to me, man. We've got $35 million tied up in this. Thirty-five million dollars that belongs to some ugly, dangerous people. You pull out, and we're both going to be in deep trouble, buddy."

"I'll make good on the money, Bernie. You tell them — "

"Ed, come on. Think this through. You're upset. I understand that, but don't let it cloud your judgment. This isn't about the $35 million any more. We've got the other side right where we want them."

"What are you talking about, Bernie?"

"They don't want this to go to trial; that's why they want you to step down. They want to put their handpicked guy in your place and settle this thing. That's what we wanted all along, remember? A settlement?"

"I thought your investors wanted to acquire Tequesta."

"That's right. We'll settle this by effectively acquiring Tequesta. They're playing right along, like they read our script, buddy. Think about it. You're going to be worth close to a billion once the dust clears."

"But they've got Cynthia."

"She'll be okay, Ed. We'll make that part of the package."

Ed remembered the video, and the raw fear on Cynthia's face. "Not good enough. I'm going to file a motion — "

"Ed, listen to me. You know what kind of people my investors are; don't play dumb. If you pull out, our leverage goes away, and they know that as well as the people who own Tequesta do. Do you think they'll let you walk away?"

"But Cynthia — "

"They don't care about Cynthia. Neither side cares about her. You said it early on; Cynthia's just a pawn. I can't believe we're having this conversation, but I'm going to spell it out for you. This isn't a threat, and it's not something I have any control over, but I'm telling you, if you file that motion, I doubt you'll live to see Cynthia released."

"I could go to the police."

Bernie laughed, long and hard. Gasping for breath, he said, "Ed, take it easy for a little while. I need to think this through, make a few calls, maybe. I'll get back to you, but don't do anything rash. You have until tomorrow night to file, right?"

"Yes, that's right, unless they change their minds."

"If you hear from them again, call me immediately. In the

meantime, let's use the time until the deadline to come up with a way out of this that will keep you and Cynthia and me alive, okay? If Gregorio's not behind Tequesta, we need to find out who is."

"Okay," Ed said. He heard a muted click as Bernie disconnected the call.

28

As soon as Bernie hung up from Ed Savage, he called the lead investor in the consortium that was funding the Tequesta suit. "They're pushing for Savage to withdraw," he explained.

"We can't allow that, Mr. Albertson."

"I agree, but Savage is rattled. They're threatening to sell the girl as a sex slave."

"And he believes them?"

"Yes. Why wouldn't he?"

"I thought you told him that we would hold the girl."

"I did, but he says someone else has her now. He told me that two men from Trinidad took her away from Gregorio's people."

There was silence on the line for several seconds. Bernie said, "That means we may have been wrong about who actually owns Tequesta, so he doesn't trust us anymore."

"If not Gregorio, then who does he think has her?"

"He has no idea."

"That's good. Whatever happens, don't let him file that motion. I'm holding you responsible for his actions. Do you understand?"

"C-certainly. I need a little tactical support to make him realize the gravity of his situation, though."

"That's reasonable. We'll take care of it right away."

"We need him intact," Bernie said, alarm in his voice. "It won't do to have him crippled or killed."

"Mr. Albertson, we don't need you to tell us how to run our business." There was a click, and the call was disconnected.

THE DRAGON LADY fingered the carving on her desk as she contemplated her upcoming meeting with the Berger woman. With Ed Savage back in Atlanta, there was no reason for the woman and her Rasta sidekick to persist in their quest to find who had taken the girl, but it would be useful to know what they had discovered so far. The more she could learn about their perception of the situation, the better she would be able to predict Savage's behavior.

She was troubled by Berger; none of her usual sources had turned up anything useful about her or the Rasta, and they had drawn a complete blank on J.-P. Berger, the woman's father. He was French, from Martinique originally, and wealthy. He had a fleet of large charter yachts in the Mediterranean, but that seemed more of a hobby than a business. It was an exorbitantly expensive hobby, though, and in her experience, men with that kind of money weren't invisible. Yet, she'd been able to learn nothing about him. The dearth of information was so severe that it was suspicious in itself. She pressed the intercom key on her telephone.

"Yes, Madame?"

"Is Wong in the office this morning, Veralyn?"

"Yes, Madame. He's reviewing some files in the conference room."

"Send him to me, please."

"GOOD MORNING, MADAME," Wong said, entering her office after knocking softly at the door. "You wished to see me?"

"Yes. Is the girl still aboard *Lion of Judah*?"

"Yes, Madame, as you wished."

"Good. Come with me to Bequia to meet Danielle Berger, and after the meeting, take *Lotus Blossom* out to rendezvous with *Lion of Judah*. I want the girl in our custody. I don't trust Gregorio's people with her."

"Are they expecting this?"

She shrugged. "Take $50,000. That should persuade them to give her up and keep their mouths shut about it. Tell them Gregorio is not to know, or you will hurt them."

He nodded, grinning. "And where do you want the girl?"

"On *Lotus Blossom*, for now, but lock her up below. I don't want her in my stateroom after she's been on that filthy little ship. Make sure they spray her down for lice before we get there."

"Yes, Madame."

"And Wong?"

"Yes?"

"Don't touch her — yet. She's not to be harmed until I give the word."

"I understand. Is there anything else?"

"Yes. Ms. Berger will no doubt have a professional interest in *Lotus Blossom*. Before he brings her to me, have Schmidt give her a complete tour. Make sure that she sees every corner. I want her to know beyond a doubt that the girl is not aboard."

SHARKTOOTH BROUGHT *Lightning Bolt* to a stop inches from the boarding platform that hung suspended alongside *Lotus Blossom*. Dani stepped across the small gap with the grace born of experience. She didn't take the implicit offer of assistance from the man in the starched white uniform who stood with his forearm extended slightly in her direction. She acknowledged his tacit offer with a smile and a nod.

"Good morning, Ms. Berger, and welcome aboard *Lotus Blossom*. I'm Eric Schmidt, her captain."

"Pleased to meet you, Mr. Schmidt," Dani said, extending her small, hard hand.

She noticed that he was careful not to grip her hand as he would a man's, instead taking it in his fingers as if he held a fragile bird. Irritated with his condescension, she squeezed his fingers together, feeling the crepitus as his knuckles were crushed together. Seeing the shock on his face, she grinned and relaxed her grip.

"Madame Chen just called from the helicopter; she asked me to apologize for her failure to welcome you aboard personally; she'll be here in just a few minutes. She suggested that you might have a professional interest in examining *Lotus Blossom* in the meantime," he said, flexing his fingers.

"Actually, I would," Dani said. "She's beautiful. Have you been her master for long?"

"Yes. I was hired by Madame Chen's father."

"I see. So you must have known Madame Chen for a long time, then."

"Since she was a child. I understand that you have a lengthy résumé when it comes to yachting, as well. You've crewed on some famous sailing yachts in the Med, she tells me. And now you have that lovely Herreshoff ketch I've been admiring for several years."

"Yes," Dani said, wondering how much Chen knew about her background.

"So, where would you like to start our tour, Ms. Berger?"

"I'm intrigued by classic motor yachts. I've always sailed. I don't know much about motor yachts, so I want to see it all. Let's start at the shaft log and work our way up to the bridge."

"As you wish. Come with me." Schmidt led her up the boarding ladder and through a watertight door into a corridor amidships. He opened another watertight door and led her down a narrow, steep ladder into the engine room. He paused and opened a locker, handing her safety glasses and ear protection. Taking a set of earmuffs for himself, he said, "You'll want these when we get to the generator room."

She put on the protective gear and followed him as he led her into the spotless bowels of the old vessel, opening every locker and door and explaining what was there. Twenty minutes later, they had completed the quick inspection and ended up on the bridge. Looking aft, Dani saw that a small helicopter had landed aboard while they were below.

"I'll take you to Madame Chen now, Ms. Berger."

"Thank you, captain. I appreciate the tour, and I commend you on keeping your ship in Bristol fashion."

He nodded tersely. "Thank you." He turned and gestured for her to precede him through a door in the bulkhead behind the chart table.

Dani stopped in the short corridor behind the door, admiring the burled walnut paneling. Schmidt tapped lightly on a heavy wooden door.

"Come in," a woman's voice said, and Schmidt opened the door and stepped aside for Dani to enter.

Dani took in the lavish appointments as she stepped through the door. She found herself face to face with a gorgeous woman about her own size.

"Thank you, Schmidt. Leave us, please," the woman said.

"Ms. Berger, thank you for coming. I'm Marissa Chen." Chen extended her hand, and Dani was pleased with her firm grasp. She felt the calluses along the outer edge of the woman's hand

and recognized that they were from the practice of some form of martial art.

"Thank you for inviting me, Ms. Chen," Dani said, releasing Chen's hand. She studied the woman's smooth, porcelain-like face, wondering how old she was. From what she knew of Chen, she must be in her mid-to-late forties, but she looked of an age with Dani.

"I apologize for being late. Thank you again for coming. It's so nice to meet another successful business woman."

Dani nodded. "Apology accepted. It gave me a chance to admire *Lotus Blossom*."

"And what do you think of her?"

"For a motor vessel, she's charming. With the engine shut down, I could forget that she's not a classic sailing yacht."

"I'll take that as a compliment."

"Good. I intended it as one. I told Captain Schmidt that I have little sea-time other than under sail. She's a beauty."

"Thank you. Let's go into the sitting area and get comfortable." Chen turned slightly and walked around a corner, leading Dani out into what could have passed for a Victorian-era sitting room.

"Please," Chen said, gesturing to a grouping of three wingback chairs.

As Dani turned to sit down, she felt the caress of soft leather under her hand. Chen took the closest chair to the one Dani had chosen; there was a small, carved teak side table between them. As her hostess sat, Dani caught a flicker of motion in her peripheral vision and turned her head to see a dwarf in a rumpled, white silk suit entering the sitting area from around another corner.

"Ms. Berger," Chen said, "permit me to introduce my colleague and old friend, Li Wong."

The short man bowed slightly and murmured, "Ms. Berger."

"Mr. Wong, I'm pleased to make your acquaintance," Dani said.

"Would you care for some coffee or tea, Ms. Berger?" Chen asked, as Wong stood, waiting.

"No, thanks," Dani said.

"Very well, then. Wong, please sit down."

He took the third chair in the group, leaving Chen positioned between him and Dani.

"I asked Wong to join us, if that's all right with you. He's my detail man; he keeps me honest, and without him to get things done, I'm not sure how I would cope."

Dani nodded and smiled, not saying anything while she studied Chen's finely sculpted features. Again, she wondered at the woman's age, thinking she must never let sunlight touch her skin. Wong's face, in contrast, looked like wrinkled saddle leather. With the angle of the light on his face, she noticed the stitches; from experience, she could tell they closed superficial wounds, although they gave him a menacing look. She saw that there was minimal bruising associated with his injuries. Someone had hit him to make him bleed, not to inflict any real damage, she thought.

As Chen began to describe the charity that she ran to teach young island women the mechanics of running a business, Dani gave the appearance of listening politely while she considered what the real purpose of this meeting might be. After describing how the women were taught the basics of finance and accounting, Chen told her about having them present business plans to her. She funded the ones that she thought had merit, and offered constructive critiques on the ones that needed more work.

"Do you ever reject any of them outright?" Dani asked.

"I haven't, yet. But I would, if it were warranted. My intention is to teach them to stand on their own, to think about business the way you and I would, not to give them handouts."

"How do you see me fitting into this?" Dani asked. "Sounds like you have everything covered."

"You're a successful businesswoman, an entrepreneur. There's a lot that you could teach them. Besides your accomplishments, you have the academic credentials, and you're from an entrepreneurial background."

"I'm not sure what you mean by that," Dani said.

"Well, your mother's family has been in the investment banking business for generations, and she's the managing partner now, so you have a strong businesswoman as a role model."

Dani smiled at that. Chen didn't know much about her mother.

"And," Chen continued, "there's your father. I understand he's a successful man, as well. I can't recall just now, though, exactly what business he's in."

Dani, poker-faced, let the silence hang.

"Was it yachting?" Chen asked, finally.

"He's a yachtsman, yes," Dani said, hiding a smile at the edge of frustration she sensed in the other woman's tone of voice.

"I don't know if that's where he made his money," Chen finally said, pausing again.

Dani didn't respond.

"Would you be interested in mentoring one of our young women?" Chen asked, at last, frustrated by Dani's refusal to be drawn out.

"I'll consider it," Dani said. "When you have something specific, some particular person in mind, give me a call."

"Very well," Chen said. "Now that our business is cleared up, I wanted to ask how your guest, Mr. Savage, is coping. Is there news of his daughter?"

"No, not really," Dani said. "But he did ask me to thank you, Mr. Wong, for your attempt to rescue her. That was kind of you. I gather your wounds are the result; it was brave of you to take such a risk to help Cynthia."

"She's an impressive girl," Wong said. "She escaped once. Perhaps she'll escape again."

"I heard that one of your crew was injured, as well," Dani said. "I hope I'll get the opportunity to give him Mr. Savage's personal thanks."

"I'm sure you will," Chen said. "We'll see that you do; Riley — that's the man — is the first mate. He can run you back to your yacht in a bit. Is Mr. Savage still with you? Perhaps Riley could meet him."

"No, he's left us," Dani said. "He needed to go back to the States to deal with this."

"Has he heard from the kidnappers?" Chen asked.

"Yes," Dani said.

"And what are their demands?" Wong asked.

"I'm not at all sure," Dani said. "He's a typical lawyer; he keeps his cards close to his vest."

"I see," Chen said. "May I offer you an early lunch, so that we can continue our chat?"

"That's kind of you, Ms. Chen. Perhaps another time. I have some things that require my attention, now that our current charter seems to have come to an unexpected end."

"Well, thank you for your time, Ms. Berger. I'll call you one of these days when the right project comes along. Wong, call Riley and have him take Ms. Berger back to *Vengeance*."

"Yes, Madame," Wong said, standing up, and reaching for a telephone.

Chen rose to her feet and extended a hand to Dani. "Thank you again, Ms. Berger. It was a pleasure meeting with you."

Dani stood up and shook her hand again, and Chen excused herself.

There was a tap on the door and Wong opened it, revealing a burly man in starched whites with his right arm in a sling. His left arm, heavy with bandages, hung at his side.

"Ms. Berger, meet Mr. Riley, our first mate. Riley, this is Ms. Berger; she's the captain of the yacht the girl was on."

"Good to meet you, Mr. Riley," Dani said.

"And you, ma'am."

"Ed Savage, the girl's father, wanted me to extend his thanks for your assistance to Cynthia."

"Weren't nothin'," the man said, with a gap-toothed grin. He ran his eyes up and down Dani's slim figure, nodding his head, making it obvious that he liked what he saw.

"Too bad you were injured so badly," she said. "Must cramp your style with the ladies."

He chuckled. "Few cuts on my arms, is all. Little bastard coulda done me some damage the ladies woulda noticed with that razor of his. Seen him do it before, but I'm okay."

"Well, it's too bad," Dani said, her ambiguous remark lost on the oaf. She had seen Wong's eyes narrow when Riley had referred to the little bastard and his razor.

"He's probably going to lose the use of that right arm," Wong said.

"That's a shame," Dani said.

"Well, hon, I got the tender ready. Let's go for a ride," Riley said, gesturing for her to precede him through the door into the corridor.

She stepped into the corridor and went through the door onto the bridge deck. Before Riley caught up with her, she stepped out onto the port wing of the bridge and let out a piercing whistle. By the time Riley and Wong reached her, *Lightning Bolt* was bobbing alongside the boarding platform.

"Kind of you to offer, gentlemen, but I have my own transportation. Watch out for the little bastards with razors, Riley. I hear they can be vicious. A guy like you might have something to lose. Outward appearance can be deceptive."

29

ED SETTLED INTO THE SOFT LEATHER SEAT OF HIS SL 600
roadster, relishing the feeling of being in a cocoon, secure from
the irritations that had plagued him all morning in his office. The
car was an outrageous expense, but one that he had allowed
himself when he had scored his first million-dollar fee. To him, it
represented not just achievement but also escape, and if he'd ever
needed an escape, he needed one today. He pressed the starter.

The blinding flash of light that enveloped the car faded in a
split-second, but the echoes of the blast persisted for a long time,
even though he could barely perceive them. He was sure his
eardrums must be ruptured as he staggered from the car and fell
to the concrete floor of the parking garage, disoriented. His vision
cleared before his hearing began to return, and he could see that
the car appeared undamaged.

He was on all fours when the security guard sprinted up. The
guard flailed about, wild-eyed, the oversized pistol in his hand
jerking around erratically. Seeing nothing amiss, he lowered the
pistol, holding it loosely by his right thigh. "Mr. Savage?" he
asked.

Ed watched him, not sure whether he heard the man call his

name, or whether he imagined it. The guard dropped to a knee and put his pistol on the floor, raising a hand to Ed's shoulder. "You okay, Mr. Savage?"

Ed thought for a second. Other than the ringing in his ears, he didn't feel anything amiss. "Yeah, I think so," he said.

"No need to shout, Mr. Savage," the guard said, drawing back, startled. "What happened?"

Ed shook his head. "No clue. Call the cops."

"They're on the way. That was a hell of an explosion. You know where it was?"

"Under my car," Ed said, still unable to judge how loudly he was speaking.

The guard dropped to his hands and knees and peered under the low-slung Mercedes. "Don't see nothin', Mr. Savage. You sure?"

Ed shook his head. "Uh-uh."

"That your phone?" the guard asked, as Ed felt a vibration in his pants pocket. He couldn't hear the ringing.

He sat back on his haunches and fumbled the phone out. "Yeah?" he barked, after he swiped the screen. He switched the phone to speaker mode as he raised it to his ear, hoping he'd be able to hear it. "Yeah?" he said, again.

There was a forced laugh from the speaker, and then he heard a rough, low-pitched voice. "That was a warning, Mr. Savage. Just to show you how it could happen if you file that motion to withdraw."

"But I ... " Ed's voice trailed off as he realized that the caller had disconnected.

"How was it?" Liz asked, pouring coffee into two mugs as Dani and Sharktooth settled in under the cockpit awning.

Sharktooth picked up a piece of the still-hot pastry that Liz had baked while he and Dani were gone. He took a bite, moaning in appreciation.

"No big surprises," Dani said. "She's still trying to figure out who I am. She asked several questions about J.-P., too." Dani took a sip of coffee.

"What did you tell her?" Liz asked.

"Nothing. She made sure I had the grand tour of the yacht; it was obvious that the captain had been told to make sure I knew they weren't hiding anything. *Lotus Blossom's* got lots of little nooks and crannies, but she's clean as a whistle."

"So they don' have the girl, then," Sharktooth said.

"Oh, I'm pretty sure they do," Dani replied. "Otherwise, why go to so much trouble to show me they didn't?"

"You shouldn't assume everybody's as devious as you, Dani," Liz said.

Dani smiled. "We should call Mario."

Liz passed her the satellite phone. "He really does seem to worry about you; it's nice that you remembered to call him."

Dani set the phone on the cockpit table and placed the call with it in speaker mode. "I want him to hear this; I'm hoping he can check a few things for us."

"Good morning, Dani."

"Morning, Mario. Sharktooth and Liz are with me."

After exchanging greetings with the others, Mario asked, "Learn anything from Chen?"

"Maybe," Dani said, "indirectly." She told him about her suspicion that Chen was holding Cynthia.

"Could be," he said.

"Anything else?"

"Yes. Wong was in the meeting. I got a good look at his injuries; he was sitting where the sunlight was on his face."

"And?" Mario asked.

"Superficial; somebody hit him to make him bleed, not to do any real damage. And the Chief Super says he's a brawler. I could buy that someone might land one sucker punch, but he wouldn't get hit in the face three times, with no other damage, unless he allowed it to happen for some reason."

"What are you thinking?" Liz asked, frowning. Her frown faded to a smile as she watched Sharktooth scoop the rest of the pastry onto his plate.

"I think he and the first mate messed each other up to lend credence to the story about the two guys in the speedboat taking Cynthia back."

"Really?" Liz asked.

"The first mate's a big, dumb bastard. He's been in his share of fights — knife scars on his upper arms and his face, knuckles all swollen and twisted." She told them about his comments about the "little bastard and his razor."

"Wow! He did everything but tell you it was Wong who cut him," Liz said.

"Yes. If you could have seen the body language the two of them displayed, you'd have no doubt."

"Why would he give all of this away, Dani?" Mario asked.

"He isn't the tightest knot in the rope, for one thing, and for another, he's pissed off at Wong, and it shows. He may lose the use of his right arm. That's probably more damage than he signed up for."

"He said he'd seen 'him' do it before," Liz said. "Do what before?"

"The strong implication was that the 'little bastard with the razor' had amputated someone's penis. This jerk wanted me to know he'd escaped that fate."

"Thought you fancied him, did he?" Liz asked, nudging Dani with her elbow.

"Hope springs eternal, I guess," Dani said.

"The mon who ran the drug squad here, he was cut like that," Sharktooth said. "Coroner say prob'ly wit' straight razor."

"We hadn't heard that," Dani said.

"Jus' hear this mornin', when I check on the plane."

"Did you get the tail number?" Mario asked, "I can — "

"No need, Mario," Sharktooth said. "Plane registered to Apex Investment Partners."

"Okay. Good work," Mario said. "And back to the coroner's discovery that Sharktooth mentioned. Don't forget Mike DiFiore was sexually mutilated as well."

"With a razor?" Dani asked.

"My source said they couldn't tell exactly what happened; the wound was cauterized — with a blow torch, probably. It kept him from bleeding to death, but it made a mess of the wound, and caused a lot of extra pain, I'd guess."

"Mario, do you know someone who can check out Apex Investment Partners for us?"

"Sure. You think there's something off about them?"

"I don't know. There's something off about Ed Savage. His reactions are inconsistent."

"Inconsistent in what way?"

"Liz noticed it; she got closer to him than I did." She turned to Liz. "Think you can explain it?"

"Well, it's just that at first, he was distraught about Cynthia's kidnapping, like you'd expect. But then, he would seem to not think about it. Not like he'd forgotten — more like he wasn't worried about her. It's hard to describe, but unless something happened to remind him that she was missing, he just wanted to try to seduce one of us."

"One of you?" Mario asked.

"First Dani, but she got too wrapped up in finding Cynthia to be bothered with him, so he shifted his attention to me."

"You said, 'unless something reminded him,' Liz," Mario prompted.

"Right. When he'd get a call from the kidnappers, or one of us would mention Cynthia, it was like a cue to play the worried parent role. Dani saw it before I did."

"I'll get my financial people to look at Apex right away, then," Mario said. "I'm hoping they'll have more on Tequesta Recycling by this afternoon. I'll call back as soon as I hear."

"That sounds good," Dani said.

"Sharktooth's expecting to hear more about *Lion of Judah* later today, too," Dani said.

"I thought it was in charter to Chen," Mario said.

"That was jus' the rumor on the waterfront," Sharktooth said. "Paperwork confusing, but no mention of Chen. I got some people lookin' into it in Haiti."

IT TOOK Cynthia a moment to realize that the roaring in her ears had stopped, replaced by a thumping, clattering sound like some demented giant was shaking an oil drum filled with bricks. She recognized that the noise must come from the anchor chain being released. It sounded much like the anchor chain on *Vengeance*, amplified by the vibrations it induced in the steel hull of the dirty little freighter. The ship was coasting to a stop, the engine at idle.

A muffled, rhythmic banging, accompanied by the raised voices of women screeching in anger or fear, resonated from across the corridor. A man yelled something in the language that she couldn't understand, and the women quieted down.

"Where de hell we at, you assholes? You damn betta lemme go o' I give you sump'n' you ain't never gon' get ovah. I know how to gi' you de virus, mon," a woman's voice bellowed from the cabin across the corridor.

"Shut up, stupid bitch; you gon' be sorry you evah born. We gotta take care a the rich little white bitch firs', then you gon' have some good time wit' us, yeah. Betta you rest now; you gon' be busy tonight. The boys all askin' fo' you an' yo' virus." He laughed.

Cynthia recognized the voice of the one man who spoke broken English.

The hand wheel in the middle of the watertight door squeaked and began to turn. She clutched the torn shift around herself and huddled in the corner of her berth, waiting.

In a few seconds, the door crashed open, swinging back against the bulkhead, and two grubby-looking men stood in the opening, leering at her. She saw that the English-speaker stood behind them. He barked something at them, shoving them into the cabin with her. They stumbled toward her, each grabbing one of her arms.

She thrashed, kicking out with her legs, catching one of them with a foot to his groin. The other one laughed and drew back his fist, punching her in the stomach. She retched and doubled over, fighting for breath, and felt an open hand explode against the side of her head.

Disoriented by the blow, she allowed them to drag her out of the cabin. She was too frightened to wonder what was going to happen to her; she focused on breathing and staying conscious. She could taste blood from where her teeth had cut the inside of her cheek when he hit her, and her vision seemed blurred as the two men pulled her through the corridor.

They came to another door, and she spread her arms as best she could, bracing her hands on either side of the door. One of the men hit her on the back of the head with something hard. She didn't lose consciousness, not completely, because she knew that one of them lifted her in his arms like a child and carried her for some distance. She felt him pass her to another pair of waiting arms, and she saw the dwarf as he stuck a hypodermic in her arm.

30

"GOOD AFTERNOON, EVERYBODY," MARIO'S VOICE CAME FROM THE speakerphone on the table in the main saloon aboard *Vengeance*. "I have some news on Tequesta."

"Well, don't keep us in suspense," Dani said.

"The actual ownership is well-hidden, but the man who runs it is Joe DiFiore. That means Jimmy Gregorio is certainly the ultimate owner. The DiFiores are his long-time underlings."

"That makes sense," Dani said. "They must have snatched Cynthia so they could put pressure on Ed Savage to change the outcome of the class action suit."

"But what about the ransom demand?" Liz asked. "That doesn't fit."

"No, it doesn't, Liz," Mario said. "Any ideas on that, Dani? Sharktooth?"

"Suppose Gregorio paid somebody to take her," Dani said, "and they saw an opportunity to freelance?"

"You mean, take Gregorio's money and pick up an extra ten mil on the side?" Mario asked.

"That's one explanation," Dani said.

"I can't see that happening. If Gregorio got wind of that, he'd make sausage of them."

"Okay, so assume Gregorio blessed the $10 million ransom demand. What would he get out of that?"

"It's small change in the context of the suit," Mario said. "I can't see any reason why he'd agree to that."

"Leave that for a moment, then," Dani said. "Several things point to Chen's being behind the actual kidnapping."

"What, for instance?" Mario asked.

"Wait," Sharktooth said. "Befo' you leave Tequesta, I got some word back from Haiti."

"Yes?" Mario said.

"Tell us, Sharktooth," Dani said.

"The mon you talkin' about, this DiFiore?"

"What about him?"

"He sign the papers for a long-term charter of *Lion of Judah*."

"That's good information, but you said it tied in to Tequesta," Liz said. "Is there a direct connection, or just an implied one?"

"He sign the paper as Managing Director of Tequesta Recycling, PLC," Sharktooth said.

"That's a direct connection," Liz said.

"Anything else, Sharktooth?" Dani asked, seeing the gleam in his eye.

"Mm-hmm," he rumbled. "Charter specified that the ship is for the exclusive use of Fragrant Harbour Spices, Ltd."

"Fragrant Harbour," Dani mused. "That's what Hong Kong means in English. Think that's Chen's company?"

"Mm-hmm," Sharktooth said. "Authorized agent of Fragrant Harbour Spices, Ltd. is Li Wong. He mus' approve all shipping documents to authorize use of *Lion of Judah*."

"That gives us a solid enough connection between Chen and Gregorio," Mario said. "Sounds like there was a disagreement between Chen and Mike DiFiore, though. What now?"

"I want to board *Lion of Judah*," Dani said. "I've got a feeling that's where Cynthia's being held."

"Dani," Mario said, "I need to let you know that the Feds have all the information that I just gave you. They'll be moving on Gregorio as we speak."

"How did they find out?"

"I asked the questions; a lot of the people I asked are involved in various parts of the government's effort to break up the drug trade. You'd better assume they'll put the pieces together as quickly as we did."

"Thanks for the heads-up, Mario. We'll just have to move faster than they do. They may not be as worried about protecting Cynthia as we are."

"That's why I told you."

"Thanks again. Sharktooth, can your people find the *Lion of Judah*?"

"They already lookin'. Soon come, we know."

"SHARKTOOTH AND I WILL BOARD HER," Dani said. "You stand off in *Lightning Bolt* and be ready to back us up if anything goes wrong."

Liz nodded. She was already at the controls of the go-fast boat. "Check the UHF radios," she said, referring to the tiny transceivers that Sharktooth had provided. He kept a small armory hidden away on *Lightning Bolt*.

"Done," Dani said, passing one of the earpiece-sized units to Liz. They were equipped with throat microphones which picked up the slightest vibration of the vocal cords, allowing near-silent communication. "They're all set for voice control. Take us in easy."

They were drifting about 100 meters away from their target; *Lightning Bolt's* engines were shut down. *Lion of Judah* was anchored off the old whaling station on the tiny island of Petit Nevis, about a mile south of Bequia.

Liz engaged the electric thrusters and moved them into position against the side of the rusty ship without a sound. Dani, cat-like, leapt onto the lowest rung of the boarding ladder that was affixed to the ship. Sharktooth grasped the ladder and held them in position until Dani had cleared the ship's rail. With a nod to Liz, he swung himself up and she backed *Lightning Bolt* away into the darkness.

Dani scrambled up the exterior steps to the bridge deck, leaving Sharktooth to clear the hold and the main deck. She worked her way down as he worked his way up; they met in a corridor that ran across the ship's main deck. They flashed each other the all clear sign. The only sign of life aboard was raucous laughter punctuated by women's screams. The noise emanated from what appeared to be a dining area that opened off the corridor near where they stood.

Dani held up three fingers and Sharktooth nodded. She folded her fingers down, one at a time. When she dropped the third one, she dove through the opening and rolled to the right, coming to her feet with a silenced pistol held down beside her thigh. The room went silent as the four men who were abusing three women noticed her.

One man grinned and took a step toward her. She noticed the others watching him, waiting to follow his lead.

"Hey, bitch! You got good timing. We jus' needed one more woman. Now you here, but you got too many clothes on. He grinned and took a step toward her, collapsing with a scream as her pistol coughed.

"Shut up," she yelled, over his wails, "or I'll pop the other knee."

The three remaining men disengaged themselves from the naked women, spreading out and moving toward Dani as if they had done this sort of thing before.

She stuck the pistol in her belt and launched herself at the closest one as Sharktooth grabbed the other two from behind. Holding each of them with a big paw around the neck, he smashed their heads together. He dropped their limp forms to the deck and stepped back to watch as Dani ducked below her opponent's punch and drove an elbow into his groin.

As the man bent over, she lunged up from her crouch, driving her head into his chin. When he collapsed, unconscious, she drew the pistol again and turned to the man clutching the ruins of his knee and moaning.

"Stand up," she said, nudging him with her foot. "Party's about to get good."

"What do you — " he screamed as she put her foot on his bloody knee.

"I want you on your feet," she said. "Sharktooth, give him a hand."

The big man grabbed a fistful of greasy hair with his left hand and hoisted the wounded man off the deck, his feet dangling as his hands flew to grasp Sharktooth's wrist in an effort to ease the pain in his scalp.

"That's better," Dani said. "Cut his pants off."

The man's eyes went wide as a 12-inch filet knife materialized in Sharktooth's right hand.

"I'll tell you anyt'ing you want to know," the man said, twisting like a fish suspended on a line.

"Not just yet, but hold that thought," Dani said. "Sharktooth?"

With two deft movements of his right hand, Sharktooth rendered the man naked from the waist down.

Dani studied him for a moment, laughing and shaking her head. "You let that little thing get you into this mess?"

As he wriggled in Sharktooth's grasp, she said, "Maybe you'd be better off without it; it hardly seems worth the trouble it's already caused you."

"No, please," the man whined.

"What do you think, ladies?" she asked, addressing the women huddled in the corner. When they didn't answer, Dani realized they were in shock, or drugged. "I'll take their silence as agreement," Dani said to the man. "Go ahead, Sharktooth."

"Wait!" the man wailed. "I'll tell you where the girl is."

Dani put a hand on Sharktooth's wrist. "Girl? What girl?"

"Young white girl, the one from your yacht."

Dani laughed. "My yacht? What do you know about it?"

"I know you run that yacht wit' the other lady. I don' hurt the girl."

"You think this is about her?"

"I kept her safe," he said.

"She scratch her name in the paint in a cabin by the engine room," Sharktooth said. "Wit' the dates."

"You had her on this boat," Dani said.

"Yes, ma'am. We keep, until he come for her."

"Who came for her?"

"The Dragon Lady's midget. He the one do this. He bring her to us to keep safe."

"Who's the Dragon Lady?"

"Madame Chen the Dragon Lady. Li Wong her dwarf. We don' hurt the girl. Tha's de trut', I swear it. Tha's all I know."

"I cut him anyway." Sharktooth said, pulling his hand free from Dani's grasp. "He don't tell us nothin' we don' know."

"I'll tell you where she is," the man squeaked, his eyes locked on the gleaming knife that hovered below his waist.

"Okay," Dani said. "But if you're lying, we'll be back."

"No lie. The midget, he take her to Dragon Lady boat in Bequia, jus' now."

"How long ago?"

"Jus' 'bout sunset, he come, with the man got he arm cut."

"Liz?" Dani said.

The man hanging from Sharktooth's fist looked confused.

"Are they here yet?"

Sharktooth, listening to Liz's reply on their earpiece radios, looked at Dani. She nodded, and he reversed the filet knife in his fist. He brought it up and used the butt of the grip to knock his victim senseless. He dropped the man in a heap.

"We go now?"

"Yes. The people Mario sent will handle it from here," Dani said.

"Who are these people," Liz asked in a soft voice, watching the black-clad figures scaling the side of *Lion of Judah* as Dani and Sharktooth settled into the seats next to her.

Dani shook her head. After they were a hundred meters away from *Lion of Judah*, she said, "I'm not sure. Mario was sharing information with some covert federal agency — DEA, DHS — who knows?"

"What are they going to do with the ship and the crew?" Liz asked.

"The deal was, they didn't care if we got Cynthia out as long as we left this bunch alive for them," Dani said. "They're going to 'find' *Lion of Judah* in international waters, acting on an anonymous tip from a reliable source. They'll claim they're smuggling drugs and people into the U.S. and take them back to the States. They plan to connect them to some mobster named Gregorio."

As Liz steered *Lightning Bolt* toward West Cay at the western tip of Bequia, they saw *Lion of Judah* getting underway, heading west. Dani said, "My bet is they'll leave her chugging away to the west and disappear into thin air just before a Coast Guard boarding party shows up."

"What if there are no drugs aboard?" Liz asked. "Or if those women are willing participants?"

Dani rolled her eyes. "I'm sure they have a contingency plan for that; they're the government. They manufacture evidence all the time."

As they rounded West Cay and came abreast of Ship's Stern Point, they saw the lights of a large motor yacht moving out of Admiralty Bay on a westerly heading. Dani picked up a pair of night vision binoculars and announced, "Perfect. That's *Lotus Blossom*. Let's just follow them. If we can let them get out of sight of land before we board, so much the better."

31

LIZ MATCHED THEIR SPEED TO THAT OF *LOTUS BLOSSOM*, TRAILING
the motor yacht at a distance of a couple of miles. They were able
to make out the motor yacht's stern light, flickering as the waves
sometimes blocked their view. *Lightning Bolt* was running dark,
invisible to their quarry.

"Think they'll spot us on radar?" Dani asked.

"Not at this distance. Too much scatter from the waves,"
Sharktooth said. "How we board them?"

"They're running at about eight knots," Liz said. "You'll have to
jump; it'll be a trick in this sea, unless we're running in their
wake."

"There's a swim platform across the stern," Dani said. "If you
take us in close, I'll jump from the bow. If I take a messenger line,
we could rig a towing bridle. Think they'd notice the drag,
Sharktooth?"

"Prob'ly not. Water's pretty rough, an' they going slow. *Lightning Bolt* not ver' heavy, slip through the water easy. Only problem
be if they got a lookout aft."

"We'll chance it," Dani said. "You pay out the bridle and I'll
make it fast. Liz, once I jump, match their speed and stay back

maybe half a boat-length until Sharktooth's rigged the towline, then ease back gradually until the bridle takes the load."

"Got it. You want me to stay here, then?"

"You're our reserve; if we hit a snag, we'll call you on the UHF headset radio. Think you can manage to close the gap and get aboard without getting the towline caught in our props?"

"Yes. Rig a light line from where the bridle attaches to the towline back to the console here; I can retrieve the bridle and towline as I close in. If I have to join you, I'll probably tie *Lightning Bolt* up short — a few feet from the platform."

"Okay. There's no access to their swim platform except by stairs from the aft deck, so once you join me on the platform, Sharktooth, I'll leave you and Liz to rig the bridle while I secure the aft deck."

"Okay," Sharktooth said. "Then what?"

"Same drill as before. Meet me on the aft deck. I'll go starboard; you go port. There's a transverse corridor amidships with watertight doors onto the side decks. We'll open the doors if they're closed and meet in the corridor; let's say 45 seconds to get to the doors, 30 seconds to open them."

"Okay."

"There's another watertight door on the aft bulkhead of the corridor that will take you below. I'll clear the superstructure up to Chen's stateroom and meet you there once you clear the spaces below deck. Crew's three men, counting the captain, and a stewardess who looks like a pit-bull. We need to take them all down, then we can deal with Chen and Wong."

"What about the bridge?"

"There's bridge access from her stateroom. We'll leave the person on the bridge for last, once everybody else is out of action."

CYNTHIA CAME AWAKE WITH A JERK; she peered around, wild-eyed. She knew this place; she was in Madame Chen's stateroom on *Lotus Blossom*. Her vision blurred for a moment; she blinked and tried to rub her eyes, but she couldn't move her arms. Looking down, she saw that her wrists were secured to the arms of a chair with duct tape. She tried to move her legs, but they were immobilized as well. She felt nauseated and tried to lean forward to throw up, but there was a restraint around her chest.

She couldn't help it; she heaved, vomit running over her chin and down her chest. She heard a soft chuckle from behind her. Someone was back there, watching her. She thought at first that she was naked; but she tipped her head far enough to see that she still wore the bikini.

"She's awake," a man's voice said, from behind her.

She thought it was Wong; but she wasn't sure until he stepped in front of her. His face was at the same level as hers as he grinned at her. He extended a hand toward her face; she flinched as he rested his fingertips on her forehead. He raised her right eyelid with his thumb and shined a penlight in her eye, moving it up and down and from side to side. He turned off the light and dropped his hand, backing away.

"She's ready, I think," Wong said. "She's going to be groggy from the shot, but we can probably go ahead."

"Is she able to feel pain?" a woman asked.

"Should be," Wong said.

"Show me," the woman said, "but no marks, remember."

Wong brandished a two-inch long sewing needle. Cynthia watched, feeling doped-up, as he lifted her right thumb and gripped it in his left hand. Without warning or haste, he pushed the needle under her thumbnail. She heard herself scream and realized that she was arching her back, helpless as he manipulated the needle, extracting repeated shrieks from her until he pulled the needle out and released her hand.

Patting her on the cheek as she whimpered, he asked "What do you think?"

"She'll do," the woman said. "Go ahead and start the camera; we can edit what we don't need."

Cynthia could hear her moving closer. As Wong stepped out of her field of view, he was replaced by an Oriental woman in a black leotard.

"Hello, Cynthia. I'm Marissa Chen; we haven't met yet — at least not while you were conscious." She paused for a moment. When Cynthia didn't speak, Chen picked up the girl's throbbing thumb and studied it briefly before she squeezed the tip between her own thumb and forefinger.

After Cynthia's scream subsided to a sob, Chen said, "You're an ill-mannered young woman. You will acknowledge my introduction."

"Y-yes, ma'am. I'm sorry."

Chen nodded. "What do you say when you meet someone, Cynthia?"

"P-pleased to m-meet you, ma'am."

"I'm sure you are. We're going to get much better acquainted over the next few minutes. I need your assistance in persuading your father to co-operate with me. Do you understand?"

"Yes, ma'am."

"Good. We're going to make a video, you and Wong and I. You will be the star. We will be doing things that cause you a great deal of pain; feel free to scream as you wish, but do not under any circumstances refer to us by name. If you do that, we'll be forced to erase the video and start over from the beginning. Do you understand?"

"Yes, but ... "

"But what?"

"Why must you hurt me?"

Chen smiled at her for a moment. "Two reasons. The first is that we enjoy it, Wong and I. The second is so that your father will know we are not making idle threats. If he had followed instructions this might not have been necessary, though we might have done it anyway. Oh, and I'm sure you're a vain young woman; you're certainly beautiful." Chen paused, an expectant look on her face.

"Th-thank you, ma'am."

"You're welcome. I don't want you to worry that we might do something to spoil your looks. Wong is an expert at causing intolerable pain without leaving any visible marks. You are quite valuable to us, and we'll get a good price for you once we're finished with your father, so rest assured that you will be as lovely after this as you are now."

"Th-th-thank you, ma'am."

"Oh, you're most welcome, my dear. Wong?"

"Yes, Madame?"

"Are you ready?"

"Yes, Madame."

"Start the sound recording, then, and let's begin."

DANI CROUCHED IN THE DIM, walnut paneled corridor outside Chen's stateroom. Sharktooth was taking much longer than she expected, and she had been unable to raise him on the UHF radio. She tried again, speaking without opening her mouth. The microphone that was fastened against her larynx picked up the vibrations as if she had spoken aloud. There was no answer.

She had seen no sign of the crew members as she had searched the vessel from the main deck up to the level of this corridor. At least one person must be standing watch on the bridge; it was possible that the other three were there as well, but she didn't want to chance that.

The sound of a ringing telephone came from within Chen's suite; it stopped abruptly, as if someone had answered it. Dani pressed an ear to the door, but the voices were too muffled for her to understand. She was considering backtracking to look for Sharktooth when she heard a scream from within Chen's stateroom.

Silenced pistol at the ready, she turned the latch on the door and burst into the stateroom. She saw Chen standing next to Cynthia, who was seated. Chen smiled at Dani as Cynthia moaned. Dani leveled her pistol at Chen, but before she could fire, she felt her arm twisted behind her with a force that she thought would wrench her shoulder from its socket. She caught a glimpse of the dwarf as he snatched the pistol from her numb fingers with his left hand. Without releasing the pressure on her right arm, he pressed the pistol to the side of her head.

"Good evening, Ms. Berger," Chen said, still smiling. "I thought we might have the pleasure of your company. Riley just called to tell me that your Rasta friend was below decks. Unfortunately, he can't join us; he's sleeping off the effects of a tranquilizer dart. That seemed the most humane way to deal with such a brute."

Dani glared at Chen for a moment and then shifted her gaze to Cynthia. "Hang in there, Cynthia. We'll have you free in no time," she said.

Chen laughed. "The girl's not stupid, Ms. Berger. She knows an empty promise when she hears one."

"I heard her scream; you pieces of shit are going to pay for that."

Chen laughed again. "Big talk, Ms. Berger. You have no way to make good on a threat like that. It's best if you behave. Just ask our young friend, here."

"Are you such a sorry excuse for a woman that the best you can do is this midget?" Dani asked. "Too old to handle a real man, I guess. This little rat turd has to use a gun to keep me from kicking his ass."

"May I prove her wrong, Madame?" Wong asked, speaking for the first time.

"As you wish, Wong. We can warm up with Ms. Berger and let little Cynthia watch, so she'll have a better idea of what to expect."

Dani felt the pressure of the gun's muzzle ease. As she readied herself to strike, Chen said, "Wong?"

He pressed the muzzle firmly against her head again, still twisting her right arm painfully.

"Yes, Madame?"

"You may cut her, if you wish, but only for pain. She's salable merchandise; don't spoil her looks. After we've had our fun with her, we'll call Abdullah. Go ahead; Cynthia and I are waiting for the show."

"Of course, Madame. Thank you."

In a blur of motion, Wong tossed the pistol across the room and released Dani's arm. Before she could move, he flung her into the adjacent bulkhead with enough force to knock the wind from her lungs.

Dazed, Dani spun and shoved off the bulkhead, launching herself at the man. Wong, a little over half her height when he stood erect, bent at the waist and took her charge by driving a shoulder into her belly. His arms swept her feet out behind her and he snapped himself to an erect position, his arms guiding Dani's flight. She sailed over his head, landing on her shoulder in the middle of the floor, winded.

Before she could recover, Wong was on her, his feet flying as he kicked at her head and chest. Stunned, Dani rolled onto her side and curled into a fetal position, protecting herself as best she could. After several brutal kicks to her lower back, he danced around, kicking her shins and hips on his way to work on her forearms.

As he drew back his right leg for a last kick at her bottom, her legs shot out. Her left leg extended behind his supporting leg and her right leg swung out in front of his. With a swift, scissor-like motion, her right ankle struck his left knee as her left leg trapped his foot. His knee gave way, bending the wrong way with a loud snap. He grunted and fell backward.

Dani rolled, his lower leg still trapped between hers. He screamed in pain as she bent his broken knee even farther. As she released her scissor hold and continued to roll toward him, she saw the straight razor appear in his right hand. Ignoring the threat of being cut, she cupped his chin in her right hand and forced her folded right knee between his shoulder and the deck. She wrapped her left forearm around his head and gave a mighty twist as he flailed at her with the razor.

There was a pop as her twisting motion met momentary resistance, and then she felt his neck give way and his arms fell, limp. She put all of her strength into a final heave, twisting his head almost to the point where he faced the floor. Satisfied that he was finished, she swept up the razor with her right hand and went for Chen.

32

LIZ, SITTING ON THE BERTH IN THE CABIN UNDER *LIGHTNING BOLT'S* foredeck, looked at her watch for the third time in the last minute. Dani and Sharktooth had been aboard *Lotus Blossom* for almost ten minutes. She hadn't been able to reach either of them on the radio after she heard Dani call Sharktooth two minutes ago.

She knew something had gone wrong; they should have taken the bridge by this time, but *Lotus Blossom* maintained her course and speed. If Dani and Sharktooth had been discovered, the crew would have seen *Lightning Bolt* by now. She moved to the companionway and used a small hand mirror to keep her head out of sight as she looked across the foredeck toward *Lotus Blossom*.

There were three people, standing shoulder to shoulder at *Lotus Blossom's* stern rail, watching *Lightning Bolt* bobbing in their wake. That left one on the bridge, plus Chen and Wong. Liz picked up the AK-47 with the suppressor that she had loaded earlier and flipped the selector to full auto. She was already wearing a Kevlar vest with inserts, two extra magazines in the pouches on the front.

She crawled through the companionway and rose to a crouch, steadying her left forearm on the edge of the hatch. One of the three people raised an arm, pointing in her direction, and she squeezed the trigger, raking them with one burst across their chests and a second at the height of their knees. She didn't think the suppressed weapon would have been heard aboard *Lotus Blossom*, but she watched for a few seconds to be sure no one else was moving on deck.

Seeing no movement, she put in a fresh magazine and moved to the helm. She started one engine and eased the throttle forward, taking in the towline as she closed the gap between the two boats. When it appeared that the bow of *Lightning Bolt* was about to hit the stern platform of the motor yacht, she backed off the throttle enough to hold her position. She scrambled onto the foredeck and cleated the towline, checking to be sure she could make the jump without any trouble.

She retrieved her weapon from the steering console and shut down the engine. Moments later, she was on *Lotus Blossom's* aft deck, surveying the damage that she had wrought. Satisfied, she moved up the starboard side deck to the watertight door and stepped into the corridor Dani had described. She saw the door that led below; it was fastened open.

She heard loud, crashing sounds from below decks. Moving to where she could peer through the door, she could see the shiny top of Sharktooth's head as he methodically jerked against the heavy chain that held his wrists to the rail of the ladder.

Leaning over the doorsill, she said, "Hey, sailor. You want to have a little fun?"

Sharktooth grinned up at her. "You got anything to eat?"

"Later. Where's Dani?"

"Don' know, but all three crew are — "

"Taken care of," Liz said. "Pull that chain out straight so I can hit the lock."

Seconds later, they were standing outside Chen's stateroom.

Sharktooth looked from the door to Liz. She nodded, and he raised his leg and kicked the door so hard that it was torn from its hinges. Liz followed the flying splinters into the stateroom as he turned and opened the door onto the bridge.

"So you think you're ready for a real match, Ms. Berger?" Chen said, assuming a graceful pose, her arms raised for balance as she stood on her left leg, the right one folded back, ready to strike. "He was, as you said, only a midget."

Chen shifted her position only slightly, barely seeming to move. Her right foot struck Dani in the solar plexus, doubling her over and knocking her off her feet. She rolled to the wall, put her back to it, and slid up to a standing position as Chen pivoted, delivering a roundhouse kick with the fluid movement of a dancer. Her foot struck Dani's shoulder, knocking her sideways toward the corner.

Dani dropped to a crouch, her back in the corner, as Chen pranced into position to strike again. "You dancing or fighting, old woman?" she said, grinning. "Think you can handle me in a clench?"

"Indeed," said Chen delivering a kick to the side of Dani's head and following it immediately with a clawed right hand which landed on Dani's left shoulder. Chen drove a knee into Dani's chest as her hand found the nerve center where Dani's neck met her shoulder. Chen dug her thumb into the bundle of muscles and nerves, paralyzing Dani's left arm.

Dani scrunched her left shoulder up, trapping Chen's hand, and snapped her head to her left, sinking her teeth into the flesh of Chen's inner forearm. Dani clamped her jaws shut, feeling her teeth grinding into the tendons, forcing them against the bone. She visualized her teeth cutting through the tendons and increased the pressure. Chen screamed and dug at Dani's face with her left hand, trying to get her left thumb into Dani's eye socket.

Dani flicked the straight razor open and took a firm grip on it, driving the squared tip into the inside of Chen's right thigh at the groin. Putting her weight behind it, she forced the razor down along the inside of the femur until she reached the knee. The blood pouring from the woman's severed femoral artery caused Dani to lose her grip on the razor as it bit into the cartilage.

She hooked her right hand behind Chen's right knee and thrust up, straightening her own legs and forcing her opponent over on her back. She dragged herself up onto Chen's chest and drove the folded knuckles of her right hand into the other woman's larynx.

Hearing a crash behind her, she glanced over her shoulder to see Liz charge into the stateroom, her AK-47 at the ready. Dani took a quick look at Chen to make sure she was out, and then said, "Nice entrance, Liz. What kept you?"

"I didn't want to spoil your fun," Liz said.

Dani said, "Sharktooth's — "

"Securing the bridge," Liz interrupted.

"The rest of the crew — "

"They lined up along the stern rail for me like tin ducks in a shooting gallery. They're finished." Liz set her weapon down and began cutting the tape that held Cynthia to the chair.

They felt the vessel slowing down gradually, and a minute later, Sharktooth stepped in from the bridge. "You ready to go? I'm hungry, Liz. You said you'd feed me later. It's later."

"We need to deal with the mess," Dani said, testing her battered muscles and joints as she slowly got to her feet.

"Did that already," Sharktooth said. "Jus' finish when that ugly woman look like a pit bull shoot me wit' the dart gun."

"You sure?" Dani said.

"Mm-hmm. Shame to see a nice boat like this 'splode 'cause of gas in the bilge. People should take more care. Gas ver' dangerous." He held up something that resembled a garage door opener. "Let's go. Liz got some cookin' to do."

He watched Cynthia struggle to keep her balance as she pushed herself to her feet. "You mus' be Cynthia."

"Yes," she said, wobbling.

"Call me Sharktooth." He lifted her in his arms like she was an infant. "Prob'ly give you the same stuff they shoot me wit'. It wear off in a few minutes." He carried her to the swim platform as Liz helped Dani negotiate the stairs, and they were soon settled in the cockpit of *Lightning Bolt*.

Liz dropped the towing bridle as Sharktooth cranked the engines. He maintained a modest speed until they were half a mile from *Lotus Blossom*. Then he throttled back, turning the boat around so that they could see the motor yacht in the dim light of the false dawn. He pressed the detonator, and the big boat disappeared in a ball of fire.

EPILOGUE

Two days later ...

"I'm going to live with my Aunt Ellen, at least until this blows over, and we see what happens to my dad," Cynthia said. She sat across the cockpit table from Dani and Liz as *Vengeance* rocked in the gentle waves that rolled through the anchorage in Bequia's Admiralty Bay.

"How do you feel about that?" Liz asked, pouring herbal tea into the girl's cup.

"I'm excited about it. She was my favorite aunt when I was little. I haven't seen much of her since my mom died."

"She's your mother's sister, then?" Dani asked, taking a sip of the fragrant tea.

"Right. She and my dad aren't close."

"But he's okay with your staying with her?"

"Oh, sure. They don't hate one another or anything; it's not like that. She just kind of started avoiding him while mom was sick."

"I can see where a protracted illness like cancer might cause a rift in a family," Liz said.

Cynthia smiled. "Dani's right, Liz. You do always try to put things in the best possible way."

"You don't think it was your mother's illness that came between them?" Dani asked.

"No. I was just a kid, too oblivious to see it back then, but thinking about it now, I'm sure he was trying to get Ellen in the sack. She's fashion-model pretty — just the type he's always chasing. For all I know, they had a — "

"Cynthia!" Liz said.

"Oh, come off it, Liz. I appreciate what you're trying to do, but I know my dad. He can't leave women alone. That's just the way he is. Some guys never grow up. I'm not sure how he got himself into this mess, caught between two mobsters, but I'd be surprised if there's not a gorgeous woman involved."

"There was," Dani said. "Marissa Chen."

"You don't think he was ... "

"No. As far as I know, they never met, but she was definitely involved, and she was gorgeous," Dani said.

"I didn't really get a good look at her the other night; I was too scared of Wong and his razor. I thought we were both goners. You moved so fast I couldn't even see what you did."

"Fear does that," Dani said. "I was so scared I don't even remember what I did to him. I just didn't want to get cut; I'm not scared of knives, but something about a straight razor makes my skin crawl."

"That didn't stop you from using it on Chen," Liz said.

"When it comes to choosing between quick and dead, I'll always choose quick. She was kicking my ass."

"Have you heard anything new from your godfather?" Cynthia asked. "About what exactly was going on. I can't make any sense out of any of it."

"I'm not sure anybody would have figured it out except for the guy who ran Apex Investment Partners."

"They were the ones funding the suit?" Cynthia asked.

"Yes, sort of. The suit had a real basis; your dad was on the up-and-up when he filed it, by the way. Anyhow, Bernie Albertson, the lawyer that was the front man for them, is co-operating with the Federal prosecutor. Once your dad confessed to his part, Albertson was kind of exposed. Your dad gave up Albertson, and Albertson told them that Marissa Chen engineered the whole scheme. She was the one who funded Apex. Her plan was to force a gangster named Gregorio to settle the suit by selling Tequesta to Apex. He owned it; it was a front for money laundering and running drugs. She was aiming to end up with Tequesta Recycling; she would have probably done away with Gregorio at some point."

"Why would she want Tequesta Recycling?" Liz asked.

"Tequesta was moving drugs all over the southeastern U.S. under the cover of hauling trash to their landfill sites. Chen was the source of the drugs, and she wasn't happy with the cut that the mob was taking, so she decided to take it all for herself," Dani said. "She figured to force the settlement, and Apex would have ended up effectively owning what was left of Tequesta after they paid damages to the people in the suit. That would have been mostly trucks and barges and employees, plus maybe some legitimate contracts and the landfill sites."

"How did my kidnapping figure in?" Cynthia asked.

"According to Albertson, Gregorio thought Chen was just a supplier of drugs. Albertson enabled Chen to be invisible; Gregorio had no clue as to the scope of her enterprise. She got Albertson to suggest to your dad that he bring you on a charter down here in Bequia, and she planned to kidnap you. Once she had you, she asked Gregorio to track down some background on your dad, on the pretense that she was trying to figure out how much ransom you were worth. She was betting that once

Gregorio discovered who you were, he would want in on the kidnapping so that he could use you for leverage to get your dad to back off on the lawsuit against Tequesta."

"You mean, my buying the grass didn't cause this?" Cynthia asked.

"According to Albertson, they were already planning to use the crooked cop who ran the drug squad to kidnap you before you even got here. Your buy played into their hands, but it didn't make any difference."

"What about the $10-million ransom demand?" Liz asked.

"Part of Chen's smokescreen, according to Albertson. She did that to make Gregorio think she was just a kidnapper. When he wanted in, she even haggled with him about how much more he'd have to pay, over and above the $10 million, if he wanted to use you to manipulate your father."

"What a convoluted mess," Cynthia said. She set her cup down on the table and sat up straight. "You guys saved me from who-knows-what-kind of horrible things. I'll never be able to thank you enough."

"We're just glad you didn't get hurt any worse than you did," Dani said.

Cynthia held Dani's eye for a moment. "Well, if it hadn't been for you, I'm sure I would have. But I need to ask you something."

"Sure," Dani said. "Ask."

"When do you think my dad knew they were going to kidnap me?"

Dani and Liz traded looks. Dani dropped her eyes and Liz spoke.

"The way you asked that makes it sound like you think he was in on your kidnapping," Liz said.

Cynthia smiled. "You sound like a lawyer, Liz, evading my question that way. I don't mean to offend you, but I've been around lawyers all my life. I don't trust any of them. I know you're just trying to spare my feelings, and I appreciate that. But I know my dad ... "

"You're asking us to speculate about your dad's motives, Cynthia," Dani said. "You just pointed out that you know him far better than either of us could. I'm not sure we're equipped to help you through the doubt that's behind your question. What could we say that would make you feel better about your relationship with your father?"

Cynthia thought about that for a moment, and said, "Thanks, Dani." She twisted on the cockpit seat and wrapped her arms around Dani's neck, tears rolling down her cheeks. "Thank you."

"Thanks?" Dani asked. "For what?" She patted the girl on the back.

"For treating me like an adult. You're right. I have to work that out for myself. I'm going to miss you guys."

"We're not going anywhere. Maybe you and your Aunt Ellen can come down for an all-girl charter," Liz said.

"And anyway," Dani said, "you've got four more days. Where do you want to go? *Vengeance* is yours."

THE END

MAILING LIST

Thank you reading *Bluewater Ganja*.

Join my mailing list at http://eepurl.com/bKujyv for notice of new releases and special sales or giveaways. I'll email a link to you for a free download of my short story, **The Lost Tourist Franchise**, when you sign up. I promise not to use the list for anything else; I dislike spam as much as you do.

A NOTE TO THE READER

Thank you again for reading *Bluewater Ganja*, the ninth book in the **Bluewater Thriller** series. I hope you enjoyed it. If so, please leave a brief review on Amazon.

Reviews are of great benefit to independent authors like me; they help me more than you can imagine. They are a primary means to help new readers find my work. A few words from you can help others find the pleasure that I hope you found in this book, as well as keeping my spirits up as I work on the next one.

Bluewater Clickbait is the latest novel in the series, and was published in December 2020.

I also write two other sailing-thrillers series set in the Caribbean. If you enjoyed this book, you'll like the Connie Barrera Thrillers and the J.R. Finn Sailing Mystery series.

The **Connie Barrera Thrillers** are a spin-off from the **Bluewater Thrillers.** Before Connie went to sea, she was a first-rate con artist. Paul Russo signed on as her first mate and chef, but he ended up as her husband. Connie and Paul run a charter sailing yacht named *Diamantista*. They're often drawn into problems unrelated to sailing, usually those brought aboard by their customers.

The **Bluewater Thrillers** and the **Connie Barrera Thrillers** share many of the same characters. Phillip Davis and his wife Sandrine, Sharktooth, and Marie LaCroix often appear in both series, as do Connie, Paul, Dani, and Liz. Here's a link to the web page that lists those novels in order of publication: http://www.clrdougherty.com/p/bluewater-thrillers-and-connie-barrera.html.

My newest series, the **J.R. Finn Sailing Mystery** series, introduces a government assassin disguised as a boat-bum lazing about the Caribbean Islands. This series is also available in audiobook format.

If you'd like to know when my next book is released, visit my author's page on Amazon at www.amazon.com/author/clrdougherty and click the "Follow" link or sign up for my mailing list at http://eepurl.com/bKujyv for information on sales and special promotions.

I welcome email correspondence about books, boats and sailing. My address is clrd@clrdougherty.com. I enjoy hearing from people who read my books; I always answer email from readers. Thanks again for your support.

ABOUT THE AUTHOR

Welcome Aboard!

Charles Dougherty is a lifelong sailor; he's lived what he writes. He and his wife have spent over 30 years sailing together.

For 15 years, they lived aboard their boat full-time, cruising the East Coast and the Caribbean islands. They spent most of that time exploring the Eastern Caribbean.

Dougherty is well acquainted with the islands and their people. The characters and locations in his novels reflect his experience.

A storyteller before all else, Dougherty lets his characters speak for themselves. Pick up one of his thrillers and listen to the sound of adventure as you smell the salt air. Enjoy the views of distant horizons and meet some people you won't forget.

Dougherty's sailing fiction books include the **Bluewater Thrillers**, the **Connie Barrera Thrillers**, and the **J.R. Finn Sailing Mysteries**.

Dougherty's first novel was *Deception in Savannah*. While it's not about sailing, one of the main characters is Connie Barrera. He had so much fun with Connie that he built a sailing series around her.

Before writing Connie's series, he wrote the first three Bluewater Thrillers, about two young women running a charter yacht in the islands. In the fourth book, Connie shows up as their charter guest.

She stayed for the fifth Bluewater book. Then Connie demanded her own series.

The J.R. Finn books are his newest sailing series. The first Finn book, though it begins in Puerto Rico, starts with a real-life encounter that Dougherty had in St. Lucia. For more information about that, visit his website.

Dougherty's other fiction works are the *Redemption of Becky Jones*, a psycho-thriller, and *The Lost Tourist Franchise*, a short story about another of the characters from Deception in Savannah.

Dougherty has also written two non-fiction books. *Life's a Ditch* is the story of how he and his wife moved aboard their sailboat, Play Actor, and their adventures along the east coast of the U.S. *Dungda de Islan'* relates their experiences while cruising the Caribbean.

Charles Dougherty welcomes email correspondence with readers.

www.clrdougherty.com
clrd@clrdougherty.com

OTHER BOOKS BY C.L.R. DOUGHERTY

Bluewater Thrillers

Bluewater Killer

Bluewater Vengeance

Bluewater Voodoo

Bluewater Ice

Bluewater Betrayal

Bluewater Stalker

Bluewater Bullion

Bluewater Rendezvous

Bluewater Ganja

Bluewater Jailbird

Bluewater Drone

Bluewater Revolution

Bluewater Enigma

Bluewater Quest

Bluewater Target

Bluewater Blackmail

Bluewater Clickbait

Bluewater Thrillers Boxed Set: Books 1-3

Connie Barrera Thrillers

From Deception to Betrayal - An Introduction to Connie Barrera

Love for Sail - A Connie Barrera Thriller

Sailor's Delight - A Connie Barrera Thriller

A Blast to Sail - A Connie Barrera Thriller

Storm Sail - A Connie Barrera Thriller

Running Under Sail - A Connie Barrera Thriller

Sails Job - A Connie Barrera Thriller

Under Full Sail - A Connie Barrera Thriller

An Easy Sail - A Connie Barrera Thriller

A Torn Sail - A Connie Barrera Thriller

A Righteous Sail - A Connie Barrera Thriller

Sailor Take Warning - A Connie Barrera Thriller

Sailor's Choice - A Connie Barrera Thriller

J.R. Finn Sailing Mysteries

Assassins and Liars

Avengers and Rogues

Vigilantes and Lovers

Sailors and Sirens

Villains and Vixens

Killers and Keepers

Devils and Divas

Sharks and Prey

Other Fiction

Deception in Savannah

The Redemption of Becky Jones

The Lost Tourist Franchise

Books for Sailors and Dreamers

Life's a Ditch

Dungda de Islan'

Audiobooks

Assassins and Liars

Avengers and Rogues

Vigilantes and Lovers

Sailors and Sirens

Villains and Vixens

Killers and Keepers

Devils and Divas

Sharks and Prey

For more information please visit www.clrdougherty.com

Or visit www.amazon.com/author/clrdougherty

PREVIEW OF BLUEWATER JAILBIRD

Read the beginning of *Bluewater Jailbird,* the tenth **Bluewater Thrillers** adventure...

CHAPTER 1 - BLUEWATER JAILBIRD

As Liz Chirac walked down the dock at the marina in Rodney Bay, she swept her eyes over the dinghies tied at the end. There was no sign of the one she and Dani used on *Vengeance*. Frowning, she unzipped the small duffle bag that hung from her left shoulder. She took out her cellphone and called Dani again, upset when her call went to voicemail.

"Dani? Where are you? I'm worried now! Call me!" Liz touched the disconnect icon and turned around, striding back toward shore as she wondered what to do.

She checked the time on the phone's screen before she slipped it into her pocket. It was about a quarter to five; she'd emailed Dani from the airport in Brussels early this morning with her expected arrival time, and Dani had responded as Liz was boarding her flight. Her email had suggested that Liz meet her at the restaurant at the head of the dock for an early dinner before they went back to the boat.

When Liz didn't get an answer to her call from the taxi a few minutes earlier, she'd thought that Dani was probably in their dinghy and couldn't hear the phone over the noise of the outboard. By the time she'd paid the taxi and gotten her bag from the back, ten minutes had passed since her call. She had expected to see Dani waiting in the restaurant's bar. Not finding her friend there, she'd walked down the dock, thinking she would meet Dani coming up to the restaurant.

She stood at the head of the dock, tapping her foot as she considered what to do. Maybe the outboard had stalled; Dani could be paddling the dinghy in from their anchorage out in Rodney Bay. Her route would have been against the brisk offshore wind, so she would have to kneel in the bow and paddle vigorously to make any progress. Although the RIB had oarlocks, the pudgy little boat didn't row well, especially into the breeze. The notion of her friend's aggravation with their balky outboard brought a wry smile to Liz's lips, but then she remembered the unanswered phone.

Shaking her head and frowning, she walked over to the concrete seawall. Following the walkway along the seawall to the area where water taxis and other local service boats tied up, she spotted the battered little flag-bedecked runabout that belonged to the man who made his living peddling fruit to the people on the yachts out in the anchorage. He was crouched in the boat, sorting his unsold fruit when Liz came within earshot.

"Good afternoon, Timothy," she called.

The man sat up and turned to look over his shoulder, a big grin lighting up his dark, whiskered face when he recognized her.

"Good afternoon, Liz. Is good to see you; welcome back. You jus' now come?"

"Yes, I just got in, but I can't find Dani and she's not answering her phone. I wondered if — "

"I t'ink she on *Vengeance* when I go by jus' now."

"Did you see her? I thought maybe she had trouble with the outboard. We need to clean the carburetor."

"No, I didn't see her, but the dinghy tied to *Vengeance*."

"How long ago?"

"Mebbe ten minutes, at mos'. I don' stop, 'cause I know you

not there, an' Dani, she don' buy the fruit. I t'ink I would wait for you to be back, 'cause you always out on deck lookin' fo' me. I figured you be back soon."

"I'm a little worried, Timothy. She knew what time I was coming; she was going to meet me up at the restaurant for dinner."

"Well, mebbe she do be comin' an' have some trouble wit' de motor. Come, we go see can we find she."

"You don't mind? I could take a water taxi."

"No need fo' dat, Liz. I happy to see you back. You come, now. We go see what she up to, that Miss Dani."

DANI APPROACHED the table that was filled with muttering women, hostile looks on their faces as they watched her. There was one open seat at the end of the bench that was closest to her. She shut out the stench of the highly seasoned, over-cooked swill on her tray and set it on the table in front of the vacant seat.

She put her hands on the table, one on each side of her tray, and swung a leg over the bench. As she sat, she brought her other leg over. Ignoring the sudden silence of her table mates, she stuck her plastic spoon into the sticky yellow mass of whatever comprised the main course.

She resisted the urge to pinch her nostrils shut before she put the spoon in her mouth. She felt a beefy hand clamp down on her left shoulder, and before she could react, she was pushed off the end of the bench and thrown to the rough cement floor.

"You in my place," a huge woman said, her voice deep and harsh. "And tha's my favorite supper, you little white bitch."

Her assailant towered over her, an ugly grin displaying her gapped and broken teeth. Dani hooked her left foot behind the woman's right ankle and drove her right foot into the lower edge of the woman's kneecap with the force of a pile driver. The woman screamed as the ligaments around her knee gave way, her leg bending the wrong way as she collapsed against the table where Dani had been sitting.

Dani scrambled to her feet and snatched her tray from the table, sending the food flying. She twisted at the waist, drawing the tray out to the side, and then whirled, swinging the edge of the aluminum tray into the woman's temple with her weight behind it. The woman's eyes rolled back in her head as blood gushed from the gash left by the tray.

Dani took two steps back, feeling the concrete block wall behind her, as the other women converged on her in a semicircle. She held the tray in front of her like a shield and grinned at the women. "Which one of you wants to be next," she taunted, measuring the distance as they approached, shoulder to shoulder. "You gutless fools," she yelled as she feinted with the tray and dropped to a crouch, delivering a powerful kick to the knee of the woman at the right end of the line.

As the woman went down, Dani threw the tray aside and grabbed the next woman's shirt, dropping her head a fraction as she lunged forward. She heard a satisfying crack and felt the warm blood run over her face as her head-butt knocked the woman unconscious. The women were backing away, throwing punches as Dani charged first one, and then another.

She paused as two matrons with nightsticks pushed into the crowd from behind, watching as the measured blows to the backs of the women's legs took them down. They curled up as the nightsticks rose and fell in a rapid tattoo of blows. After thirty seconds or so, the larger of the two matrons looked at Dani and said, "Your turn, missy."

Dani steeled herself, knowing that if she fought, she would inevitably be made to pay. The matron gripped her nightstick in two hands and thrust the end into Dani's solar plexus. Dani doubled over and the two women delivered a flurry of blows to her ribcage and lower back. She slipped to the floor, covering her face and head as best she could with her arms.

To her surprise, she heard one of them say, "Okay, Amaryllis. I 'tink she done had enuff." The matrons grabbed her under the arms and frog-marched her from the dining room.

"Don' be feelin' too easy, now, little white girl. The warden, she want to see you while you can still talk. You don' tell her what she want to know, then mebbe we work on you some more. Or mebbe she want us to sof'en you up some, firs'. We see."

"DINGHY STILL THERE," Timothy said, as he and Liz approached *Vengeance*.

Liz studied the RIB as it bobbed in the chop behind *Vengeance*. "It's still chained to the big boat," she said.

"Mebbe Dani take a nap," Timothy said.

"I don't know. The phone would have awakened her, I think."

"Less'n she have it set to vibrate," Timothy said, as he shut down the outboard and stood up to fend off from *Vengeance's* side.

Liz scrambled aboard. "Dani?" she yelled, as she stepped back to the cockpit.

Alarmed to find the companionway doors locked, she fumbled for the key that they kept hidden in the small locker on the port side of the cockpit. She unlocked the doors and swung them back, reaching in to undo the barrel bolts that held the sliding hatch cover closed. She leaned against it with both hands, using her weight to push the heavy teak hatch open. "Dani?"

"I wait," Timothy said, "case you be needin' some help, mebbe."

Liz nodded. "Thanks, Timothy."

Liz went down the companionway ladder, noticing that the interior was in disarray. Her eye fell on Dani's iPhone on the chart table, next to the canvas briefcase that she carried instead of a purse. She touched the phone's screen and saw the notifications for the two missed calls she had placed earlier.

She checked the cabins, noticing again that someone had rummaged through the boat, but that nothing seemed to be missing. Things were just slightly out of place, as though Dani might have tried her unpracticed hand at housekeeping. Liz would have been amused by that except that she was too worried.

Dani's bed was unmade, but the others were undisturbed. That did bring a brief smile to her face; she knew that Dani would have made some attempt to make the bed before going ashore. She wouldn't have wanted Liz to catch her being sloppy.

Dani always felt a little guilty that she was a slob at heart, but Liz found her lack of domestic skills charming. It was one of the things she teased Dani about. Still, something was wrong. She contemplated what to do, her thoughts interrupted by Timothy's call.

"Liz?"

"Sorry, Timothy."

"You want me to take you back ashore? We go look for she?"

"No, thanks, Timothy. I've imposed on you enough. I know you need to get home to your family. I'll be okay; I've got the dinghy, and I'm home now. I'll call around and see if anybody's heard from her."

"Mebbe she go off wit' some frien's an' lose track of de time."

"Maybe," Liz said, stepping onto the companionway ladder and poking her head out. "Thanks again for your help, Timothy. Have a good evening."

"You, too." Timothy released his hold on *Vengeance* and bent over to start his outboard as his ragged little boat began to drift away into the gathering dusk.

ONE OF THE matrons held Dani with her right arm locked behind her back, the tip of a nightstick in the crook of her elbow and her wrist up between her shoulder blades. Dani stood on her tiptoes to keep her arm from breaking. The other matron stood beside her at attention in front of the warden's desk.

"Berger, this is not some waterfront tavern. We don't tolerate that kind of behavior. Do you have anything to say for yourself?"

"Yes, ma'am. I've been here for hours, and I haven't been allowed to call my lawyer."

"This is not the United States, young woman. You have whatever rights I decide to give you, and that's it. What's the meaning of your behavior in the cafeteria just now?"

"Why don't you ask the woman who tried to take my food? I was just defending myself."

"That's the kind of statement I'd expect from a killer. That why you knifed Herbert Watson? Defending yourself?"

"I don't know what you're talking about. I want to call the U.S. Embassy in Barbados. I have nothing further to say to you until I see my lawyer."

"Oh, my. You have a lot to learn, Berger, and this is just the place to teach you. Start behaving like a lady and answer the Detective Constable's questions right now. He's waiting in an interview room. Are you going to cooperate?"

"I want to see my lawyer."

The warden turned to the two burly matrons who still held Dani's arm twisted behind her back.

"Give her the full treatment. And then put her in the hole. We'll see just how stubborn you are when you can't stand up by yourself, Berger."

———

Read more about *Bluewater Jailbird* at www.clrdougherty.com